DESMOND CORY
Dead Fall

WALKER AND COMPANY · NEW YORK

First published in the United States of America
in 1965 by the Walker Publishing Company, Inc.

This paperback edition first published in 1984.

ISBN: 0-8027-3062-0

Library of Congress Catalog Card Number: 65-22137

Printed in the United States of America

10 9 8 7 6 5 4 3 2 1

... For what are worldly gains but emptiness, and wind, and the fear of falling?

St. Augustine

Dead Fall

1

JEYE had had two-one-two from the beginning, all to himself, and had never wanted to change it. It wasn't the best room in the building, but it was better than most. The windows were wide, and gave on to the rough stubble plain beyond the river; on a clear day he could see the mountains of the Guadarrama, white-tipped, jewel-like, on the rim of the horizon, and on the high Castilian plateau most winter days are clear. At times there came light rains that tinged the distance with grey and blue undertones; but then a brittle, sparkling sunshine returned and with it that uniquely Spanish sharpness of colour and contour, invading even the subdued green shades of the sanatorium. Outside, and in spite of the sun, it was very cold, but two-one-two was always the same, its temperature controlled by thermostatic central heating. The bed had a clean white coverlet, the walls were painted grey and orange and the chromium taps in the adjoining bathroom were always polished and shining. It was like a room in a first-class hotel. Jeye was comfortable there.

He knew that Dr Delgado was pleased with his progress, and so, for that matter, was he. The ugly rasp in his throat had long since disappeared; Jeye was a man who traded in silence, in utter silence, and at one time that roughness in his breathing had almost alarmed him. Now it had gone, as had the slow jitter in his hands, the nervous tic that had

11

curled up one corner of his mouth. "In fact," Dr Delgado said, "your course of treatment here has virtually ended. With complete success. *Enhorabuena.*"

"Thanks," Jeye said. "Thanks very much. I certainly feel a great deal better."

"Should you wish to leave, you know, there's no reason at all why you shouldn't. I hardly think you'll be coming back to see us in a hurry."

"You've all made me very comfortable," Jeye said.

"Well, I'm glad to hear it. We do our best. But——"

"I feel I should like to stay here a little longer."

"As you wish," Delgado said. "That's entirely up to you."

He could, of course, have said nothing else. It was no part of his job to kick out paying customers who wanted to go on paying. If what he did, in effect, was run a home for drunks, it was nevertheless an exclusive home for well-born or well-heeled drunks; Jeye, who fell into the latter category, was able to appreciate the distinction between being treated as a victim of nervous disorders rather than as a simple alcoholic with the screaming willies, and it was in preserving precisely that distinction that Delgado had made his reputation. Jeye was in what many people might have called good company. He shared a corridor with Robert Warner Warren, eldest son of the conventional oil magnate from Texas; with Manuel Alvaro, who owned the greater part of one of the biggest wine-exporting firms in Jerez and had last year come close to exhausting the company's reserve stock singlehanded; and with Juanito Salinas, whose wife was the Condesa de Arpo and whose father was a millionaire and well-known connoisseur. Juanito was in his early twenties. He and Jeye were much the youngest of the assembly, and they often took breakfast together; having been accustomed in the past to breakfasting mainly on a bottle of cognac with a water chaser, it was between the hours of eight and ten that Juanito found himself most in need of moral support, and this Jeye did his best to provide. He quite liked Juanito.

"That bastard Delgado."

"Yes?" Jeye would say.

"First thing I'll do when I'm out of here, I'll buy this bloody place up and give that nit the sack."

"Oh, I don't know. He's only doing his job."

"Man's nothing but a beastly sadist."

"Oh, I don't know."

"Bastard," Juanito would say, concluding the conversation. Salinas might have formed the Spanish prototype of the Angry Young Boozehound and in some sense the refutation of the English, since his origins were obviously anything but humble. Virtually the only direction in which his ill-aimed fury and ill-informed contempt did not extend was towards his own person; unlike many of the sanatorium's other inmates, and notably Robert Warner Warren, he was invariably smoothly shaved, impeccably barbered and exquisitely dressed. Perhaps it was this unlikely combination in him of Jimmy Porter and Bertie Wooster that amused and interested Jeye, since Juanito's was not otherwise an immediately likeable character; it is also true, of course, that had Juanito not been a patient at the Delgado sanatorium Jeye would never have gone near the place either.

Still, this consideration may not have weighed as much as one would suppose on Jeye's somewhat unordinary mind. Whatever Jeye did, professionally or otherwise, held little element of the masquerade. He had not simply assumed the rôle of an alcoholic in order to gain admittance to the sanatorium, as a less gifted man might have done: in the space of a shade under three weeks he had instead *become* an alcoholic, had developed the symptoms, medically recognisable and otherwise, that normally appear slowly, gradually, throughout some five years' constant misuse of the human frame, and this while retaining, at the back of his mind, that diamond-hard sense of purpose that guaranteed him, all the time, his continued membership of the human race. It might be argued that such a form of sanity passes all the recognised limits and becomes, in its turn, a kind of obsession. Argued by others, though. Never by Jeye himself.

"No privacy," Salinas said. "No place for just being oneself, if you know what I mean. That's what gets on my wick."

"I suppose they have to watch us. That's part of their job."

"Know what it all reminds me of?" Salinas said, staring moodily into a cup of black coffee. "The time I was around seventeen and failed my exams. Oh, I failed 'em in style, I did. Not just one. The flipping lot. And you know what my father did then? . . . Ups and fills the house with private tutors. Fifteen or twenty of the sods, I swear you couldn't walk down the stairs without tripping over half a dozen of 'em. Drove me bats, or dam' nearly."

"That was in Málaga?" The Salinas winter residence was in Málaga. Juanito didn't like Málaga. Jeye had heard quite a lot already about the Salinas winter residence. And Málaga too.

"Yes. That was in Málaga. You'd think you'd be able to hide yourself away somewhere, wouldn't you, in a dirty great shack like that? . . . Well, not a hope. Any time I'd hide myself away for a quiet smoke and a look through some dirty

14

magazine or other, they'd be shouting up and down for me like a pack of deerhounds. 'Hey, hey, Juanito! Come and be killed!' Then it'd be two solid hours of logarithms and I don't know what all. Just one place they could never find me, else I'd have been ripe for the loony-bin, I honestly would."

"I can guess," Jeye said. "In the library."

"Eh? . . . Oh, I see what you mean. Least likely place, and all that." Juanito nodded vigorously, acknowledging the subtlety of Jeye's reasoning, then stopped nodding and shook his head instead. "No, but in point of fact you're not so very far out. It was a sort of balcony place just beyond the library, end of the passage, it'd all been nailed up but I pulled a board loose and that was it. A bit dodgy, because what you had under it was a drop of fifty odd feet. But I didn't much mind *that*, I've never been scared of heights. Looking back," Juanito said reflectively, "I'd say I spent some of the happiest hours of my whole dam' life on that old balcony. Doing damn-all, mind you. Just sitting and thinking and smoking and maybe getting the odd drop of vino inside me. Nice view of the mountain, I remember. I *loved* that place."

"Getting away from it all," Jeye said. "I know the feeling. Like having escaped from . . . something or other."

"*Exactamente*. I suppose most kids have their secret places, haven't they?" Juanito sighed and, visibly steeling himself, took a mouthful of coffee. "I was a bit old for it, maybe. But there you are."

"Well, you're still looking for one, aren't you? A secret place? It's not a bad idea at that. Someone ought to suggest it to the management."

"Fat lot of good that'd do," Salinas said gloomily. Then, "It's all right for you," he added unexpectedly. "You're not married."

Jeye sipped at his own coffee and considered for a while that last remark. He thought he could see the connection, but he wasn't sure. He had met Juanito's Condesa on several occasions —she visited the sanatorium twice weekly on the official visiting days, Wednesday and Saturday—and privately thought that Juanito had little to complain about in that quarter. He had noticed, of course, that she talked too much, in one of those sprightly knees-*bend* voices, and he also knew that it was principally at the Condesa's instigation that Juanito had wound up as one of Delgado's patients; he didn't know exactly what form of concealed blackmail the Condesa had employed to secure that end, though the interesting tautnesses of her superbly-cut black dresses made it a fairly simple matter to guess. But in any case, the husband's point of view is bound to differ from that of the outsider; and though Jeye's brain was packed with items of information relating to Juanito Salinas and the Salinas family, there were certain aspects of that subject into which he found it unnecessary to enter.

He himself had no complaints to make on the matter of personal privacy. His mind was, as it had always been, unquestionably his own, and of recent weeks he had made some effort to improve it, slogging his way conscientiously through a number of the heavier volumes in the library and making painstaking notes in a loose-leaf exercise book. These related, for the most part, to Spanish architecture and modern methods of house construction. His body also he had subjected to an intensive course of exercise; his two months in relative confinement had softened the muscles of his thighs and stomach, but his shoulders, arms and wrists remained as supple and powerful as a trapezist's, belying from the very first that constant nervous tremor of his hands. Delgado, who was no fool, had been puzzled by that anomaly. "Now yours is a *remarkable* body, Señor Jeye."

"Oh? In what way?"

"Magnificently developed. Why, you might have been a professional acrobat. Alcoholism is always a lamentable weakness," Delgado said severely, "but in your case it amounts to a crime. This kind of body," he said, punching Jeye painfully in the solar plexus, "hardly ever comes our way. Much too good to be wasted."

"Ow," Jeye said. "Well, yes. At one time I was something of an athlete."

"So I imagine. We'll get the masseurs on to *you*."

And they had done a very good job. They were still doing it, three times a week. Jeye had by now accepted—or had perhaps been accepted by—the sanatorium routine; he was comfortable—very comfortable—and secure; yet not so comfortable and secure as to forget that comfort and security carry, for men such as he, an element of risk. He was learning much that he needed to know, and he was out of danger in the sanatorium; as effectively out of danger as he might have been in prison, for the entries and exits of patients and visitors were very little less carefully guarded. But an awareness of the permanent possibility of danger was always there, somewhere at the back of all his thinking. The thing that men like Jeye must always, while they live, remember was dormant in him, yes, but not forgotten.

And it came to life with a sudden jump the day he had the visitor.

"To see *me*?"

"Sí, señor."

"*Bien*," Jeye said. "*En seguida estoy.*"

Fé Carbonell Rodriguez de Moreau, the visiting-card said; and gave the address of a flat in Madrid on the Calle Serrano. An expensive-looking card, with wavy gilt edges. Jeye left it on the writing-table.

At the Delgado sanatorium were both public and private visiting-rooms. Señora de Moreau had asked for one of the private ones. She was sitting erectly at a table in the exact centre of the room, with both her hands resting, knuckles upwards, on the table's polished surface, rather as though she were surveying an invisible hand of patience spread out in front of her. She didn't look up until Jeye, too, had seated himself on the opposite side of the table. "It's Mr Jeye?"

"That's right," Jeye said. "And you're the Señora de Moreau. We haven't met." He was looking careworn and didn't smile.

"We've a mutual friend, I think. The Condesa de Arpo."

"Oh, yes. Yes, I've met the Condesa."

"And I understand from her that you may be leaving the . . . this place shortly."

"Nothing definite has been decided."

"But we should like to."

"To. . . ?"

"Decide something definite."

"I'm afraid I don't quite follow," Jeye said.

"No. Of course it's rather a delicate matter." She didn't seem particularly uneasy, though. "About work, you see, I mean taking up employment."

"Good heavens. You're from the Old Lags' Reclamation Society, or something? Alcoholics Anonymous?"

"Oh, no. Nothing like that."

"No," Jeye said. "You don't look the type."

"*Work* I'm talking about. I'm in the same line of business as you are, Mr Jeye. Well, or almost."

"But I don't run any kind of business."

"You take things, don't you?"

"*Take* things?"

"Certain things."

She has a beautiful neck, Jeye thought. Long and slim. Just right for pearls. Or, from another point of view, for throttling. The danger was here right enough, had dropped on him out of the blue. It could hardly be worse.

"I'm sorry," the girl said. That was all she was; a girl. Twenty-two or twenty-three. "It's a bit of shock, I know—or I can imagine—to have a stranger come in and. . . . There doesn't seem to be any way of doing it tactfully, though. Does there?"

"I'm not rated all that high on tact myself," Jeye said. "All right. Let's assume I take things. I take photographs, say. What comes next?"

"In the first place, you have a photograph I can sell for you."

"You're sure of that?"

"Quite sure."

"Sure I have it? Or sure you can sell it?"

"Quite sure of both."

"Go on," Jeye said.

"Then we need your help in taking more photographs."

"We?"

She looked down her nose towards the table. It was a long and thin but in no way unattractive nose. "There'd be a three-way split."

"I see," Jeye said. "You let me keep a third of what I've

19

got. That's very generous."

"Not at all. What we have, we hold. Just a three-way split on future deals, is what I meant. And if I run for you, then it's 20 per cent."

"Again," Jeye said, "you don't look the type."

"That can be an advantage. You know that."

"Yes. I'll have to think about this."

"But not for too long."

"How long is too long?"

"That photograph you have—its price won't hold. The client may fill his album from somewhere else. As for the new shots, well, we have some very handsome sitters lined up who obviously won't stay sat. May I come and see you again on Sunday?"

"Yes. All right. And what's the alternative?"

"How do you mean?"

"I mean that I've always been very happy taking my snaps by myself. What happens if I decide to go on that way?"

"I don't know," the girl said. "I hope the eventuality won't arise." Her neat silver-painted fingernails rattled briefly on the surface of the table, then were still. "Kruger wouldn't make you as good an offer, though, would he?"

"I doubt it."

Jeye felt a little tired; mentally fatigued, as though his spell in the sanatorium had slowed down the speed of his brain's responses even while sharpening certain of his senses. He was aware, after so many weeks of the hygienic, disinfectant, pine-woody smell of the sanatorium, he was abnormally aware of the scent of the girl's perfume; there was sandalwood in there somewhere; Vent Vert, maybe?—and of subtler scents behind it, of clean lingerie and of her body; and behind them something that was subtler still, salt water maybe, a tinge of ozone that seemed to be clinging to her hair. His eyes, too, were alert to points of detail, picking up, for instance, that fractional shortness to the hem of her ash-grey skirt that placed it as a French cut, not Spanish or American. All this, and yet his brain seemed unable as yet to correlate the detail into a whole, a coherent pattern. She was probably right about one thing. It *was* time for him to leave. He should have left already.

She began to pull on her gloves, white kid gloves without buttons; her wrists were narrow, smoothly tanned; she wore no wrist watch. "How was Africa?" Jeye said, and watched the big violet eyes come swerving up at him again. No reaction, other than that, but the eyes were speculative. "Africa?"

"Tangiers, was it?"

"A point to you. If you wanted it. How did you guess?"

"It's February," Jeye said. "There aren't many places in Europe where you can bathe in February. And I can smell the salt in your hair. It's hard to get rid of."

"I could have bathed in Spain."

"Then you'd have travelled here by car, or in the train. But you don't smell of travel. You must have come by air."

"Amazing," she said, and stood up. "I thought that kind of thing went out with Conan Doyle. Though of course he was on the other. . . . Sunday, then?"

"I'll expect you," Jeye said. "I'm fond of swimming myself."

"If you want to get in touch with me earlier, you have my number."

"I have?"

"It's on my card."

"Of course."

Jeye stood up when she did, but she didn't offer him her

21

hand. "*Hasta pronto*, Mr Jeye."

"I'll be expecting you," Jeye said again.

There was nothing to pick up. She had no handbag. Jeye went to the door with her, watched her walk down the parqueted corridor which echoed the sharp click of her stiletto heels. He felt no easing of the tension now that she had gone. He felt tireder than ever. He walked—more slowly than she had—down the passageway and back to his room. It didn't seem as comfortable as it had seemed before.

For a while he stood looking out of the window, across the plain and towards the mountains that today were veiled in shadows; the cloud was building up over Navacerrada, and long grey-white streamers were moving eastwards. Beyond the river, a row of glinting poplars marked the line of the road, the road that ran down to Cercadilla and then turned south towards Madrid; the shiny beetle-backs of cars moved along it from time to time, driving slowly, avoiding the ruts, seeming at that distance to be feeling their way with outstretched antennae; passing the trees, they picked up speed and, swinging slowly to the left, disappeared into the brown Castilian immensity. ". . . Spain," Juanito Salinas had said. "Now there's a lousy country for you. I mean, you're English, aren't you? Why the hell should you want to live in a dump like Spain?" And Jeye: "Because you can be rich here without people asking too many questions." And that was true. There were other reasons, certainly; but that was as good a reason as any. Juanito had laughed, sardonically; then had fallen silent.

But Spain, Jeye was now thinking, is also a big country, a very big country; an easy country in which to disappear, providing you have the use of more than one passport. You drive past a row of poplars, you turn left; and that's it. North, south, east or west; you take your choice. Jeye's choice, of course, had already been made; it would be west, west to Salamanca; then down to Badajoz and maybe into Portugal. Travelling by train, naturally. Hired cars are too easy to trace. Travelling by the slow train, and mostly at night. Things could have been worse, much worse. The sanatorium job, after all, was completed. The lemon had been sucked dry. And it could have been Kruger; oh, yes, things could have been worse.

It was simply having been rumbled that was bad. Jeye had been rumbled only once before in his life; the man who had done it was dead, not with Jeye's connivance or even with Jeye's foreknowledge; his death had been a lucky break, no more than that. He had died at least five, no, six years ago; that had been another reason for Jeye's having settled in Spain . . . though "settled" hardly seemed the right word. Well, and now it had happened again. It was something you had to be prepared for; and now it had happened. That was all.

All he could do now was run.

And so he ran.

They picked him up five minutes before the train drew into Principe Pio.

. . . It's difficult to understand the mentality of men like Jeye. Criminal projects may be, and often are, carried out in ways that resemble very closely the ordinary methods of business practice; but the difference between the criminal and the commercial mentality is very evident. And of all criminals, it is the jewel thief who is the farthest removed from the comprehension of law-abiding persons, perhaps because he is the farthest removed from the complex of modern civilisation, the nearest to the so-called "law of the jungle".

Naturally, it is the circumstances of the crime itself that focuses the average newspaper-reader's attention. But the crime itself is nothing but a means to an end. And it is by what happens *after* the strike that the curious mentality of the thief is shaped. For from that moment on, he is vulnerable; he has become a property-owner, has become rich, yet he has none of the means of defending his property which its former owner enjoyed. The law will give him no protection; he must defend it himself, alone.

And if the position of the ordinary thief is vulnerable, that of the jewel thief is horrifyingly so. His property is uniquely valuable in relation to its bulk; it is easy to handle, though difficult to dispose of; and its worth may be such as to compel him to defend it, if necessary, almost to the death. *Almost*. Never quite. That's the trouble. Because the man who twists the wire round his forehead knows that, in the end, he'll sing, though the end may be a very long and unimaginably painful while in coming. Yet he can't give way at once; he *can't*. Torture to the point of death is never a pleasant prospect, but it's a prospect that the successful jewel thief faces virtually every day of his working life.

It is in this that the real weakness of the gang strike lies, since the victim may sing, not just for himself, but for all. To the jewel thief, anyone who knows his name and where he may be found is an enemy. That enemy may even be a member of the gang; because unlike most of the great killers of the animal world, the jewel thief is often a cannibal. There's always something unsatisfactory about taking a mere share of a strike, especially when that share may be months

24

in coming. To be a member of a successful gang of jewel thieves is not, therefore, a life that many people would enjoy. And often, for this reason, some—like Jeye—prefer to hunt alone, though Jeye was not the kind of man to have just one simple reason for doing anything.

There may or may not be more glamour attached to the career of the solitary. It depends on how you look at it. From a safe distance, you may think a tiger to be rather more glamorous than a pack of wolves; from a shorter range, it may be harder to decide. The solitary is also the name of a kind of tapeworm, a parasite that murders, by slow degrees, its host; and curiously, the nearest parallel one can easily find to the solitary thief's weird parasitic psychology is that provided by the wartime traitors . . . William Joyce, John Amery, others unnamed. . . . Men, like the solitaries, of widely varying individualities, sharing only that peculiar kink or twist which makes them able to live their lives, so to speak, at an angle to the perpendicular, seeming to parallel the normal yet never doing so.

On the other hand, the solitary is not very like the gang thief. His victims are chosen on a quite different basis. He doesn't pit himself against the banks and the big jewellers; he would be foolish to try. He is an individual, and his victim is an individual; a rich individual; it would be tempting to say rich and stupid, but rich people are not often stupid, at least where their riches are concerned. Nor are they often careless. But it is on that *not often* that the solitary's career depends. As far as he is concerned, they have to be stupid *once*, careless *once*. That's enough.

Much more than the gang thief, he is sensitive to the laws of supply and of demand. He tends to be sure of his market before he strikes, and his strike will indeed usually be aimed at filling a specific demand. He will take a good price for a poor set of stones rather than a bad price for an excellent set; indeed, the really good sets have no other. The solitary is as good as his intelligence service. And that is the snag, because that is his weakness. It is only through some slip-up on the part of his intelligence contacts—or through, of course, some act of boasting or comparable lunacy on his own account— that the solitary is ever rumbled. To be rumbled need not be the end, if he acts quickly and if he has made the right plans. But the danger, while it lasts, is as acute as any that he can experience. The act of crime may be dangerous in itself, but it is always as safe as he can make it. On a strike, he knows where he is. Being rumbled is quite different. Then he doesn't.

It is necessary to explain all this at some length, since otherwise Jeye's behaviour must seem strange. A normal person would not, on seeing a harmless and decidedly attractive girl enter a first-class railway carriage, experience that sensation of near-suffocation that overcame Jeye, nor his subsequent impulse to leap past her and out of the door of the train to impale himself upon the passing railings. Jeye was not, as would from this appear, an abject coward. Indeed, his physical bravery was—some would have said—his only really admirable quality. The danger that the girl represented to him was a real and a terrifying one; much more terrifying, in fact, than even a full understanding of the solitary's manner of thought might suggest. Because Jeye was something other than an ordinary solitary, something different. In the criminal as much as in the law-abiding world, there is room for abnormality; and Jeye was abnormal. He was, as the word is commonly understood, a genius.

Which is to say that he did things that nobody else could

have done, mainly because, for doing them, he had the wrong reasons.

. . . All that the girl did was sit down opposite him and cross her knees. Of course she didn't have a gun, or any nonsense of that kind. And obviously, she was alone. Only to Jeye's imagination was she "they", was she one of the name-less, one of the others in that civil war Jeye fought against the greater part of humanity. All she did was sit down and cross her knees. Then, after perhaps a minute,

"Hullo," she said.

"Well, hul-*lo*," said Jeye.

Standing before the mirror, he put on his coat; adjusted the set of his rolled-gold cufflinks; straightened his tie. It was a regimental tie, navy blue with stripes of red, green and gold; the Royal Marines. Jeye had never been in the Royal Marines (the cad). But he liked the colours. He was still admiring them when the telephone rang, and he crossed the hotel bedroom to answer it.

"Jeye speaking."

"Room 324," the girl said.

"Now?"

"As soon as you're ready."

"Right," Jeye said, and hung up the receiver.

Sitting by the half-open window, the girl looked a little different to his recollection of her, just as her voice had sounded a little different on the telephone. More fragile, more finely-spun. Like porcelain. The man who was sitting beside her got up and stretched out his hand. "So *you're* Mr Jeye."

"That's right."

"Pleasure to meet you. My name's Moreau. My wife I think you know already."

"We've met," Jeye said, turning towards her. The hand that until then he hadn't touched was narrow, like her wrists, and firm. They were both drinking whisky, he noticed; Moreau with a water chaser and the girl, straight.

"What'll you have to drink, Mr Jeye?"

"The same," Jeye said.

"Whisky? . . . I don't suppose Dr Delgado would be very pleased." A faint, a very faint twist of malice appeared at the edges of Moreau's smile. "Still, as this is something of a special occasion. . . ."

An older man, certainly, than Jeye had expected, maybe in the late fifties. A big man; heavyish, a pound or two short of thirteen stone, a little of that weight being fat. His strength, like Jeye's own, would be mostly in the arms and shoulders. It was the face, however, that focused one's chief attention; strong-boned, austere, Roman; the forehead high and the hair above it a pure and silky white. Most of the power of that head lay in the mouth and chin, which were uncompromisingly solid; the creases that marked the contours of the lips were deep and decisive, reminding Jeye somewhat of the portraits of Beethoven. But the eyes, turning now in his direction, were by contrast mild and hesitant, pale blue counterparts to the gentle, almost effeminate tenor in which he spoke. "Of course you're a difficult man to *get* to meet, Mr Jeye."

"Brains are better than legs," Jeye said. "I wasn't quite difficult enough."

"Oh, I hope you'll have no need to reproach yourself. I can assure you that in coming to meet us you haven't committed any kind of mistake, though it's natural that you should think so at the outset. Last time, I mean, it *was* a mistake."

"Last time?" Jeye held the bubble-glass lightly poised in his fingers.

"When you agreed to work with White."

"Oh, *that*," Jeye said.

"Kruger thinks you pulled a fast one there. Both of you."

"He fell," Jeye said. "He wasn't pushed."

"I don't think anyone's worried about White overmuch. It was the job itself that got Kruger wild."

"We got in first," Jeye said. "That was all." Then, "How well do you know Kruger?"

"Oh, not well," Moreau said softly. "Hardly at all."

"The Carnival stones weren't Kruger's. Not ever. They were mine."

"They are now."

"Go on," Jeye said.

"I repeat, they are now. And all the others. This isn't a shakedown; you'd be a hard man to shake. White had an accident, just the way you say. The fact remains that he's dead and you're alive." Moreau moved his great head negatively from side to side. "Shakedowns are in Kruger's line. He's a big man now, I'm told. They're not in ours."

"All right," Jeye said. He reached over to hold his glass to the syphon, splashed in the sodawater one-handed. "No shakedowns, then. So what is it you want?"

"First of all," Moreau said, "to talk about the Medina job. The Medina miss. That was bad. Wasn't it?"

"All misses are bad."

"They don't have to be as bad as that one was. It was an FPA set-up. You didn't realise?"

"I realised it, yes. When it was too late."

"Well, that's when *everyone* realises it. But not everyone

29

can do a drop of thirty-odd feet, run fifty yards and clear a twelve-foot wall in fifteen seconds. I've worked out the timing carefully, and you couldn't possibly have taken very much longer. So it wasn't too late after all. That's the whole point."

"Legs have their uses," Jeye said, and smiled.

"They do, indeed. But brains are better. You know what a pyrostat is?"

"I've heard about them."

"Perhaps you should have gone into the matter a little more closely."

"Perhaps. But I've never gone in for arson."

"You're missing the point, if I may say so. A pyrostat is a devilishly complicated device, because nowadays it does much more than simply detect fires and sound the alarm. It actually puts fires out. It points any one of a series of extinguishers at any given focus of heat and sprays it with chemicals. It can work to as little as one-foot radius. And our friend Medina has one of the most up-to-date models available installed at that place of his. If you had studied the exterior of the house a little more carefully, you'd have seen the fittings on the corner of the roof. You didn't, though, did you?"

Jeye sipped at his whisky-and-soda. He said nothing.

"There again, a reference book would have told you that, among his many other activities, Pepe Medina's the president of the Kinemesa electrical engineering outfit at Reinosa. Electronic devices are his favourite hobby. Now even in the ordinary way, you could safely assume that anyone who has a pyrostat in his house is going to have a floor pressure alarm as well. They operate on the same circuit. And when the owner's main amusement is playing about with switches and miniature transformer units—why, nobody in his senses is going in. It was suicide, Mr Jeye, professional suicide. It really was."

Jeye nodded slowly. His expression remained withdrawn, contemplative. "There were reasons," he said.

"Of course. But no reasons could be good enough." Abruptly, Moreau cracked his fingers. "Forgive me the lecture, please. It's just that I've been in the removals business for some little while now, I've built up my files with great care and I wanted to prove to you that, at least on occasion, what's in those files might be well worth your knowing. That's what *you* might hope to gain. As for us . . . well, now." The corners of his eyes crinkled up engagingly. "As I say, I've been in the business for a long time. Perhaps too long. I'm nearly sixty; I have the brains, but I don't have the legs. So I need some help. That's all there is to it."

"And it has to be me?"

"Yes. It has to be the best."

Moreau took from his inside pocket a brown manila envelope, took out a blue slip of paper. "This is why," he said. "You'll realise that by no means all our assets are included. It's still a respectable figure, you must agree."

An account slip from a Madrid branch of the Banco de Bilbao; the name in which the account was held was Richard Moreau. The credit figure it showed was a little short of eight million pesetas. Jeye, who held five different accounts himself, didn't imagine it was the only account that Moreau ran, either; and it looked to be unquestionably genuine. He jerked his chin in acknowledgement and approval, handed the slip back. He was now more than a little perplexed.

"A lot to lose," he said. "As much as most."

"Exactly," Moreau said. "That's why we choose to be fussy about taking on a new partner. It has to be someone as good as we are. Or very nearly."

31

"Some people would think of retiring, with that much in the stash. Some people would."

Again that faint twist of malice at the corner of Moreau's mouth. "And when one retires, of course it's convenient to find someone else to take the rap—as the vulgarians says—just so as to make sure of being left in peace. Yes, I follow your line of thought, Mr Jeye, and I can't blame you for being suspicious. I should feel the same way in your place." He sighed windily and stared upwards for a moment at the ceiling, the rueful gaze of an elderly don faced with yet another cleverish undergraduate ... *good brain, but over-imaginative....* "And what do *you* think, Fé?"

"I think you're talking too much philosophy," the girl said, "and not enough business."

"We don't need to *rush* things, do we?"

"Yes, I know you'd rather talk round the subject for hours and hours. But so far as I'm concerned, the only way to build up a business relationship is to do business. *Talk's* no good."

"You may have a point there," Moreau said.

There were red carnations in a tall vase by the window, and Moreau's empty glass stood beside them. As he refilled it, a slow stain of scarlet grew on the upper surface of the glass's glowing bell, widened as he added water from a yellow beaker. A freak of the light, Jeye thought, and angled in such a way that he alone could see it; the girl in any case was no longer looking towards the window, but at him. "You've some kind of a concrete proposition? ... or so I think you said."

"It's concrete all right," Fé said. "There's an offer for a twenty-six carat pendant, eight of them matching blues. To make up a set, as seems obvious. So of course I thought of the de Chaviri stones. They'd do very nicely."

"Two-carat blues, yes. But ten of them."

"We'd try and go over the price mentioned. But it's a good one."

"How much?"

"Eighteen thousand dollars American."

"Not bad," Jeye said. It wasn't.

"And for the de Chaviris, maybe twenty."

"They were mentioned?"

"Oh, yes. They were mentioned."

"Um," Jeye said. He bit his lower lip.

"So were the Pavannes."

"The Pavannes went in London, for God's sake. They'll have got back to Holland by now."

"Quite so," Fé said. "That one's hopeless. Which means the market's clear. It's an offer I like."

"Where's the client?"

"I thought you could have guessed." At the corner of her mouth, an uncanny little replica of Moreau's crease of malice; it was there for a second, then was gone.

"Tangiers."

"Yes."

"No problem there."

"No. Just the time factor."

"When by?"

"Saturday week. At the latest."

". . . Look," Moreau said. "I feel we should give Mr Jeye a little more time in which to consider the proposition we've made. Why don't you two have lunch together tomorrow and talk it over? Then—if you reach an amicable conclusion —you could bring him back to the flat and we'll discuss some projects. *Interesting* projects. And exchange reminiscences, perhaps. That'll be great fun."

"Two o'clock?" the girl said. Her face held such a lack of

expression that it might have been either a statement or a question.

"All right," Jeye said. "Where?"

"You know the Gallego?"

"Yes." He got up. "I'll see you there."

Again the cool, even pressure of her hand; then again Moreau's, warmer and slightly moister, a ball of muscle swelling at the base of the palm. In silence they watched him leave the room; he went out without looking back. Still in silence, Moreau reached out for his glass of whisky.

Eventually,

"I suppose I *do* sound a little like a theorist," he said. "It's just that we've never done anything like this before, have we? But I'm pretty sure that everything will work out right."

"I hope so," the girl said. "I still don't like it."

Jeye didn't much like it, either. No one likes being held, as the saying goes, over a barrel; but he had made the wrong move and he now had no choice. What puzzled him was why Moreau and the girl (as he still thought of her) should think it worth their while to pretend that he had, that this was a proposal of honourable partnership rather than a takeover bid. The alternative was Kruger; not an alternative that any reasonable person would fancy. Kruger was far away in Paris, but Paris was nowhere near far enough. So it would be the Snowy White business all over again; one of those *watchful* partnerships, a game of poker with the table going over at the first and slightest suspicion of a stacked deck. And very much worse, because Moreau looked to have forgotten more about fixing the deal than Snowy White had ever learnt. In short, the odds weren't right. Jeye would have to do what he could to even them up.

In the morning he hired a car from the Hertz garage and drove out to El Escorial. The car was a new Floride, recently run in, and handled nicely enough. There was a strong wind and plenty of cloud, but spring was creeping up from behind the mountains, softening the bite of the air and filling the pine woods with sounds and with scents; in the village, the chestnut trees were coming into leaf already and were loud with sparrows. It had been a mild winter, even outside the sanatorium.

Jeye celebrated his escape from the Delgado regimen by sitting in the gardens of the Victoria Palace and drinking black coffee with Fernet-Branca. Four Madrid businessmen (carefully casual open-neck shirts, silk scarves knotted round their soft brown necks) sat at the next table, and four pretty girls sat opposite them and chattered in their harsh, brightly gay voices that sounded, from a distance, very like the noise of the sparrows. The men argued meanwhile amongst themselves as to who was going to pay the bill; obscure points of honour appeared to be involved. A satisfactory enough escape, Jeye considered; sitting there in the sharp-toned sunlight, aware of the birds, the trees, the wind, the pleasant acridity of the coffee, the sound of Spanish being spoken, the swift but approving glances of the girls at the other table. Escape? . . . Well, a holiday, then. The fact that he had hired a car was sufficient proof that he had planned nothing else; though likely as not that blasted Fé hadn't even bothered to check. Why should she? He was over a barrel now, and she knew it. And if this was a holiday, it was still a holiday with a purpose.

When he had paid his bill he walked slowly downhill to the Banco de Santander; where Hernandez—who seemed delighted, in the usual Spanish way, to see him—got out the keys and opened Jeye's private safe deposit. Jeye slipped into his pocket the brown paper envelope that contained the de Chaviri pendant, returned the keys with thanks, and accepted an invitation to more coffee in the manager's office—this time with cognac. Business was undergoing a recession, Hernandez said, cashing Jeye's cheque for forty thousand. Yes. Again. Foreign investment was what was needed. A stabilising influence. Otherwise, who could tell? Maybe devaluation of the peseta. Yes. Again.

"Well, if you hear of anything good, Enrique, you can always let me know. Our Gredos shares aren't doing all that badly."

"Um," Hernandez said gloomily. "Let's say they're holding up as well as any. Yes, we're always at your service here, Señor Jeye, as I'm sure you know. A drop more coffee?"

"Thank you," Jeye said. "I must be going."

He went back to the Victoria Palace. The table that had been next to his was now empty; but one of the girls stood at some five paces' distance from the car, gazing towards the mountains with an air of great concentration. Jeye watched her for a few moments, his hands resting on the steering wheel.

"I'm going into town," he said. "Can I give you a lift?"

"*Qué amable,*" said the girl.

She got in.

Jeye's was normally a mobile face, even an expressive one; he might easily have passed for Spanish, but for his accent. But that mobility often concealed rather than revealed what he was thinking; he was in no way an easy man to read. He might even have seemed to exist in two dimensions only, like the cardboard cut-out figure to which many Spaniards, through their evident lack of imagination, approximate, had it not been equally evident in his case that a third dimension was not simply present but was apparent in his every action; it was there and at the same time it couldn't be probed, it moved away as one tried to approach it, yielded like elastic. "At first," said Moreau, pulling contemplatively at his thin black cigar, "I thought it had to do with his being English. The English tend to hide themselves behind a brick wall—don't they?—and then nine times out of ten there's nothing behind the wall other than a garden full of cabbages. They're competent all right, but simple and direct and—oh—uncomplicated. But I don't feel that about Jeye. Now that I've met him, he puzzles me even more than he did before. He's unusual."

"Would we be interested in him, if he wasn't?"

"No. That's true."

Fé stared out of the taxi window. Her fingers drummed soundlessly for a moment against her knee. "Look," she said. 'No more amateur psychoanalysis, Richard. *Please*."

"Don't come the acid," Moreau said equably. "He interests me, that's all. Doesn't he interest *you*?"

She sighed. "Oh, yes. If you say so."

"Attract you, even?"

"I don't often find men attractive. That's one of the main differences between you and me."

"You *are* in a bad mood today," Moreau said, remaining, however, genial. The taxi stopped outside the Gallego, swerving and braking simultaneously for no other apparent purpose than to demonstrate the driver's Iberian *joie de vivre*; Fé swore at him under her breath while getting out. "I'll do what I can," she said. "I'm modest, is all. I just wouldn't claim to be irresistible. Meanwhile you can stop dropping hints, they're

37

quite unnecessary."

"Hints?"

"Yes. Hints. I'll see you tonight, at the flat."

She turned and walked past the line of shrubs that masked the restaurant entrance. She saw Jeye at once, at a table to her right, under the pergola; not, however, before he had seen her. He was on his feet already. At least he had nice manners, she thought reluctantly; polite without being smooth. The smooth ones were four a penny, the discards from the well-worn pack of high society; Queen Charlotte's, hot towels at Germers', lunch at Vincent's and all that caboodle gone to waste, something funny having happened to them on the way to the Foreign Office, something to reveal a chink, a fault, a flaw, a hole in the wall and through that hole, yes, a plot of wormridden cabbages; Jeye wasn't one of those, anyway. Richard was right. Richard, when it came to the point, didn't make mistakes. She crossed the cobbled floor, swaying delicately on her high white heels; accepted first Jeye's hand and then the chair he proffered her. "I thought we might eat out here," he said. "It's quite warm under the pergola."

"Yes. I'm a little late—I'm sorry."

"That's all right," Jeye said.

"*M'sieu?*" said the waiter. At the Gallego, all the waiters talked like that.

Jeye leaned back in his seat and ordered lunch. He ordered *almejas a la marinera* and *noix de veau braisée* with a bottle of Arbois '45 and with *poires flambées* to follow. With the shellfish, he asked for dry toast and a bowl of celery. The waiter, sticking out his tongue, scribbled furiously in his notebook and went away. "They don't hover, you know. Not really."

"What?" Fé said.

"Well, you're always reading in books about hovering waiters. But they don't. Either they're there or they're not there and there's nothing you can do about it."

"You sound like a philosopher."

"Stoic or Epicurean?"

"Oh, Epicurean."

"Greedy pig's another way of putting it. There's nothing like a few weeks in a sanatorium to sharpen the palate."

"I was thinking. . . ." Fé said.

". . . About what?"

"That time you said you smelt the salt on my hair. You really *did*, didn't you?"

"Oh, yes," Jeye said. "You smelt very nice. Much nicer than the fellow I had next door. *His* hair smelt of brilliantine, mostly."

"And do you *taste* things the same way?"

"I have to be concentrating," Jeye said.

"I see. Yes, I appreciate the compliment."

"I've been thinking about that myself."

"About. . . ?"

"Our interview."

"Well. We hoped you had."

"Not so much about what you *said*."

"No?"

"No. More about why it was you."

"I don't understand."

"Why it was you who came. Not Moreau."

"That was *his* idea."

"He seems to be a clever man."

"Yes, he is."

"He's a queer, isn't he?"

"What?" Fé said.

"He's a homosexual."

". . . I didn't think that was so . . . obvious."

"I didn't say it was obvious."

"You don't *like* queers? Is that it?"

"I don't have to," Jeye said. "I'm not married to him. You are."

"But——"

"The thing is, was that why he sent you? Are you sort of thrown in with the deal? It'd be nice to know."

Fé didn't say anything. She was blushing; she knew it. It took her a moment longer to realise that she was also almost in tears. Then the gleaming white of the tablecloth, the sparkle of the cutlery, suddenly dimmed over; she lowered her head even further. ". . . Because if you're not," Jeye said, his voice as from a distance, "what the hell are we going to do about it?"

"It's not like that at all," Fé said.

"It is. It has to be."

"I don't see why everything always has to be the way that Richard——"

She stopped.

". . . Plans it?"

"Oh, be quiet."

"You hurt too easily," Jeye said. "I don't like that."

Her eyes were clearer now, and she looked up at him. He was crunching a small piece of celery and wiping his fingers on a paper napkin, all with an air of thoughtful impersonality. Another bloody analyst, she thought; oh God, oh God. "Of course I can be hurt, I'm human, I*'m* not a bloody diamond."

"Yes," Jeye said. "He would know that, though. And he's fond of you. *That'*s what I don't understand."

"Maybe human beings mean a bit more to him than they

do to you. That's possible, isn't it?"

"That's not what I meant."

"What *did* you mean?"

Jeye shook his head. "It doesn't matter."

"No, come on."

"I mean that it's not his being *fond* of you that puzzles me, it's why, *being* fond of you, he should . . . take the risk of hurting you. That's all."

"Oh, I *see*. When you cast me aside like a worn-out glove."

"Don't be silly," Jeye said. "It's *he* who's hurting you, not me. Casting aside is one thing; offering in exchange is quite another."

"I've already told you that it's not——"

"That's right," said Jeye. "We're talking at cross-purposes. Try a little celery, it's excellent."

"No, thank you."

Instead she went to work on the shellfish. On the far side of the pergola, behind Jeye's right shoulder, another young couple were deeply engrossed on what seemed to be much less mutually baffling a conversation; Fé focused her eyes on the silver medallion that hung between the other girl's breasts and found that she could see it clearly. The moment had passed quickly enough, but it had been a bad one while it lasted. She wasn't disposed to forgive Jeye for having provoked it.

The other girl threw back her head (affectedly, in Fé's opinion) and laughed; ha, ha, ha. The moron.

"The truth is that you and Richard are rather alike. You should get on splendidly."

"It seems we're in the same profession. That might account for the resemblance."

"You call it that?"

"A profession? . . . Why not?"

"In your case, he seems to think it's more of a special gift. Or a talent. *That one talent which is death to hide* was how he expressed it. Not very original, but there you are."

"*Paradise Lost?*"

"No. But you're not far off."

"I like reading," Jeye said. "I read a good deal. But I've a lousy memory. He's a clever man, though, is . . . Richard." He spooned the last of the *caldo* into his mouth, reached across for another paper napkin. "And what *is* my talent, according to him?"

"Diamonds," Fé said.

"Stealing them?"

"No. He didn't mean that. Just a talent for diamonds, for little bits of rock. What I'd call an obsession."

There was a moment's silence. Jeye was wiping his mouth. "And Milton?"

". . . What about Milton?"

"He was blind, wasn't he? But he went on writing poetry. Keeping his daughters up half the night getting it all written down, they probably thought he was potty. Had *he* an obsession?"

"A talent. A gift. That's what Richard meant, I suppose." She shrugged. "I'm not interested in that. In giving names to things."

The waiter took the plates away, Fé's half-empty.

"How long have you known him?"

"Richard? . . . Oh, five or six years."

"He's never been in prison?"

"Never."

"I have," Jeye said. "In England. I was just turned twenty."

The *noix de veau* arrived, steaming exquisitely in the still air. Very palatable. Fé wondered if she might not, after all, be hungry. Jeye poured out the wine.

"It's not so very different," he said, "from being in a sanatorium. In one way I didn't mind it. In another, I did." He lifted the wine-glass, tilted it in his brown and powerful fingers. "You think about them is the trouble. You think about them all the time. It's not enough just to *have* them. Unless you can see them and touch them. . . ." A narrow wrinkle of reminiscence appeared just above his eyebrows. "You can't smell them, of course. They never smell. Never. They never tell you anything, so whatever it is they've got, they never lose it. They accept nothing. Nothing. Not even light. They throw it straight back at you, all broken up into colours. And they last, you see. That's *how* they last. For ever. Or very damned nearly." He had put down the wine-glass, its contents untouched, and now his fingers moved quietly in his lap, breaking open the seal of the brown paper envelope, their power converted into an unexpected delicacy. "Here they are the way I remembered them, the same as on the day I went in. Here they are. You see? . . . *Paradise Regained*. . . ."

His hand rose to table level, spilled a stream of liquid light over the stiff white linen, a twisting frozen stream, thousand-edged, curved like a snake and as wickedly, as dangerously alive. The de Chaviri pendant. Fé's lips came open; her tongue moved between them, damped their sudden dryness. "You *brought* them."

Jeye's hand fell over the jewels, closed to pick them up, opened again to show them nestling in his palm. "I saw her wearing them once," he said. "A fat little woman—I don't know if you've ever met her—with a fat little neck. A kind of blasphemy, really. Though I don't think I've ever seen a woman beautiful enough to wear diamonds. Pearls, yes. Pearls die just like people do. But not diamonds." He rolled the stones over with the ball of his thumb. "These little things, they never change. Some people in prison think about women, but women change while you're in there. It's not the same."

"You must be mad," Fé said. "Put them away."

"They're for you."

"But not *here*, for heaven's sake."

"Why not?" Jeye's fingertips rubbed together like a conjurer's and the pendant came swinging out from them like a pendulum, twelve inches of diamonds and muted gold. "Girls get offered all kinds of things in a place like this. Go on. Take it."

"Not things as recognisable as these are." She took it all the same, the stones spilling across her wrist and fingers. "No one recognises diamonds," Jeye said, almost mournfully. "Not one man in a million. Not any more. They recognise film stars and pop songs and Milton quotes, but they don't recognise diamonds. Not even the people who own them, sometimes. If they could, things might be different."

She took paper tissue from her red Swiss-silk purse, screwed the pendant up in it. Jeye watched her closely. "Don't *you* ever wear jewels?"

"Hardly ever."

"Try it on," Jeye said suddenly. "Try it on."

"No. You wouldn't like it, if I did."

"Because of what I just said?"

"And because they're not mine. They're yours. I'm just an agent. You hate having to sell them, don't you?"

"Yes. But it's what they're for. They shouldn't ever stay too long with just one person. And I won't think about them any more, once they've been sold."

"There'll be others."

44

"That's right. There'll be others."

He picked up his knife and fork and returned to the veal. The brown envelope, empty now and crumpled, lay beside his plate.

"Is that how you tend to think of things? In terms of what they're *for*?"

"I suppose so," Jeye said. "I'm a complex person, in some ways. So I like to keep things simple."

"And women?"

"How do you mean?"

"Do they count as *things*?"

He considered the point for a moment, leaning back in his chair; she noticed, for the first time, the touch of grey at his temples. "That might not be so bad as you make it sound," he said. "In the first place, it might be safer. For them and for me. Then again, it's a thing that women themselves tend to forget, so from time to time they like to be reminded of it. Even a purely physical want can be better than no want at all."

"What about the corollary?' '

"Corollary?"

"You said that you never thought about them any more once they'd been sold."

Jeye nodded. "Yes, that's true. It's like I said—I like to keep things simple."

"In other words, you're only at your best in a brothel, isn't that it?"

"The world *is* a brothel," Jeye said. Then, having crossed his knife and fork on the empty plate, "I didn't make it. I just live in it."

"I'm sorry," Fé said. "I shouldn't have said that."

"That's all right. I like angry people."

"I *am* angry," Fé said. "You know, I came here in the hell of a bad temper to start with. And now that I feel actually *angry*, I feel much better. Odd, isn't it?"

She looked down at her plate and started to laugh; ha, ha, ha. And why not? she thought. What's wrong, when it comes to the point, with being a moron?

That's what causes all the trouble, having to think. Jeye could be right about that. But look at him now, smiling politely like the nice man he isn't. Why, he doesn't even know what the joke is. I didn't live in the joke; I just made it.

She went on laughing. She couldn't stop.

The lift came smoothly to a halt. The doors whirred open. Jeye followed her out into the green-carpeted corridor, and the polished wooden cage sank downwards again with a soft hydraulic almost feline moan. She took the key from her bag and opened the door of the flat, swinging her shadow-nylon overcoat down from her shoulders as they entered. The study door was ajar, and a faint wave of heat came through from where, in the far corner, a one-bar electric fire was burning. Moreau was sitting at the big desk, smoking another of his black Pantera cheroots; a glass decanter of whisky and a bubble glass three fingers full stood on the desk in front of him. "Ah, good. This is splendid. You've come to an agreement."

"I wouldn't say an agreement." Fé dropped her coat over the back of an armchair, sat down, adjusted her skirt. "He's a philosopher like you. He splits hairs."

"Sit down, Mr Jeye, sit down. I've always taken an interest in philosophy."

"But even more interest in practicalities, I imagine."

"Oh, but how very wrong you are. I'm a metaphysician. I think of myself as a fixed point of sanity in a world of

46

illusion. I deal in——"

He stopped short. Fé's purse was open; she took from it the scrap of tissue paper and tossed it on to the desk. Moreau reached for it one-handed and teased it open. "That's beautiful," he said. "Really charming. Exquisitely matched. I'd be sorry to have lost this, very sorry indeed, if I were the Señora de Chaviri."

"She liked the insurance money just as much," Jeye said. "If not more."

". . . Though of course a purist might think them . . . yes, beautiful, of course, but a minor piece from the coarsely financial viewpoint."

"I don't think I'm a purist. Not really."

"No, you're a philosopher, as Fé says. You and me, Mr Jeye, we've a hold on reality. Whereas the people who traffic in these things are handling illusions. Nine times out of ten, they don't even think these gems are particularly beautiful; they just take someone else's word for it. In the same way, they take someone else's word for it that they're valuable. All they know is that they've got hold of something they don't really understand, and so they're afraid, and because they're afraid they bury them in dark safes and in blue velvet boxes. Then they wear replicas made of paste and they're happy, because with paste they know just where they are."

He leaned forwards to drop ash meticulously into the big red Murano glass ashtray; the light from the bay window snatched at his great head, picked it out in instant detail—the mop of bleached white hair, the heavy cleanshaven upper lip, the painstaking mouth. Then he leaned back; the light evened out, the face lost contour. "Do you ever read Dostoevsky?"

"No," Jeye said. "Not yet."

"Well, in one of his stories there's an interesting passage in which he claims that what people really long for is to have themselves defined—no matter how unpleasant the terms. To be a sluggard or a glutton—that's wonderful—but what's unpleasant, what indeed is unbearable is not to know what one is at all. And that's what diamonds do, you see. . . . They remind people of their essential insecurity. They buy them, maybe, to feel secure—protect themselves against inflation or whatever—yes, and what happens? They look at them. They think 'What the devil is there in *these* to give me security? In these little chips of stone? I'm told they're valuable, yes, but can I believe it?' Yet they *are* valuable, they are, if people only knew." Moreau's chest and cheeks began to shake, were convulsed with a sudden silent tremor. He was laughing.

Jeye flicked his thumb irresolutely against the side of his chin; he wasn't at all sure that he understood. He felt, for some reason, uneasy. "You may be right. I'm not all that strong on psychiatry."

"You're not? Well, after all, what do psychiatrists do that *we* don't? We listen to people, don't we?—we find out what their worries are, how much money they have, how well they sleep at night, what servants they keep, whether they're fond of dogs, whether they're always imagining they hear footsteps on the floor, at what time they expect their lovers, all these things and hundreds of others . . . then one night we come along with our little scalpels and cut away the seat of all their neuroses. Painlessly, quite painlessly. It's true, isn't it? Of course it's true."

With a vaguely self-congratulatory air he drank most of his whisky.

"It's one way of looking at it," Jeye said.

48

"But not yours?"

"Not really, no."

"Then how else would you account for the fact that a jewel thief is the one kind of criminal with which many respectable people seem to sympathise?"

"I don't have to account for it. Why should I?"

"As a scientist," Moreau said. "As a philosopher."

"I'd say, if anything, it was just the Robin Hood element. You know. Robbing the rich to help the poor."

"The poor?"

"I'm poor," Jeye said, and smiled.

Moreau laughed again, this time allowing a soft chuckling sound to escape his lips. "Yes. That theory has the merit of simplicity. You know, I think ours is going to be a profitable association, both materially and intellectually. You *are* coming in with us? That's definite?"

"Yes," Jeye said. The word cost him no appreciable effort.

"Wonderful," Moreau said. "Wonderful." He reached for the decanter. "Then we'll drink . . . the three of us . . . to future success. . . ."

"You've been drinking too much," Fé said.

"That's nonsense."

"I said drinking too much. Not drunk."

She had changed into a nylon housecoat with a blue-and-white printed pattern, and she was eating the leg of a fried chicken. While she ate she moved round the study; nervously, one might have said; and when she spoke, her eyes remained fixed on what she was eating. "I'd better put that call through to Stresemann."

"He'll be pleased."

"Yes."

". . . How did it go, Fé? Really?"

"It went all right," she said. "He probably doesn't believe he has much choice."

"That wasn't what I asked."

"Wasn't it?" She sat down, somewhat abruptly, in the big leather-backed chair with the lion's-head carvings. "Oh, he gave me what's probably the usual treatment. Bags of charm to start with. Then a frank and open discussion of his boring little sex life. You know, giving me to understand it'll be all right with *him*. But all in a *very* impersonal way, to make it seem a bit more discreet, like I said with philosophy and suchlike. He forgot about it soon enough when we got down to business."

"You're being a bit hard on him, aren't you?"

"He's not exactly a cream meringue himself."

She dropped the chicken bone on the plate; took a fold of Kleenex from her pocket and began to wipe her fingers. Moreau watched her all the time; closely, attentively. "Perhaps we should separate our feelings for our business partner from . . . well, what we feel for the male sex in general."

"I don't see why," Fé said.

"It may make things a little difficult otherwise. You'll be letting him know, will you? . . . about the call to Tangiers?"

"No need to worry." She spoke over her shoulder, on the way now to the kitchen. "I don't doubt he'll be on the 'phone tomorrow morning with some bright idea or other. A stroll in the park, maybe. Oh, no need to worry."

"Good," Moreau said. "That's all right, then."

Fé Carbonell Rodriguez de Moreau, the visiting-card said. Fillmore held it thoughtfully between his pudgy fingertips; "Oh, yes," he said. "I think so. This'd be old Carbonell's daughter. She married Moreau some time back."

Jeye took the card and slipped it back in his wallet. "Who is Carbonell?"

"Foreign Ministry. No, he died, oh, must've been in the late fifties. Rather a pal of Serrano Suñer's and a bit of a Hitler fan. Well, more than a bit. He never got anywhere near the Cabinet, but people said he was quite a power behind the scenes. I never met him."

"That's interesting. Rich?"

"Married money. Quite a big spender, though, from all accounts. Gambling, drinking, women, the lot. Of course that sort of thing used to be fashionable till Franco clamped down on it; they're a much sedater lot nowadays. In fact Pablo Jordano was telling me only the other day——"

"What about Moreau?"

"Yes, I've met *him* somewhere. Peculiar chap. Vichy Frenchman, you know, got out of it in '43 if I remember rightly and came down here, probably had a lot of pals in Madrid. In fact I have the idea old Carbonell was one. He'd be much older than the girl, of course, *much* older, but then that's becoming. . . . Peculiar chap."

"What d'you mean, Vichy Frenchman? A politician?"

"I don't think exactly a *politician*, no. I have an idea he had something to do with the police." In Jeye's admirably-trained face not a muscle moved. "But of course, collaborationist as all get-out. Hasn't a hope of ever getting back there. I even believe there was a move to get him extradited at one time, but you know the old Spanish motto. What we have we hold. Besides, I don't think they had anything very serious against him, not a war criminal or anything like that—just might have stepped over the margin here and there."

"Quite," Jeye said.

Fillmore was something on the British Council. He had been there for donkeys' years; he was the Old Spanish Hand. He was acquainted with a vast circle of people, nine-tenths of whom would run like rabbits at the sight of him; this because his main purpose in life seemed to be, as the American Ambassador once remarked in an unguarded moment, to bore the pants off anyone who couldn't get away in time. Fillmore's mind was a well of interminable anecdote undefiled, and from it endless chains of buckets rose unceasingly to the surface. Once in a while Jeye would draw a chair up to Fillmore's table at the Café Gijon and would tune in on the broadcast, occasionally deriving the expected ha'p'orth of bread from this intolerable deal of sack; but even for Jeye, once in a while was quite enough. Tonight he had Fillmore all to himself. Which was hardly surprising.

He found that he had momentarily lost the wavelength.

". . . To which," Fillmore was saying, "the Minister replied, 'I must ask for notification of that question.' Hey? Dam' good, eh? Dam' good." Jeye leaned forwards in his chair and started, metaphorically, to twiddle the knobs.

"That," he said, "reminds me. You were talking just now about Carbonell. . . ."

"I mean it all goes to show," Fillmore said. "I always say the Minister's not such a fool as some people think."

Tuning in to Fillmore could be a trying business, at times. A matter of remarkable accurate adjustment. "By the way," Jeye said, "would you fancy another cognac?"

"You know, I think I would. That's very kind of you. Oils the wheels, as I always say. Oils the wheels. Miguel? . . . Miguel?"

"*Dos coñacs, sí señor, ahora mismo.*"

"Yes. Primes the pump. Now where was I?"

"You were telling me about this chap Carbonell."

"So I was," Fillmore said. "So I was."

". . . And old Juanito? *He* was there?"

"Had the next room to mine."

"Well, good God. *Ma're de Dios.* What a screech."

"He didn't seem to like it much."

"I'll bet."

"Perhaps," Jeye said, "I shouldn't have mentioned it. I don't suppose he'd want *everyone* to know."

"Oh, it won't go any farther. You know me. After all, we're old pals and all that. So not a word. Lips are sealed. You can trust old Pepe."

"Have another drink?"

"No, this one's on me, old boy, absolutely on me. Have to watch it, though, won't I? Be ending up behind bars myself. What's it like, though, in these places, I mean is it really so utterly foul?"

"No. It's not too bad. Cheers."

"Cheers. You know," Pepe said, focusing his eyes on Jeye's tie with determination, "s'wunnerful to see you back, Michael. No, it really is. Wunnerful."

". . . Pepe?"

". . . Tell-me-tell-me-tell-me?"

"A girl called Fé Carbonell. You ever met her?"

"What? No, I don't think so. Which one does she work in?"

"Not in a *cabaret*, for God's sake."

"You mean she's OCD?"

"OCD?"

"Our Class, Darling?"

"Yes, of course, you clot. Father was some kind of a

53

politico. *Asuntos Exteriores.*"

"Oh, *that* Carbonell. Why, she got married. Some nit of a Frenchman. *That* Carbonell. Oh, yes. A smasherina. Yes, yes, yes. But anyway. What *is* all this?"

"What's all what?"

"I mean, you better watch it. That's all."

"Why? Because she's married?"

"Gahhhh," Pepe said, nicely mixing savagery and contempt. "I don't *know,* mind you, but she used to be one of the tightest bitches in town. Old Santi Quevedo had a go, I seem to remember. You could knock all you liked, he said, but you couldn't get in. There again," he said more thoughtfully, "one hears of marriage working wonders in these cases. And the husband's about *ninety* from what they tell me. You think she's about ready to. . . ? I mean, well, you fancy your chances, do you?"

"I don't know about *that,*" Jeye said. "Santi knows more than I do, probably."

"Oh, yes, he had a go. I don't know how serious he was about it, though. Poor kid didn't have any money," Pepe said cheerfully. "That was *her* trouble."

A quarter past ten, said the clock over Puerta del Sol. At the door of the Negresco, Jeye took out his handkerchief and mopped his brow. This was Madrid and the evening had barely started; but, as far as Jeye was concerned, it had been a hard day's night already.

All to some purpose, though. The pieces gradually were falling into a pattern; not a significant pattern, as yet, but

54

maybe that would come. Some night club or other off the Calle de la Pez; that was where Santi Quevedo would be; if not now, then before long. Jeye swore to himself, and shivered, and started walking.

2

IN the flat at Serrano, Moreau was writing a letter. The lamp
that stretched its metal arm across from behind his shoulder
poured warm light on to the paper, on to his big pale hands,
glinted on the gold strap of his wristwatch; while his head was
bent downwards into the shadows. He seemed to be sitting in
the midst of a pool of stillness, to be centred in it as his hands
were centred in light; the noises that Fé heard coming from
the street below—the perpetual growl of the traffic punctuated
by the sudden racket of a motor-bike, the recurrent grinding
clang of the trolley-buses—seemed unable to penetrate the
aura of oblivion he cast around him, built up through the
force of his concentration. Fé herself sat on the floor in front
of the electric fire, propped up on one arm, her legs folded
beneath her. She was aware of the fire's warmth as a gentle,
sensual tickle against her shoulder, her relaxed arm, the outside of her thigh, and also as a slow and comfortable wave of
laziness ebbing and flowing inside her. She sat there without
moving and without thinking, unless the mere awareness of
physical sensation be considered thought. She and Moreau
were perhaps six feet apart; yet they each sat in their own
little worlds of self-absorption, so adequately insulated from
each other that they might equally well have been sitting in
different rooms; or, for that matter, in different countries. Their
mutual rejection of each other's existence was such as to suggest their awareness of a kind of conflict between them; not a

57

conflict of wills, nothing so obvious; a conflict of intangibles. Whatever it was, it seemed to disappear when Moreau lifted his head into the narrow circle of light and looked towards her; she turned, as though she had sensed the movement, and smiled at him tightly. ". . . Finished?"

"For the time being," Moreau said. Carefully he screwed the cap on to his fountain pen, placed it in his inside pocket. "It's a reasonable precaution, you know. No more than that."

"A week," Fé said. "It's been a bloody *week*. What d'you suppose he's been doing?"

"Walking."

"*Walking?*"

"A stroll in the park. Remember?"

"Very funny."

"Walking, though. Here and there. Asking questions. That's what I should be doing in his place. After all, we know a lot about him and he knows next to nothing about us. Not a situation to appeal to our Mr Jeye."

"That could be dangerous."

"I don't think so. Jeye's not a fool."

"He *can't* have run away. Not and leave us with the pendant."

"I agree. As I say, one merely takes precautions."

"Well, he'll have seen the last of it, that's for sure, unless he rings through today. That 'plane leaves in the morning and whatever else happens, I'll be on it."

"I'm sure he'll call. Meanwhile I'd rather like a glass of sherry. The oloroso."

Fé sprawled out her legs, rolled to her feet. "Oh, I'm sure he'll call," she said disgustedly. "I'm sure of everything. You know what you remind me of sometimes?"

"Guessing is so fatiguing. You'd better tell me."

"An actor-manager, that's what. Of the old-fashioned school. Setting the scene just the way you want it. Left of sofa, right of sofa." She paused by the sideboard, selecting a bottle. "On the sofa. Oh, yes, the show must go on, the play's the thing. Even though you're the only one who's read it."

"I didn't mean to irritate you, Fé dear."

She put bottle and glass on the desk, by his right hand, to one side of the tray that already stood there. "It's all right. I suppose I'm nervous. God knows why."

Moreau raised his hand to her hip as she stood beside the desk, squeezed until he felt the hard jut of the bone against his fingers. Between them and her flesh there was only the blue-and-white housecoat; he released her abruptly. "The thing is," he said, "you sound as though you're blaming me for something. I wouldn't say you were being altogether fair."

"Women aren't fair," Fé said shortly. "We didn't invent them, you know—fair play or justice or any other of those things you talk about by the hour. Why *should* I be fair? That's a perfect example of what I mean. You try to plan other people's lives for them, and yet you don't understand something about women as obvious as *that*."

"You don't get the effect you want by understanding people, you know. You get it by willpower, mostly. And nothing weakens the willpower so much as the effort to understand. That's one thing at least that I learnt from the Occupation. We French tried to understand; it's a national mania. The Germans didn't bother."

He moved his hand now down the line of Fé's thigh and

59

past the swell of her buttocks, following the modelling with the possessiveness of a sculptor rather than of a lover. ". . . The effect you want," Fé said, not moving. "That's the aim, is it? To secure an effect?"

"To secure the effect you want—yes, I think so. And what I want—among other things—is for you to be happy. You believe that, don't you?"

"Yes. You're kind to me. You always have been."

"And, I hope, always will be."

"I believe that, too. But always is a long time. And it could be that all you're doing is keeping me from really growing up. . . . Had *that* ever occurred to you?"

Moreau withdrew his hand; poured himself out a glass of sherry. "I don't like it when you talk that way."

"Poor old daddy-oh," Fé said, and slipped her arm round his shoulders. "So much for the wisdom of the Sphinx. Well, none of us is perfect."

"I do need you, Fé."

"I know."

"In fact, if it weren't for you. . . ."

Moreau stopped speaking. For a moment or two, neither of them moved. Then,

"There you are, you see," Moreau said.

Fé took her arm from his shoulders, reached across the desk for the silver cigarette-box. She took out a cigarette, dropped it, picked it up again. Moreau remained motionless, slumped in the chair.

"Well?" he said. "Aren't you going to answer it?"

Fé put the cigarette in her mouth and walked away. In the next room, the harsh ringing of the telephone stopped.

Moreau began the slow transfer of his full attention from

her to the glass of sherry on the tray before him. After a while, he tested it on his palate; then sighed heavily, this although the sherry was excellent. *Mon chér M Kruger,* he thought. No. Not this time. Setting down the glass, he took wax matches from his pocket and, leaning forwards again over the desk, over the big red ashtray, set sudden bright flame to the edge of the letter. In the next room, quietly, Fé went on talking.

"I suppose," she said, "I was hoping that it wouldn't be any good."

"It?"

"Well, *this.*"

"There's no *it* involved," Jeye said. "Just you and me. That's all."

"No. That's never true."

"Anyway, I'm glad you enjoyed it."

"Oh," Fé said. "It was quaite naice."

She lay face downwards on the stripped bed. The pillow had fallen to the floor and so she had turned her head to rest it on her folded arms. A glow of fading sunlight came through the slatted window to dapple one side of her body, outline in shadow the smooth curve of her rib-cage; the line of her spine was deep and clearly-marked from between her flattened shoulder-blades down to the final steep hollow at the small of her back. Jeye, who lay in the shade, traced that line with his index finger, feeling the warmth of the sun on his hand and wrist in pleasant contrast to the coolness of the bed linen; the evening in Africa was hotter and hazier than in Spain, hotter and as though tinged with gold. Or was that nothing, he thought, but the reflection of the smooth tan of Fé's body?

61

". . . And anyway," Fé said, "what else *is* there?"

He wondered for a moment what she meant. He looked down briefly at her closed face with its closed eyes, at the long dark curves of the eyelashes merging into the darkness at her temples, at the corresponding curve of her wide mouth, the lips still slightly swollen with sexual gratification; then looked away again.

"You know, I once thought of becoming a nun. When I was fifteen or so. It's not the answer nowadays, is it? . . . And yet practically everybody thinks they'd like to, at some time or other. It's crazy."

"I read a science fiction thing not long ago," Jeye said. "Set I think two or three hundred years from now. After the Bombs had fallen. And everyone had gone back to living in monasteries again and it was all superstition, you know, like in the Middle Ages. I suppose it *could* happen."

"Why not?" Fé moved her arm a little, lifted her head. "A return to medieval monasticism. With me as Justine. Oh, it ought to sell."

"You mean Justinian."

"I certainly don't. Oh, ask Richard. *He*'ll tell you all about Justine. He'll lend you a copy. That, and Dostoevsky. You'll find we take a lot of living up to."

"I do my best," Jeye said.

"You'll find it pretty damned tiring. *I* do."

"It'd help if you liked him more."

"He's not an easy man to like. Loving's not so difficult."

"Loving, hating. Yes," Jeye said. "That's my own experience. But women usually make . . . I don't know. Another kind of demand."

"The thing about Richard is, he's real. In a way that not

many people are."

"Real to *you*."

"Real to me, yes. How can I possibly speak for anyone else?"

"And that's why you married him?"

"I suppose."

"But you don't have to run for him, too."

"Why shouldn't I?"

"It's a dangerous job," Jeye said, "pushing diamonds. Some people end up striped. Some even end up dead. You must know *that*."

"When something's real to you, you have to go all the way."

"All the way?"

"Yes. Richard taught me that. You know it already. I don't know how, because you've never been poor. But you know it. Other people don't. They're only half alive. That's the way I look at it."

"Have you been poor?"

"Worse than poor," Fé said. "Despised." She rolled inelegantly over on to her back. "Talking about it reminds me. What's the time?"

"Why ask me?"

"You're wearing a wrist-watch, aren't you? If nothing else."

"Yes, but you're lying on top of it."

She clicked her tongue in annoyance and sat up drawing up her smooth brown knees till they touched her breasts. "It must have gone five."

"It has. Just."

"We have to meet Stresemann at six."

Jeye swung his own legs off the mattress, reached for his shirt. "Sounds like a German."

"He is. That's why Richard deals with him. One of the old firm, you see."

"What old firm?"

". . . I just mean they're old friends."

"Ah, yes," Jeye said. "From Occupation days, no doubt."

"So you've been finding things out?"

"It's allowed."

He had turned away to pull on his trousers; now, struck not so much by her silence as by a certain quality of it, he turned back again. She had moved only to lower her head on to her lifted knees, the knuckles of one hand beneath her chin. Again it was the long curve of her back that caught at Jeye's attention, and at this moment he realised, for the first time, that her body was not only beautiful but was beautiful in a most unusual way; there was that in it that might create, in a painter or a sculptor, a new aesthetic image and in other men a new carnal ideal. The realisation did not, of course, come to him in those terms, but simply in terms of a need— a need that almost frightened him because, if he had ever experienced it before, he had long since forgotten it; a need to reach out and touch the girl and in touching her to reassure her. He said,

"It doesn't matter, you know."

"What doesn't?"

"All that side of it. In those days I was still at school and you hadn't even been born. I'm interested in today. Not in the past or in the future."

"Except," Fé said, "in science fiction."

"That's different. That's imaginary. This chap's real."

64

Possibly, however, Stresemann was not altogether real in the limited sense in which Fé had used the word. It was not so much that he lacked individuality; some attempt at the assumption of a personality was evident in the Don Juanesque pencil-line of his moustache and his carefully-trimmed side-boards. Rather did he seem to wish to withdraw into himself until he knew exactly where he stood, a condition very rare of fulfilment; such an attitude is very common among certain animals who spend most of their waking life sniffing at the wind, as among men who are brought into daily contact with one manifestation or another of human greed. Jeye was familiar with it as with anything else in his professional existence and remained, as far as he could, a discreet spectator. He had no wish to provoke unnecessary alarm.

Their business was transacted in Stresemann's apartment at the city end of the Marsha'an. The room that he used as an office was air-conditioned and had black Granadine rugs on the wall; there was a desk with two red telephones on it and beside it there were two very modern chairs, none too comfortable to sit in. Stresemann himself sat beside the desk in a strange rocking-chair contraption and examined the de Chaviri pendant very carefully with a jeweller's lens, stone by stone, patiently, scrupulously; his fingers were pale and quite remarkably steady. Probably a cleaver, Jeye thought, before going into the trade. He would know his stuff. He looked, however, at Fé rather than at Stresemann; she sat a yard to his right, hands resting in her lap, composed as a figure of porcelain. Again, that deceptive impression of fragility. Fragile she certainly wasn't.

Eventually Stresemann leaned back, let the lens drop from his eye down into his hand. "Yes," he said. "Most perfectly matched. Very satisfactory."

65

"In that case we needn't haggle," Fé said. "We'll take you up on your offer. I assume it still stands?"

"Of course, of course." He opened the sliding drawer of his desk, put the lens away. "Your material is always up to the mark, Fé. Always. Never any trouble. How's Richard been keeping?" He spoke in Spanish and his Spanish wasn't bad at all, though the German accent was noticeable. "Must be ages since I saw him last."

"He's very well," Fé said.

"Good. I'm glad to hear it. Though neither of us, I'm afraid, is getting any younger. Indeed, where you're concerned, my hopes are fast disappearing." His very white teeth flashed briefly under the thin dark moustache. "But then your stays here are always so short."

"Your place is much too elegant for me, Otto. I lack refinement."

"I could always have taken you down to the souqs, you know. I keep a perfectly revolting room there for girls who share your attitude. Ah, but soon, as I say, it will be too late. Such is life. I have my own business and, needless to say, I mind it. Eighteen thousand, did I say?"

"You did," said Fé; and made a sudden unexpected grimace at Jeye. Stresemann stood up to roll back one of the black rugs; the wall safe was behind it. ". . . Someone'll crack that job if you're not careful. It's too damned easy."

"Very possibly," Stresemann said pleasantly. "Very possibly. But I keep nothing of value here anyway. Only money." He swung back the safe door to reveal neatly-stacked piles of paper notes. "And here, since I was expecting you . . . eighteen thousand precisely. Used bills, of course." He slapped the folders of dollars down on to the desk, one after another. "You have a case?"

66

"Yes. Here," said Jeye. It was his sole contribution to the conversation; but, he felt, a good one.

Stresemann sat down, having already dissociated himself from the money on the desk; Jeye shovelled it quickly into his Revelation travelcase, clicked the locks shut again. Stresemann, meanwhile, had taken a chamois leather bag from his coat pocket. He lowered the pendant delicately into it; a last wink of the stones in the overhead light; they were gone. Jeye felt a sudden emptiness in his stomach, like that which precedes the onset of panic. He looked down at the case again. Stresemann pulled the cord of the bag tight, replaced it in his pocket; then smiled and lit a cigarette. "There," he said. "Now everyone's happy."

Moreau sat down at the desk; adjusted the arm of the desklamp and switched it on. The desk was strewn with papers, folders, files, typewritten flimsies, photographs; four sharpened pencils stood in readiness in the tray, and the whisky decanter was conveniently to hand. The curtains behind the desk were drawn; it was six fifteen. Moreau took a pencil, opened the uppermost folder; inside it were three closely-typed foolscap pages. JEYE, *Michael Stuart*, was the heading.

"That didn't take long, did it?"
"No," Jeye said. "What's next?"
"Coffee?"
"If you like."

Born 1932, Kensington, father Peter Jeye, jeweller and diamond merchant, (the last four words had been neatly underlined in green ink) *premises in Victoria Street. Parents killed, bombing, 1943; child evacuated to Southwick, near*

Brighton *(Mrs Allerton, mother's elder sister)*. Educated local Grammar School, withdrawn 1945 subject to medical report of nervous disorders. 1945-48, staying with various other relatives in Birmingham, Bristol, Cheltenham, attending various schools and/or receiving private tuition. Reports indicate a "difficult" child of exceptionally high intelligence; estimate confirmed by School Certificate examination result of nine distinctions, notable aptitude in foreign languages. Worked briefly in Cheltenham branch of Lloyd's Bank; military service 1949-51, private, Royal Army Service Corps. Returned to post as bank clerk until conviction, 1952, for part in payroll robbery; foregoing facts emerge from transcript of trial. Sentence of two years "in view of youth and previous good record," served at Strangeways with six months' remission, good conduct.

Associates in robbery: William Cray, George "Tiny" Baxter, two others unknown.

Associates in prison: John "Snow" White, John Fox.

Upon his release travelled to Paris, France. . . .

"Does it hurt so much, Michael?"

"What?"

"Selling them."

"Oh, *that*," Jeye said. "No. It was just the safe. I don't like safes."

"Of course not. Nobody does."

"I didn't mean from that point of view. No, I can handle safes as well as most. It's more like what Richard was saying the other day—it's the *idea* of safes I don't like."

"That's just a theory of his. Something about a safe being like a womb, he has this thing about psychology."

"Like a room?"

"No, a womb."

"I don't see any resemblance. All the same," Jeye said, "it's rather odd you should say that."

"Why?"

"Because it's almost the earliest thing I can remember. A big green safe in my father's office. It had a brass handle. I don't know why it should have struck me so much. But it did."

"The earliest thing. . . . No. I'm not sure. I think it may have been the sunlight. Coming through a window."

"That's nice," Jeye said. "That's much nicer."

"He has this theory that it's like an illness. Sometimes. You can be cured of it, I mean. He doesn't like prisons."

"Of course not," Jeye said. "Nobody does."

Fé laughed. "Sorry."

". . . Do you believe that?"

"I don't know," Fé said. "I just think there are two kinds of people. Some are real, like I said, but most people aren't. They're the ones I think are ill."

"In what way?"

"Well. . . . Not complete. I was like that once, or nearly. That's how I know."

"But Richard completed you? Is that it?"

"Yes, he did."

". . . Cured you?"

"If you like."

"The trouble with you," Jeye said, "is that you use words in a different way to other people."

"Let's not talk."

"All right."

"Let's go."

There were other files, other folders. Moreau, pencil in

hand, turned the pages through a heavy silence; the air was redolent now of cigar smoke; his forehead pained him slightly. The decanter that had been full was now one-third empty; Moreau replenished his glass. Then he went on working.

"I thought," Jeye said, "you were going to try for twenty thousand."

"I did. He wouldn't wear it."

"Well, didn't you argue?"

"I never argue."

"Why the hell not?"

"You said it was a dangerous job," Fé said sleepily. "So it is, if you make it so. Satisfied clients don't cause you any trouble."

"I suppose that's what Richard says."

"I say so, too."

On the hotel bed, they had just made love again. Now they were disliking each other, rather.

"We don't have to go back tomorrow," Fé said. "We don't even have to get up. Not till late. I'm glad. I'm tired."

"When's the job?"

"Soon," Fé said. "It's being lined up now."

"I won't be seeing much of you, then. When we get to Madrid."

"It'll soon be over. Then we can take another holiday. If you want."

Jeye grunted. "Where?"

"Anywhere. Casablanca's nice this time of year. Or Málaga. Do you like sailing?"

"Not as much."

"As much as what? . . . No, don't tell me. I've got it. Still, it might do for a change, mightn't it?"

"We'll probably need it. What about *him*?"

"Who?"

"You know who. Your . . . Richard."

"If we go to Málaga, he'll probably come too."

"That'll be jolly," Jeye said.

"Yes. Quite good fun."

Jeye gave it up.

"We've got a yacht in Málaga. He belongs to three or four yacht clubs, Richard does, but that's just in the line of business. He doesn't really like it. I do, though."

"You meet the right people, of course. But it's a damned expensive way of going about it."

"It's worth it."

"If you're lucky. Like everything else."

"Tina Cespedes was there a month ago."

"I've never seen her," Jeye said. "Not even in the films."

"Oh, she's a lousy actress. Hasn't a clue. But she's got a necklace that I wouldn't mind. . . . Cape stones, but damned good ones. Braguette cut. Salinas chose it for her, of course, which accounts for it."

"Pedro Salinas?"

"*He* was there last month, too. At a discreet distance. Well, fairly discreet." She turned her head abruptly on the pillow. "What's the matter?"

"Nothing," Jeye said.

"He's a collector, you know."

"Yes, I know," Jeye said.

"You haven't been thinking. . . . I mean, you're not *mad*, are you? No one in his senses'd take on Salinas."

"Is she attractive?"

"Who?"

"The Cespedes."

71

"Oh, she's lovely," Fé said. "Really lovely."

She closed her eyes. Only the dregs of the pallid African moonlight were seeping into the room, and she couldn't see him anyway; nothing of his expression; just the blur of his head and shoulders on the whiteness of the pillow. And Jeye, whose eyes were open, saw only the ceiling, the dim white-plastered ceiling above the bed.

Lovely, he thought. No, Fé isn't lovely. Lovely is just a word. But Fé, Fé was here before all words, before all language; there was no word for her and never would be. *You use words in a different way*, he thought; that's why. Love, then, she feels for Richard. She says that; she means something else. And what about this? Love, lust, fornication? Yes, those are pretty words, too. Pretty, like stars in the Spanish sky, with light years yawning between them, *les éspaces infinis*; but the spaces between words, aren't they just as frightening? The gaps, those murderous gaps, that horrible vertiginous gulf that opens when two and two make four. . . . Fé lived in those spaces; was happy there, needed no explanation. The rest of us have to use words, words like stepping-stones over infinity; we miss a step, we slip, then falling, falling. . . .

(Jeye's eyes were closed now)

. . . falling. . . .

Moreau rubbed his eyes, squeezed the bridge of his nose. He looked at his wrist-watch. Two o'clock. There was a faint yet insistent buzzing in his ears, and slow circles of pain radiated outwards from his forehead. The work was finished; now he would go to bed and perhaps, after taking nembutal, sleep. The pain was bad tonight. He took his head between his hands, pressed tightly his brow, the high dome of his forehead. His hands, when he took them away, were trembling.

3

BY three o'clock the conference seemed to have run its course. Fé had gone out, ten minutes earlier, to make some coffee; Moreau sat at the desk, Jeye by the open window. The fresh evening air touched his face, lifted the strands of soft fair hair that had fallen over his forehead. Since Fé had left the room, neither of them had spoken.

". . . Anyway," Moreau said eventually, "the Lagranja job is the one to tackle first. That's clear as daylight. That's the only one where the main difficulty is the time factor, right?"

"Right," Jeye said. He ran his fingers through his hair. "Let's hear those dates again."

"They go to Paris every year," Moreau said. Slowly, patiently. "Always at the end of this month. They've never left before the 25th, never later than the fifth of March. So next week, obviously, is the operative one. When they start the packing, she gets the chinos out of the deposit, that's in the Banco de Bilbao off the Calle Sevilla. She takes them home. When she does that, we'll know we have two or three days to work in. Not more."

Jeye leaned forwards to look past Moreau's bulky shoulder at the paper he held, at the glossy photograph clipped to the top sheet. "Second floor bedroom, you said."

"Second floor bedroom. At the head of the staircase, first

of five. That's in a sixteen-roomed house. That part of it could be worse."

"Three maids, one living in, a chauffeur living in. A cook living out. That's two there at night."

"They're married, you'll have noticed."

"So they are. Yes, that's good. Okay."

"It smells right?" Moreau seemed suddenly anxious.

"Yes, it smells right."

"You'll look into it, then? And we'll keep an eye on the bank."

Jeye raised his eyes from the paper, the photograph, to look through the window, through and down to the street beneath. Serrano on a fine February evening, the sky clear and clean behind the rooftops, the traffic moving down the wide grey roadway, unhurriedly but noisily. And in the evening, in that contrast of movement and stillness, that intangible something that one senses in Madrid when winter is definitely over, spring at last on the way. I ought to be down there, Jeye thought suddenly; I'm not doing anything here that's worth while. Down there, that's where I ought to be.

"Yes," he said. "I'll look into it. And next week, if things are right, we'll hit it. Fair enough."

"Not before." Moreau was smiling; Jeye wondered why.

"Right. Now I'd better be going."

"I knew you were going to say that. You're an *odd* fellow, Michael, you really are. If I didn't know your method of working, I'd say you were ruled entirely by impulse. You look out of the window—you think, I must be going—and so you go. It's as simple as that."

"Well, leaving a room," Jeye said. "It's not all that difficult."

"The point is that the idea just doesn't occur to you until our little discussion has reached a satisfactory conclusion. Then bingo, that's it. I wish my subconscious were as reliable as yours seems to be."

"I don't know about reliable," Jeye said. "I trust it, anyway. We'll keep in touch by 'phone then, shall we?"

"Yes, but look, Fé's making the coffee."

"I don't want any coffee," Jeye said.

He heard the clock of San Ildefonso striking six, and glanced down to check his wrist-watch; then looked back towards the gravel drive with the wrought-iron gate. The chauffeur was wearing his off-duty clothes that evening; flat linen cap, fur-lined jacket, grey flannel trousers. Dead chulo. Past the gates, he turned sharp left and walked some fifty feet along the pavement to the postbox in the wall; Jeye could see the letters in his right hand. He flicked them casually through the slot, then went on sauntering casually down the street. Jeye got out of the car.

Six o'clock on a Wednesday evening in a quiet Madrid suburb. Just like Tuesday evening, Monday evening, Sunday evening, Saturday evening; the chauffeur had already turned out of sight; the street was deserted. Jeye crossed the road, his hands pushed into his pockets, and paused before the postbox. He leaned against the wall for a moment, his shoulders slightly hunched; the probe found the spring of the lock, pushed it back. Inside there were no more than a dozen envelopes; Jeye took the top six, pushing them inside his coat, then pressed the door of the box back into place with his elbow. It was colder, he noticed, than it had been on the Monday and the Tuesday. He strolled back to where the car

77

was parked, lifting the collar of his coat against the wind.

On the floor of the car a miniature burner glowed with a quiet, steady flame. Sitting in the driving seat, Jeye took the letters from his inside pocket, glanced at them briefly and discarded two of them. He knew the Señora de Lagranja's handwriting by now; too bloody well, in fact.

The first envelope was addressed to Don Martin Hinojosa, Lafcadio 11. Jeye stooped, passed it over the steaming metal cup that rested over the flame of the burner. Then he opened it, read the contents thoughtfully; re-sealed it. He worked his way conscientiously through the other three; then, when he had finished, he blew out the burner flame and went across the road to post the letters once more.

He drove away towards Cuatro Caminos, stopped at a bar in the Rio Rosa and went in to telephone.

"You're sure about the bank?"

"Quite sure."

"Then it looks like tomorrow."

"You'd better come round," Fé said.

"I'll be there at eight."

"Eight?"

"Yes, I want to shave and change."

"All right."

The receiver clicked against Jeye's ear. He put it down; went through to the bar and seated himself at the counter. He asked for another cognac. The radio was playing something by the Cinco Latinos, one of their slower numbers with a pleasantly insistent, soothing beat. Jeye listened to it, trying to let his tiredness be drained away by the music but not succeeding. The Soberano tingled in his throat. One thing, anyway. The waiting was over.

He had had enough of reading other people's letters. Especially those written in Leonora de Lagranja's unformed, backslanting, convent-schoolgirl's script, all twisting curlicues and violet ink; all so dull, so monumentally dull. She wrote at least three a day, long ones at that. She herself was bored stiff, obviously, or she wouldn't have the time. The day after the robbery she'd probably write at least thirty; it would cheer her up enormously, brighten her life. But Jeye wouldn't be reading them, thank heaven.

Even that one to Finojoso, dull, dull, dull. The emotions it tried to convey were manufactured, synthetic, false. And yet she was certainly prettier than the average, pleasing face and excellent figure, and young, too, hardly thirty yet. Good family, rich husband, no children; a background not so very different, outwardly to Fé's. Why, then? Why, why, why?

Jeye rested his chin on his hands. It was true, what Fé had said; these people weren't real. It was always the same, always, whenever he came into contact with that kind of an existence—you couldn't call it a life; with the mind—you couldn't call it a soul—of any of The Others. What he felt was always the same; neither hatred nor despair; something between the two and quite different from each; something that was almost fear, almost terror. A sense of loneliness, of deprivation, of being cut off; a sense of eternal and irreparable wrong; a sense of need. Need for what?' . . . He didn't know. Perhaps for another loneliness of a wilder and more penetrating kind, the loneliness that lies in the five-foot swing from drainpipe to gutter rail and in the fifty-foot drop that snatches up at you when the gutter gives way. When, not if.

79

Sooner or later, it has to happen. Trust is irrational; hence you can trust the gutter and still know that one day, sooner or later, one day it will break. Either way, diamonds are immortal.

Jeye paid the barman, got up from the uncomfortable plastic-topped stool and went out. In the wide street it was almost dusk. He paused a moment to button up his overcoat; an unknown singer on Radio Madrid commenced another song.

Siempre,
quierame siempre,
tanto . . . que yo a tí. . . .

Perhaps Leonora de Lagranja was listening to the radio, too. With one neat stiletto-heeled shoe beating out the time. *Siempre* would be a long wait for her, a long, long wait; what would she do in eternity, where no time would exist to tap her foot to? Poor little sod, thought Jeye. She's human, that's her trouble, she's made of flesh and blood. Only diamonds can stand the awful vacancy of *always*. For her, for me, for everyone, a something else called death.

Good old death, Jeye thought; the one and only deterrent. That's what keeps 'em straight. What's a spell in bird compared to it? A vote for death is a vote for decent living. Choose your candidate now.

Or, no. Not now. Now is life. Fé. And tiredness. The coolness of the evening. A quick shower, a shave, a clean shirt. The surge of power in the motor of the Citroen. He turned the ignition key and drove off. In the bar, the radio went on playing; but the barman had gone into the back room and no one was listening.

"Well," Fé said. "What have you found?"

"Acknowledged two tickets for the Menuhin concert and sent a cheque. It starts at eight-thirty."

"Anything else?"

"Not unless we're going in for blackmail."

"Well, and are we?"

"I don't think so. It's a Cabinet Minister."

"Really? Which one?"

"Finojosa."

"Yes, Public Works, there you are. The chances are that dear Arturo knows all about it. He can use a contract as well as the next man."

"Finojosa's a bachelor," Moreau said. "I'd have thought he could have done rather better."

"Oh, no, she's madly decorative. Very good family, too, which God knows Finojosa isn't."

Moreau sighed. "That's as may be. A pity it's the Menuhin, though. I've a ticket for that myself."

He rubbed his neck abstractedly, the plain gold ring on his fourth finger brimming with captured light.

"They leave on the day after," Jeye said. "Friday evening. At least, that's what she told Finojosa."

"Thursday, that's Juana's evening off."

"The house'll be empty," Jeye said. "It's a real old doddle. We can't miss."

"For how long, though? How far away is the theatre?"

"Seven minutes, driving fast. I timed it."

"*Does* he drive fast? The chauffeur?"

"Yes."

"There'll be a bit of a crush, though, with Menuhin playing. Still, you're right to be cautious. That gives us fifteen minutes, say."

81

"Right," Jeye said. "Just enough."

"For two of us, yes. If we're damned quick. We'll both go in, then, and Fé'll do the driving."

"What car?"

"The Citroen, I think. We have the plates to hand. You can leave all that to Fé."

"Eight o'clock? Or earlier?"

"Let's say eight o'clock here. Your watch keep good time?"

"Yes."

"That's it, then." Moreau sighed again, this time with satisfaction. "We'll take a glass of sherry, shall we?—and then I expect you'll be wanting to get some sleep. You've been pretty much on the go these last three days."

Fé got up from the armchair, walked towards the sideboard where the sherry bottles stood. Jeye, watching her, thought that she, too, seemed to be tired; mentally, though, rather than physically. Moreau said,

"No guns, of course."

"Good God, no," Jeye said. "I haven't even got one."

"I was quite sure you hadn't."

Going in together then, Jeye thought, for the first time since Snowy White. With Richard. With someone I don't know and don't begin to understand. Yet it doesn't seem so strange. Because of the way he takes it all for granted, perhaps. Because of his self-confidence. That's a good thing to have.

. . . And the odd thing is that he might be sensitive. Moreau might. Behind the façade. Something delicate, something easily wounded. *Caracol, col, col, pon tus cuernos en el sol.* Moreau's words were like that, like the horns of a snail, with their perpetual, seemingly meaningless probing. And beneath that armour of intellectuality, perhaps, a grey soft body like a slug's, trembling, pathetic. Oh, there was *something* there; something that Fé could love, after a fashion; she'd said so. Something to be loved, yes, but nothing palpable enough to be liked. At any rate by Jeye. Yet the prospect of going in with someone, that sets up a certain link, a certain empathy. Like marriage, in a way. Though *that*, no, he still didn't understand. . . .

No. He was too tired, anyway, to cope with that kind of a question. Better to drink his sherry and go. Fé had placed the glass on the table to his right, almost as though to avoid the touch of his fingers on her own; he picked it up and drank. The wine tasted smoky and slightly bitter, coating the surface of his tongue. "I'll be going, then," he said.

Fé went with him to the door of the flat. He took her hand, lightly, as they passed through the hall; then, before she had opened the door, he put his arm round her shoulders and kissed her. Her lips felt cool; unresisting but unresponsive. "You're tired," she said. "And when you're tired, I feel it. Strange, isn't it?"

"Eight tomorrow."

"Yes."

He went through the door, and she closed it behind him and rested her head for a moment against the varnished wood. That way, she could hear his footsteps fading away down the corridor. Her mouth felt numb, yet tickled her, as though the nerves there were crawling back to life after an injection of cocaine. She went back to the study and carried Jeye's empty glass over to the sideboard. Moreau's glass, only half-empty as yet, was still in his hand; he held it musingly, as though he had forgotten its presence there. In the end he raised his head and said,

"What's the matter? Afraid?"

"Yes. A little."

"Butterflies?"

"Yes. Not for the job, though. That's all right."

"Then what?"

"I don't know," Fé said.

Moreau reached up again to rub the base of his neck with his forefinger. The lapels of his dressing-robe opened with the movement—it was of heavy blue silk, cut loosely, Italian style—to show the loosened collar of his pale blue shirt. "Does he talk much?"

"Michael? . . . To me, you mean? . . . Yes, quite a bit."

"He's coming out, you see. Out of the shell. There's an interesting creature called the hermit crab." Rub, rub, rub. A faint red patch on the loose white skin of the throat. "It has no shell of its own; it lives in shells discarded by other animals. And as it grows, it has to change, to move from one shell to a bigger one. And to do that, it has to come out. Just for a few seconds, it has no protection at all; it's a nasty moment. But it has no choice."

"And that's Michael?"

"That's Michael. That's all of us. But Michael in particular."

"He's afraid, then?"

"Not of the job. But of us. Of having to change. And fear is very contagious."

"Yes," Fé admitted. "Yes. It *could* be that."

"There again, it's mostly *you* he's afraid of."

"Why?"

"Because one always tries to give fear a definite object. Because you are the agent, so to speak. There'll have been plenty of women in his life, of course, but all the others have

84

stayed outside the shell. He hasn't *talked* to them; he isn't a fool. But he can talk to you. And he will. Because everyone wants to. Self-discipline has its limits. But there won't be room for two of you in that tight little shell of his. So he'll have to change. He'll have to come out."

"And then?"

"Then we'll see," Moreau said. "Won't we?"

Fé sat down, crosslegged, by the electric fire. It wasn't warm that evening. She felt cold.

Jeye wore dark grey terylene trousers, brown cotton shirt, grey cotton jacket and black crepe-soled shoes. Moreau wore black tie and dinner jacket, with a black silk scarf knotted loosely round his throat. He sat by the electric fire, carefully applying nail varnish with a nylon brush to the underside of his fingers, then holding them towards the filament for the heat to dry them. Jeye had spread over the desk the wide slotted canvas belt that held the tools; they gleamed in the overhead light, not brightly but dully; squat, blunt, arrogant instruments, radiating not heat but power. Now he picked up the belt and fastened it to the inside of his raincoat, passing it through a series of flanges; when he had done this he put the raincoat on, clipped the belt shut, buttoned and belted the raincoat. All the while he frowned; a frown of concentration. "It's time we moved," he said.

Moreau nodded; pressed fingertips cautiously on thumbtips, testing the dryness of the varnish. "Shall we check?"

"Coming up to nine minutes past eight," Jeye said, his head lowered over his cocked wrist. "Six, five, four, three, two, one, *now*."

"Right."

"Right."

Moreau slipped on his dark overcoat, inspected himself briefly in the mirror, then stooped to switch the fire off. They left the flat, leaving the lights burning, and walked downstairs together. Outside the car was waiting. It had been a fine day, but the gathering night had brought with it low, dark cloud brimming over from the west; Jeye lifted his face as they crossed the pavement, felt the feathery touch of the raindrops on his cheek. The street was luminous with reflected light, the road swimming in the sharp metallic glitter of the headlights. He slumped back in the seat beside Moreau, feeling the familiar hard encirclement of the toolbelt around his waist. Moreau glanced towards him. "All set?"

"All set."

"Right, Fé. Let's go."

Nothing wrong. Nothing wrong at all. Why should there be? You watch and you plan, you allow for every contingency. You wait and you wait and you wait. Then it comes. The moment of carelessness; the victim drops its head to nibble at the grass; then all the signals are already set and there's nothing to do or say but to make the hit. Ready, steady, and go-go-go. The odds are right. As good as they ever are. So right, that's it. The worrying's over.

Jeye rested his head on the cushioned seat. Closed his eyes.

She parked the car a hundred yards or so from the front gate; let the engine tick over for a few more seconds, then killed it. There was silence then, except for the almost inaudible walking the raindrops over the roof. Above the high brick wall and mingled with the swirling of the rain, a faint glow; the lights of the house, burning strongly. Jeye watched that glow for a moment; looked right, looked left; then sat back in the seat again. He could feel, rather than hear, the slow rhythmic vibration of Moreau's breathing; Fé, in the driver's seat before him, sat still as stone. Only once did he sense her foot moving, not more than a couple of inches across the floor; accelerating into the getaway, perhaps, in her imagination. A car went by, travelling fast, its tyres whirling up spray as it rounded the corner at the end of the street; then another, coming from the opposite direction. Moreau looked at his watch, then at Jeye. Jeye grimaced.

"He's running it a bit fine, wouldn't you say?"

"He wouldn't get there early," Moreau said. "That'd be infra dig."

"I was forgetting it'd be just another bloody concert."

Jeye stopped. They had all heard it. The note rose to a high pitch as the motor revved up, then fell; a silvery brightness shone for a moment on top of the wall, then disappeared. "Nineteen minutes past," Moreau said. "Just about dead right. Couldn't be more punctual."

In the distance behind the wall, a door slammed. Fé turned the ignition key; the motor of the Citroen began to quiver expectantly. A wide splash of silver yawned across the street in front of them; grew wider and wider, splintered with black shadows; the Lagranjas' car emerged slowly from between the wrought-iron gates, turned away to the left, thrummed off down the street, picking up speed. The Citroen was rolling forwards now; already Moreau had freed the door handle. Then, as the car swung past the gates, the door was wide open and he was outside, his feet gritting on the rough gravel; Jeye out too, a second later; the car travelled on, the sound of its engine no more than a gentle whisper, and the two men were walking, not running but walking fast, up the drive towards the front door. The rain was falling more heavily now;

Moreau's fingers touched his neck, pulling his overcoat collar
more tightly about him. The house was blazing with light;
light shone at them from all three of the big ground-floor windows, silhouetting their shadows harshly on the ground behind them. The house was also silent; silent as a tomb of brick
and glass. Everything was as expected, even to the air of slight
uncanniness; it was as though they were arriving as honoured
guests—like Don Juan—to a party of phantoms. Jeye's nose
wrinkled as he mounted the damp steps, stood in the shadows
of the porch. Moreau, a pace behind him, turned to look
slowly over the grounds, glanced back in time to see Jeye's
shoulders bunch and thrust, the front door jerk open with a
faint protesting whine. They went in together.

There were three side lamps in the long hall, each of which
was burning. Centre and overhead, a huge and elaborate cut-
glass candelabra broke the glow of the bulbs into fragments,
made the skin of their upturned faces seem pallid. They
mounted the stairs two steps at a time; paused for a second
at the landing, then turned left. Jeye tried the handle of the
bedroom door; it wasn't locked. He made straight for the tall
Colonial-style wardrobe in the corner; Moreau, at his heels,
swung right and passed through into the adjoining dressing-
room.

The wardrobe was locked. Jeye's gloved hands tested the
strength of the bolt, paused for a moment in bafflement; his
eyes became suddenly fixed, intent, as the resistance of the
lock to his fingers built up the familiar wave of savagery in
the depths of his brain, released into his muscles the slow
charge of carefully-hoarded energy. He bared his teeth, jerked
at the handle with all his strength; the lock bent, twisted,
gave way. He went through the wardrobe in thirty seconds
flat, leaving behind him a havoc of crumpled suits, of ex-

quisite Parisian dresses torn from their hangers, of costumes
dangling from their pegs like broken-necked corpses; turned
in a flash to the dressing-table; yanked out the top drawer
and hurled it on the bed, spilling its contents over the carpet
and counterpane. His eyes detailed the items dispassionately
while his hands were tearing out the next drawer; in fifteen
seconds the dressing-table was totally gutted, left raffish and
leering like a toothless mouth. Jeye began to pace round the
room, searching the walls, the floor; his breath was rasping
now in his throat; he moved anti-clockwise, missing nothing,
touching nothing twice; rifled hatboxes, shoes, ties, lingerie,
joined the maelstrom of twisted clothes on the carpet. The
rasp of his breath, the beat of his blood began to shape themselves into words. . . . *Bitch, bitch, bloody bitch. Bitch, bitch,
bloody bitch.* . . . He snatched the pillows from the bed, pulled
aside sheets and blankets, ran his hands over the mattress.
Nothing. Nothing.

Moreau, in the dressing-room, moved with the assured calm
of a distinguished clinician. Everything he touched he
touched with apparent distaste, barely disturbing it. He had
found Leonora's jewel-box in the first thirty seconds; but not
the right one, not the one they wanted. It was small stuff;
pendants, brooches, ear-rings. He slipped it into his pocket, all
the same. Now he was checking, as Jeye had done in the
bedroom, the walls and floor, tracing the electric points and
probable course of the cables with a lack-lustre eye and hear-
ing from the next room the sound of Jeye's barely-muffled
curses. . . . *Where are they? Where've you put them? Bloody
bitch.* . . . Seeming to be floated aloft on a vast impersonal
fury, wrecking the room with cold and systematic crudity,
with a devastating thoroughness. The only item of furniture
left was the little walnut escritorio in the other corner; un-

likely, very unlikely; he tilted it over, letting the drawers slide out and on to the carpet; nothing, nothing. Secret drawer? . . . He turned it round, kicked the back in. Spintered wood; nothing. No. *Nada. Nada.* He swung round once more, the hot floods of hatred coursing through his body; *Where've you put them, coño? Dónde están?* . . . Frustration, sheer and utter; unbearable. Oh, to kill, to rape, to ravish; the bloody sadistic well-dressed smiling shiny-magazine social-swim bastard bitch of a woman, she's hidden them but where, where, *where?*

Moreau came through the door, eyebrows raised in puzzlement. "Nothing?"

"Nothing."

"We'd better try *his* room."

"No. They're here."

"You're sure?"

"Yes. I'm sure."

Forehead, cheeks, neck, chest all wet and sticky with sweat. He lifted his head mournfully, standing with his feet apart in the centre of the room; twelve minutes, twelve blasted minutes gone out of the fifteen. It was no good. He was wrong. They were somewhere else, in some other room, there wasn't time. And it was too hot. He was too hot, with this blasted central heating. It was on. That was why. Or was it?

He jerked the glove from his right hand, touched his knuckles to the radiator grille. Cold. Stone cold. He pulled on the glove again, seized the top of the grille, braced both feet against the base of the wall. . . . A tearing, a rending, a buckling; the metal collapsed. Behind the grille, a recess. In the recess, a safe. "Torch," Jeye said, unbelting his raincoat. Moreau stooped down beside him.

"... Well?"

"I think so," Jeye said.

The tool-belt was spread out on the floor beside him. Hairline chisel, mallet, muffle. The gloved hands moved at controlled speed; he breathed deeply now, evenly, in silence. The chisel slipped. He paused to steady his wrist with the prop of his elbow.

"Fourteen," Moreau said.

The mallet rose and fell. There was a snap little louder than a click. "Cane," Jeye said. Moreau had it ready in his hand. Jeye slid it into place, adjusted his grip; put on the pressure. The safe door flicked open.

Inside there was nothing but a grey-painted safety-box. Jeye scooped it up, smashed the lock to pieces against the twisted shards of the grille, three terrific, resounding blows. A tooled-leather jewel-case; he twisted open the clasp, snapped back the lid. He looked at Moreau. Moreau nodded.

They walked down the stairs, Jeye adjusting the tool-belt as they went; crossed the hall, went through the front door to pause on top of the steps. The black shape of the Citroen edged in through the gates, shining suddenly as it entered the circle of light from the windows. The side door swung open; the car came almost to a halt, then accelerated away. Gravel rattled against metal; then there was the road hissing comfortably under the tyres and the street opening out before them. Jeye, collapsed into the front seat beside Fé, peeled off his gloves in two abrupt, jerky movements; took a handkerchief from his pocket to wipe the mingled rain and perspiration from his face.

Headlights blinked into his eyes as they turned into the main road, were instantly dimmed. The Mercedes hummed past them, slowing down to make the turn; Jeye had a brief glimpse of the Lagranjas' chauffeur at the wheel, black peak cap tilted back on his head, a cigarette slanting from his mouth. Driving back alone to a cold supper and a glass of beer. Jeye leaned over towards Fé to watch the red rear lights curve away and vanish from the driving mirror; heard Moreau's voice from behind him,

"We timed that nicely. Just the way I like it."

. . . Jovial with a huge, all-encompassing enjoyment. He put his handkerchief back in his pocket. Fé was using that same perfume again tonight.

"Straight to the concert?" she said.

"Certainly. I won't have missed more than the opening." A sound underlying the voice, a rattle, a pebble-like chink but harder, sharper in tone than any pebble; the sound of jewellery sliding, pouring from cupped hand into open bag. "I wouldn't care not to be in my seat for Menuhin, you know He hardly ever comes to Spain these days."

"Is everything there?" Jeye said.

"I fancy so. Fé'll check the list. I'll leave the bag in the glove compartment, as usual."

Fé didn't trouble to nod. They were in the main stream of traffic running down to the Castellana now, and she was driving carefully, with tight-lipped concentration. Past the Hilton, she pulled in to the side and halted the car; Moreau got out without a word and began to walk up the slope towards the pool of bright neon lighting that, some fifty paces away, marked the foyer of the theatre. The Citroen rolled forwards once more; Fé began to whistle under her breath. The lights at Colón were green; she drove on. Jeye turned his head.

"Aren't you dropping me here?"

"No," she said. "What for?"

"I was to take the Métro. That's what we arranged."

"Oh, God, do we *always* have to do what Richard says?"

"Not if you don't want."

"Let's go back to the flat, then."

Yes, but it had to be wrong. You plan for after the hit as well, because you know that that's when you're vulnerable. When you're feeling good, that's just when you're weak. You know that before, and you know it after. But after, you just don't care. It doesn't matter any more. Fate cannot harm you; you have robbed today. So up with the old two fingers. All right, it's wrong. So let's do it.

Jeye turned his head again. His tiredness was going, was gone. This was the good feeling; this was what it was all *for*. Fé's profile; long nose, full upper lip; the hair brushed straight back from her forehead. Again, in his imagination, he smelt the sea. Her profile dark against the yellow glow of the passing street lamps. Now it would be back to the sunlight.

His fingertips were just touching her shoulder.

On the desk, in apparent disorder, the Lagranja jewels. Jeye sat in the deep chair; Fé on the edge of the desk itself. Figures circled, clicked together in her brain: four and twelve and four. twenty thousand, and forty, call it sixty thousand dollars at Tangiers rates. Maybe more. And surely not very much less; nothing there was great, but all of it was good. The small stuff could go through France; would make another five, maybe. In any case the list was complete. That was the main thing. They'd got what they'd gone for.

Fé had made coffee, but hadn't changed; she still wore the suede jacket, grey shot-silk blouse and tight brown slacks she had worn on the job. Her calculations complete, she reached

93

for the coffee-cup that as yet she hadn't touched; looked at
Jeye. ". . . Unwound yet?"

"It wasn't so tough," Jeye said, and smiled. "I was a bit
slow in finding the safe, though."

"A good one?"

"No. She wouldn't have needed the bank, if it had been.
What about the stuff?"

"Sixty thousand, I'd say. Your cut'd be twenty, less ten
per cent to me if I run them for you, say eighteen, anyway,
not bad at all for a fast job."

"Yes, but how *good*?" Jeye got to his feet. He had relaxed
for fifteen minutes and now he was ready, ready to look. He
leaned the palms of both hands on the desk. He looked. Fé
found that her own hands had clenched themselves tensely
against her thighs; unobtrusively, she let them go limp again.
It was all right. For once, Jeye hadn't noticed.

". . . Not so good," he said in the end. "About what I'd
supposed. Pretty vulgar, really."

"Well, you've seen the photographs."

"You can't tell from photographs. The people who wear the
stuff, they get in the way."

"Still, look at the centrepiece. There's a diamond for
you."

"A Marquise."

"Yes." Fé picked up the necklace, dangled it from her
fingers; the centre stone dripped a cold wild splendour, an
intangible blueness, a blueness that turned to purple out of
sight in its very depths. "I see what you mean, though. The
setting's awful."

"Hard to set a stone like that," Jeye said, "unless you've got
a lot of Crown Jewels to play around with. It's a good piece,
all right. I don't like it, that's all."

"Too good for the Lagranja . . . between you and me."

"I don't know," Jeye said. "That's a greedy stone. I'd say it was about right."

She swung her feet down to the floor, walked over to the far door and went through. Jeye, in abstracted mood, continued to eye the jewels, finishing off his coffee as he did so. ". . . Hey."

". . . What?"

"What're you doing?"

". . . Trying it on."

Her voice coming from the next room, slightly distorted by some acoustic effect of the panelling. Jeye put down his cup. "Good God, don't do *that*."

He followed her into the bedroom. She was standing in front of the wardrobe mirror, adjusting the set of the great pale star at the base of her throat. ". . . I just want to see how it looks."

"It looks lousy," Jeye said. "Take it off."

"It's all right for Leonora, you say. Why shouldn't it be all right for me?"

She narrowed her eyes, staring at the other Fé at the back of the full-length mirror. Her shoulders moved to and fro, helping the diamond in its search for the light; but as though they themselves were trapped, her body trapped, in soft brown suede, in the shining gunbarrel grey of stiff silk; inside the vee of her blouse the diamond shone, enormous, hostile, indifferent, all those things and many others; even absurd. Well, yes, absurd. And how, she wondered for a moment, had she *expected* it to look? It needed an evening dress, low cut, a background of cool and colourless flesh. Diamonds don't go with suede.

"You're not Leonora," Jeye said.

"You know, I like it."

"You don't. You can't. Take the bloody thing off."

He took her by the shoulders, swung her round. He was angry. Really angry. She hadn't realised. His fingers, where they gripped her, had the strength of pliers. "You're not greedy," Jeye said. Only his voice was calm.

"Please. You're hurting me."

"Then take it off."

"But I *am* greedy. No, please. *Please*."

She twisted backwards as his hand came up at her throat; the tautened fingers clawed at the necklace, missed by a fraction, ripped open the top of her blouse. The breath jerked out of her lungs in what was almost a laugh; "What the *hell* are you doing?"

His eyes on the torn silk, on the trembling diamond, murderously intent. ". . . No. No, *don't*. All right, I'll take it——"

A burning pain on the back of her neck as the clasp of the necklace snapped; it slithered down to the carpet, lay there at her feet, a spilled pool of frost, lost and forgotten. The suede jacket fell on top of it, its dark folds hiding it from view. And the blouse pulled back now from her shoulders, his mouth following the course of the raptored necklace past her neck and down towards the stiff flowered cups of her brassiere; and she was laughing now as she had laughed that time in the restaurant, unable to stop. "You're mad. you're *mad*. Oh, God, no. Not that as well." Turning in his arms she saw herself, Fé-in-the-mirror again; her eyes wide open now and shocked, long brown back arched and tensed as though diving outwards, diving away through the yielding mists of the mirror, away into freedom; Fé-through-the-Looking-Glass, yes, with the smashed glass of the cage broken at her feet, broken and washed to and fro by the waves that lapped there. Her breasts in sudden profile as the hook snaps loose, her breasts, their risen nipples between his fingers; her eyes close in instant reflex and nothing is left but her own body, naked like a pearl and diving, always diving. "Mad. We're mad." Diving or falling, what was it? Into the abyss. The slacks coming open with a faint whisper, a whisper of reply; cloth brushing her thighs, her knees; his hands, how could they be so gentle? On the floor, dead, lifeless, her clothes, like the broken cocoon of a chrysalis. "Have you finished?"

His voice within her head like the echo of her own.

"Finished? We haven't even started."

"No, I meant have you finished? . . . undressing me?"

". . . Don't you know?"

"I don't want you to finish. Not ever."

His hands touching her ankles. She lifted her feet from the floor, one by one. "There. Now I've finished."

"Carry me, then."

"It's all of ten feet away. We'd never get there."

His hand closed over hers, pulling her downwards. Down to the floor. It took her a long, long time to join him there; it must have been even farther than the bed. Three seconds, maybe? She lay stretched out by their crumpled clothes, beside the diamonds. All the clocks stopped.

He hooked the black silk around the knuckles of his left hand, played it out softly with his right; while the violin caught at the theme and swept it effortlessly into its compass. Then the raised right hand of the conductor beckoned the orchestra in once more, and the solo violin hovered on the edge of soundlessness, dipped and disappeared. The restless murmuring of the horns became muted, and there was the

97

theme again, rising around Moreau like the warm vector that sustains a glider on its course, easing the pace of its giddy swoop, lapping it in air; the end of the scarf came loose from his fingers, slipped from his lap to trail unnoticed on the floor.

It was all there, he thought; all of it. *Music for servant-girls*, Dubos had called it, that time in Paris. In those days, nothing German could be good. Not Beethoven, not Furtwangler. Yet in those days, what else had there been? It was simply that Dubos hadn't cared to learn. That was why he was dead. And this music unchanged, the same as before, and he, Moreau, alive to listen, though not perhaps for very much longer. There were things about Dubos' death that couldn't be proved; better, then, to think of them as false. And from his death all the rest had followed. Moreau had had many other friends but, truly, no other lover.

Many enemies, too, in those days. Now he was almost sixty, and had none; none, at least, while he stayed in exile. And he would never see France again. France had gone. It wasn't the same. Only the violin remained, pirouetting wildly at the uppermost octave of the register; Menuhin, knees bent, head bowed in the pensive arrogance of genius. Moreau *was* the violin, *was* Menuhin, all the other instruments had faded and left him alone with the great cadenza. Genius, he thought; yes, Dubos had had genius, but genius involves weakness; that's the only thing that makes its destruction possible. Destruction, the exercise of power. For there's nothing else left.

The arrangement of notes in sequence to a certain end; that's music. That's power. The notes don't turn round and say, *And then? . . .* No, the question was meaningless, she should have known better. Once the crab is out of the shell, then you can destroy it. Or let it go. It hardly matters. Either way it's power. The power to secure an effect. What else is there? Only power is immortal; this music, unchanged.

The violin, he thought, brings back the past. For me, the future is clear; it's the past that is confused. For me, to think is to plan, to arrange, to ordain; only when I look back at the past do my thoughts begin to circle, coalesce, drift into chaos. I *imagine* that past; not the future. So my rational mind can rest. That, then, is why I need music, for everyone needs to rest. Sooner or later. Sooner or later. Sooner or later. . . .

4

THERE was nothing on the radio about the robbery, and after the news there was music. Jeye flipped through the pages of the *ABC* and *Arriba* while he breakfasted on coffee and rolls: a new space satellite launched by the Americans, a new missile developed by the Americans, more trouble in the Congo. The rain had drifted eastwards overnight and, beyond the open window, the morning was warm and clean-washed, alive with spring. Fé whistling quietly in the kitchenette, coming through the door with more coffee, wore an apron over her dressing-gown.

"Have you ever heard of Kasai?"

Fé put the coffee-pot on the table, sat down beside him. "Never."

"It's in the Congo. Says here that eighty per cent of the world's industrial diamonds come from Kasai."

"Industrial," Fé said. "I hate that word."

"Well, and everyone there's dying of famine. Or so it says."

"Ironical?"

"Ironical. Wouldn't you say so?"

"It's all the Belgians' fault—if you ask me."

"It doesn't have to be anyone's *fault*," Jeye said, folding the newspaper. "It's just the way the goddam chips are stacked. I didn't say it was anyone's *fault*, did I?"

"You sound like Holden Caulfield."

"Who's he? Dying of hunger, though, that's a lousy deal any way you look at it. Especially sitting on top of a diamond mine."

"It's no fun at all wherever you do it."

Silence, for a few moments. Except for the radio, the traffic, the birds and the whole of Madrid outside the window. Silence, anyway. They looked at each other in mutual puzzlement.

"Breakfast conversation," Fé said slowly. "God, we might as well be *married*."

"We could always go back to bed. Dispel the illusion."

"Filthy brute."

"You know what I'd really like to do?" Jeye said.

"What?"

"I'd like us to go out. You know, just for a walk."

"A stroll in the park?"

"Well, what's so funny about that?"

"Nothing," Fé said. "I'll go and get dressed."

She got up and went through to the bedroom. She left the door open, and after a little while he heard the sound of her whistling again. He didn't remember ever having heard another woman whistle.

He finished his coffee and walked over to the window. Fé had already cleared the desk; the jewellery had been put away, in a drawer, in a safe, he didn't know where and didn't much care. Madrid in the morning; green trees, warm mountain-scented air, the sputter and sparkle of the passing traffic. He watched for a few moments, then turned to the rows of books in the long, varnished shelves behind the desk. Dostoevsky, he thought. It ought to be worth reading. *Crime and Punishment*, he'd heard of that one, and the *Brothers* something. Richard would probably have them somewhere.

Half-way along the top shelf, another title caught his eye; or rather the name of another author. Carbonell: Juan Carbonell. The title of the book was *La Esperanza*. Jeye reached up for it, took it over to the desk; eyed the frontispiece briefly, then rifled through the pages.

They had at least all been cut. Fé had been to that extent a dutiful daughter. It was hard to believe that she'd read it, though, or read it all. Jeye had never seen the book before, but he had seen others very like it; Carbonell's little effort looked to be almost an archetype of the usual inflated memoir of the Falangist years, seasoned with political pseudo-aphorisms after the style of José Antonio and with innumerable completely pointless anecdotes. Juan Carbonell had been handsome enough, if his photograph in the frontispiece were anything to go by, and had worn a Civil Governor's uniform with admirable grace; but his intelligence could hardly have been outstanding. Even if the whole thing had been compiled by some earnest secretary of his, which was highly probable. Fé, of course, must have seen clean through that façade right from the beginning; it would be hell, thought Jeye, soberly, to have a father like that. He would have made a cynic of her from birth.

She wasn't, though. Was she?

. . . He didn't want to think about that, about last night. Not just yet. Something had happened, yes, all right, but it was much too early to think about it. He turned the pages more swiftly, in search of photographs. None, of course, of Fé; none, perhaps more surprisingly, of her mother; though Carbonell himself appeared in almost every one. A detail in the last photograph of all attracted his attention; he peered at it closely, then looked down at the caption . . . *Herr von Ribben-*

trop's visit to Paris, 1943; an informal meeting at the Spanish Embassy. . . . There was Carbonell, tall and erect like Douglas Fairbanks, Junior, and conceivably aware of the resemblance, advancing his hand; there was von Ribbentrop in position to receive it, the famous crooked smile much in evidence, the eyebrows cordially raised. And there, behind Carbonell's outstretched hand, was a man who was not Moreau and yet quite certainly was. A younger Moreau with a subtly different face, wearing a uniform that Jeye didn't recognise. The eyes were watchful, alert; their expression, Moreau's whole posture was so familiar to Jeye that he knew at once exactly what Moreau was doing there. He was the police officer in charge of a personal bodyguard. Von Ribbentrop's, obviously. So the uniform had to be the Gestapo's, or that of whatever had been the French equivalent. Fillmore had been right, then. *Something to do with the police*; yes, indeed. Fillmore was very rarely wrong.

Jeye picked up the book and went into the bedroom. Fé, stooping forwards, one foot raised, was putting on her stockings, her skirt lifted; the round brown smoothness of her thighs emerging briefly, crisscrossed by the black suspender straps; Jeye sat down, heavily, on the bed.

"Look, I found this book."

Legs, he thought, they're only legs, what *is* there about her legs?

"Oh, *that*," Fé said. "Isn't it grim."

"There's a photograph of Richard."

She straightened up, smoothing her skirt. "Yes," she said. "They knew each other *very* well."

"Really?"

"The greatest of chums."

"What exactly was Richard *doing*, at that time?"

"Shouldn't you ask him? Rather than me?"

"He might not want to tell me," Jeye said.

"Well, that's his business. Besides, you told me once it didn't matter."

"It doesn't. To me."

"Well, then."

"It's just that. . . ." Jeye flipped the book shut, tossed it down on to the pillow. "It might not be very tactful to leave the book lying around."

"It wasn't lying around, exactly."

"No. That's true. I was nosey."

"And you think other people might be?"

"It's possible."

"Well, he's not a war criminal, if that's what you were thinking. There's nothing anyone could do. Besides, I'm surprised you recognised him from that photograph. He's changed a lot."

"It was a long time ago," Jeye said.

He lowered himself back on the bed, pulled the pillow under his head.

"You know, I thought Richard *lived* here."

"No. He just stays here, sometimes."

"Sometimes? Or often?"

"Not often," Fé said. "You're asking a lot of questions."

"It does to pass the time," Jeye said.

Passing the time. That can be a genuine problem.

There are comparatively few people who, like Jeye, have to face it. The standing complaint of most professionals is that they have too little "free" time; the truth is that without that vague sense of purpose their work provides, time for them would become an aching vacancy. That is why the mile-

105

stones, as one might call them, of a professional career assume so great an importance; degrees, doctorates, diplomas; rises in salary; promotions, directorships; they grant that appearance of individual progress which the task itself, irrelevant of outward circumstance, fails to provide.

Thieves have no diplomas, no directorships, no means of deceiving themselves that things are otherwise. All they can do is live in the present, think of the next strike, and pretend that if there are no milestones, then neither is there road or landscape. In some, this is a natural gift. For others, a painful struggle.

It is after the strike that the trouble begins. The thief's chief enemies are other thieves. A really successful operator like Jeye has comparatively little to fear from the police; he holds too many cards, even if he is caught red-handed. He has enough money, in the first place, to have a chance of bribing his way out; in which case he will go to court, but the case for the prosecution will unexpectedly collapse. A good policeman knows that to get a jewel thief into court is to ensure his moving on somewhere else, and very quickly; another country, from the law's point of view, is quite as good as prison and cheaper to the taxpayer. And if the law should be five hundred or a thousand pounds in pocket as a result, so very much the better.

Secondly, if he can't bribe, he can still bargain. Insurance companies are much more interested in the recovery of stolen property than in the conviction of criminals, and the game of playing off the insurance agents against the police is one of great fascination to the expert, often giving remarkably satisfying results. Thirdly, and if all else fails, he can blackmail. Some very interesting things, apart from jewellery, can often be found in safes; things that many eminently respectable people will go to almost any lengths to prevent from emerging in court. And of course, if the Señora de Fulano can be prevailed upon to swear that *this* isn't the man who jumped out of her wardrobe, doesn't even *remotely* resemble him, the case for the prosecution may find itself, not unnaturally, somewhat cramped. Much stranger things than that have been known to happen.

A good operator is covered, then, against both other criminals and the police. He has built, as Moreau would have said, his shell, and while he stays within it he is safe. His only remaining enemy is himself.

A crab may have no trouble in passing the time pleasantly within its shell. But men are different. Men are social and sociable animals. After the strike, the thief has nothing to do until the next; which, if he is sensible, won't be for another year or two. He is free to do anything he likes. But freedom can be a most exasperating gift; and freedom in a shell is a form of prison. A few, a very few can stand up to it; mostly men like Jeye, like Moreau, who are not without intellectual resources. Others find that freedom is simply inaction. Even the clever ones, the ones who keep their shells around them wherever they go; those who are content to satisfy their needs for social experience on the lowest and simplest of levels, to make of physical contact a substitute for mental. Sex, for them, is the thief's best friend. Where would they be without it?

"I don't see much point in my getting dressed if you're going to. . . . Well, do *you*?"

"That wasn't what you said last night."

"But I thought we were going *out*. Oh, God. I-yi-yi."

Well, maybe you pay for it, yes. But the fiver on the

mantelpiece doesn't turn her into a machine. It's always a human being underneath you. And a thief is less likely than a businessman to forget that obvious fact. That's why he's there.

There are some crummy rooms off the Bayswater Road and some crummy things going on there. You can say the same of the Suikerrui, of the Boul' Haussmann, of Via Veneto, of the Calle de la Pez, of any of a number of streets from Istanbul to Tokyo. Animal lust, some people call it; with all the variations. But girls aren't animals, either. So along with whatever it is that's served, you get all kinds of odd things thrown in. Affection, certainly; tenderness, even, maybe. The most important bonus, though, is loyalty.

Even so, even then, the shell stays clamped on. Birds are human, and human beings are stupid. They let things slip. And of course the coin of loyalty has another side; jealousy has put more men in the dock than the whole of Interpol put together. And sex, bought and paid for, has many more subtle disadvantages. The immoral earnings lark, for instance. Full many an honest thief has ended up in flowery through being, naturally, unwilling to explain where the money *really* came from. The sentence is lighter than for robbery, so no one but a fool is going to cough. Yes, but oh! the *indignity* of it all.

Even worse, you may actually have done it. It's the hell of a temptation. Besides, so serpentine are the wiles of women that, on occasion, you may not even realise that this is what has happened until it's too late. And by no means is it only the law-abiding and respectable who look upon the fancy-boy with contempt; the fall from thief to ponce is a dreadful one, involving a loss of prestige that is well-nigh irrecoverable. The list of the dangers that birds bring with them would be very long indeed; and amateur tarts, of course, are far, far worse.

Marriage? Oh, yes, that would do. But what kind of freedom is that? A jewel thief's wife, a jewel thief's children make hostages to fortune of a kind that doesn't bear thinking about. Marriage is for when you retire . . . if you ever do.

And if women, paid and unpaid, are out, that leaves you with the poufs.

"What happens," Jeye asked, "when Richard stays here?"

"You're not really worried about that, are you?"

"Not exactly. I suppose I'm curious."

"Maybe he does it to stop me feeling lonely."

"Oh, come off it," Jeye said.

"He has his chums, you see."

"Yes, so I'd guessed."

". . . You think it's odd?"

"Well, of *course* I think it's odd, it's about the weirdest damned set-up I ever came across. I mean, what does he *do* to you? Whip you or something?"

"Yes. Well, he has these thigh-boots."

"He *what*?" Jeye, jerked up on one elbow, stared down at her. ". . . You silly coot. For a moment, you had me worried."

"All right. Joke. Not altogether, though."

"How d'you mean? Not altogether?"

"Oh, I don't know. There's all kinds of ways of being a pervert. Does it really matter?"

"Well, yes. If you'd got used to that sort of thing, I'd . . . I don't think I could *do* it. I've never tried."

"Oh, Michael."

"What?" Jeye said, his mouth in her hair.

". . . Your way suits me fine."

"That's all right, then."

He looked at her again. She was crying.

"No. . . . Fé? No, don't. . . . What's the matter?"

"Nothing, nothing at all. I'm being a fool."

Of course, in many countries all homosexuals are criminals, in the sense that the practice of homosexuality is proscribed by the law. It doesn't follow that all criminals are homosexuals; naturally not. But the knowledge that homosexuals are, in that one essential respect, very like themselves is bound to have an effect—to establish, if you like, an identification. It's quite true that many "straight" criminals resent this identification bitterly, and the homosexual may well find as outraged and savage an opposition within prison as in court. But even this response, in part, involves the recognition of an affinity. The struggle in the criminal's mind is against authority, against all established order and custom; and in that struggle, the homosexual and the pervert are also joined.

All over the underworld, then, they play their part; the poufs, the nancies, the fairies, the jotos, the cancos, the adelaides, the pajaros, the mignons; and as to the part they play, one can only generalise. Here again affection and tenderness and loyalty can be, and often are, involved; and many will admit that a fairy is safer than a woman, can be trusted further, if only because his own position makes him cautious. Poufs constantly level a curious indirect form of blackmail one upon the other; often it is this that gives their relationship its peculiar piquancy. But no one takes up with a pouf because it's *safer*. It's not a matter of trying women and finding them wanting, so. . . . Nothing like that. No one has reasons. No one knows why.

In prison, where men have time to spare, this topic among others is endlessly discussed. Criminals, like other people, find in themselves a subject of enormous interest. Unfortunately, though not at all surprisingly, they say two quite different things. Some say that the homosexual is essentially aggressive; some say just the opposite. It's always been an upper-class vice, a vice of the governing rather than of the governed? . . . No, not at all. It's a *refusal* to dominate. It's an insistence on equality, even in sex. . . . But doesn't it involve the humiliation of another person? . . . Yes, but *self*-humiliation, as well; it's like a non-religious act of penance. . . . Oh, balls. What about young Mortimer, doing seven years on a GBH? What's a savage little bastard like that know about self-humiliation? . . . Well, that's just the *point*, it's his better self, you see. It's got to have some means of expression, hasn't it? . . .

"But most of the queers I know are pathetically gentle."

"Ah, well, there you are, you see. *They* do it so as to release all their pent-up aggression. Saves them going round the bend."

"But then you just can't win. It goes round in circles."

"No, well, no one wants to *win* an argument. Not in prison. You'd only have to think of something new to talk about."

"I never thought of that," Fé said.

The real trouble with bird isn't just that it encourages homosexuality, but that it encourages homosexuality among people who are already criminals. And two men who are able to share—so to speak—both their work and their play are in an enormously strong position; both socially and professionally, they're a self-contained unit, they've built a shell that's big enough for two. They've eliminated almost every weakness.

When that happens, the police can only hope to catch them in the act of pulling a job, or else to wait until, for some reason or other, they split up, coming crawling one by one out of the shell. Sometimes the cops can hasten the process a little, perhaps by nicking one of them on suspicion or on some trivial charge, such as loitering with intent: there's always a chance then that the other one will panic. Nerves, that's the trouble. Queers are temperamental. It's a very small weakness, but an important one.

"Why couldn't it be a man and a woman? If they were both criminals?"

"It's hard to say why not," Jeye said. "It hardly ever happens. That's all."

"You think that women don't make good criminals?"

"They do sometimes. No, I think there's more to it than that. A permanent relationship between a man and a woman —well, that's marriage, whether you call it that or not. That's something that society *approves* of. And you've got to be against society all the time, or the . . . your will-power sort of softens up on you. You start to play it *too* safe, and that's as dangerous as driving too slowly. Besides. . . ."

"What?"

"Men and women have children."

"Yes," Fé said. "So they do."

"It doesn't help."

"No."

"There has to be something *wrong*, you see, from a social viewpoint, or it just won't work. That's what I meant when

I said it was odd about you and Richard."

"We're not wrong enough for you?"

"You're married, aren't you? He sleeps with you some-times. You say you love him. The only thing is the difference in your ages. No, it's not wrong enough."

"Now I'm asking too many questions."

"I don't think so."

The other question (Jeye said) that has no answer is the question of why you do it at all. The people on the other side, they ask that question; the thief can't tell them. If anything, it's because there is another side; the other side is what he's against. It's not poverty he fears; he probably knows it too well for that. It's running to catch the 8.17; not just once, but day in, day out. His is a life without milestones; he can't understand how other people can believe in them. To him, the ordinary daily routine of the average citizen seems a hell of insupportable monotony. To him, perhaps, it would be.

He, in contrast, has a full and interesting life. Or so he believes. He believes this through an act of faith. He may spend a third of his life in prison; the other two-thirds, he sincerely believes, is still packed with living, with *real* living. And those who don't *really* live, they themselves aren't real.

"I'd say that was true," said Fé.

Yet if you ask him such a question as, *Who's the most in-teresting person you've ever met?*—he'll probably name some-one whom none but an infantile mentality would consider of any interest at all; some pathological liar, perhaps, or spinner of yarns; or someone with an unusual physical trait, a limp or a hunchback. He may very well never have met with a genuinely interesting person in all his life; and should

113

he have done so, he'll probably have been completely un-impressed. The criminal is a self-deceiver, as much as the man on the 8.17 he so much despises; and because of his false sense of superiority, he himself is notoriously easy to deceive by others. He doesn't care about that. He just doesn't care.

"What about you, then? Don't *you* care?"

"There are so many ways of being deceived and of fooling yourself. . . . Like you said, you just can't win. It's a matter more of resigning yourself to it, sort of. There's nothing else to do."

"Richard wouldn't agree."

"Probably wouldn't."

"All the same, he never talks about it like you do. He looks at it another way. Much more abstract."

"I've been talking too much," Jeye said.

"It's my fault, asking all those questions. I never do, usually. I don't know what's got in to me today."

"I have."

"I didn't mean . . . *this* horrid thing."

"Hey," Jeye said, recoiling. "Be careful."

"Though I daresay a girl could grow quite fond of it, in time."

"An encouraging thought."

"The trouble with you," Fé said, "is, you talk too much."

Jeye was to remember, much later, that day and that con-versation. That was when he would say to himself, I knew it all, I had it all there. Yet somehow, I failed to see the impli-cations of what I was saying. Why? . . . Perhaps because of the many many ways there are of fooling yourself, I chose the most obvious; I chose to see no farther than Fé's body. And that may have been the right choice. For possibly, it would have made no difference. . . .

5

THE sharp, smoking ray of the projector jerked across the darkness of the room. On the dim screen, colour grew; flooded across the retinas of the watching eyes. "This gives the general background," said Moreau from behind the sofa. "The trees screen most of the west wing from the road, and the building you see behind them is the college I mentioned. It's a kind of training centre for the FETS girls, doing their Servicio Social. The building to the east is the servants' quarters. Four maids, a cook, a chauffeur, two gardeners and a general dogsbody. The front door is ninety-four yards from the east wing wall."

He took the slide from the projector. Fé's cigarette-end glowed suddenly to Jeye's right; then the projector clicked, another photograph came sharply into focus. "Now here's the main section. You see the drive runs up to and along the inner wall, which is about twelve feet high. Cement and broken glass. At my age, that kind of thing is beginning to present a problem. Once we're over, though, the trees give an excellent screened approach right up to the house itself. The main difficulty will obviously be the entry." A pause. "What d'you think, Michael?"

"It looks a bit dodgy," Jeye said.

"It does, does it?"

"Let's see the side elevation."

"Of course." Moreau's fingers moved quickly in the semi-

117

obscurity, changing the slides. Then the house came up again on the screen, this time closer, evening sunlight glittering on grey quartz.

Jeye grunted. "These old buildings are the devil. Still, it's climbable."

"Not very much in the way of aids, certainly."

"No. And it's no good using pitons if I can't trust the stonework. But that ledge above the window might be useful. What room is that, anyway?"

"The kitchen. We might do better to try the other side, though, further from the servants' quarters. The house is symmetrical, as you'll have noticed."

"I can have a light that side? If I need it?"

"I think so, yes. With the wall and the trees, that wing is almost completely cut off from the road. What's more, the hills behind it break up the skyline."

Jeye got to his feet and moved forwards, his shadow momentarily blacking out the screen. Even from a range of a few inches, he found the image startlingly clear, with hardly a trace of fogginess. "These are damned good shots," he said.

"Oh, well." Moreau came forwards, also, to stand at his side. "I wouldn't like you to think that you were the only one to do any work, last week."

"Is that when they were taken?"

"Last Tuesday evening."

"Couldn't be much more recent than that, could they?" Jeye ran his finger along a hairline of darkness crossing the grey stone. "See that? That's where the mortar's crumbling and the structure's shifted. Probably come down as much as half an inch. It's pretty hopeless."

"Wouldn't that give you a grip?"

"Oh, yes. For ten feet or so. Then it comes away in your hands. No, thanks. Still," Jeye said, "the other side's much better sheltered, obviously. Things might be in better condition there."

"If you like I'll get the plan out and we'll run over it together."

"Just a minute," Jeye said, stooping down once more.

In fact, it was more than five minutes before he had finished his inch-by-inch examination of the screen. During this time Fé finished her cigarette and ground it out in the ashtray; Moreau sat down in Jeye's place on the sofa; but neither of them spoke. In the end it was Jeye who broke the silence, pointing to a narrow oblong etched high up to the right of the wall. "What room's this? Inside?"

"Second and third guests' bedrooms," Moreau said. "The first is farther to the left."

"Yes. Well, if the main cable runs where it obviously ought to, they'll have had to run an extra cable to cover those two rooms. That looks to be as good a bet as any."

"I agree, I definitely agree. Olmedos did the wiring, you know, and they often make a very skimpy job of it. It might even be a simple interior wire, no more than that."

"Can we check on that before we go any farther?"

"Yes. Right away."

. . . So it went on. And on. And on.

". . . Now this is the old system. Completely conventional, of course, put in back in the thirties when the place was renovated. The master switch has to be here, you see, with the main cable running down the hallway. But as you point out, there are some rooms that weren't covered then, so when the present alarm system was installed. . . ."

119

". . . You know the *Hogar*, don't you? Man called Gutier-rez edits it now. Well, he did an article on the place last year, with quite a few good photographs of the interior. You can see them later. The point is that when I rang him up last year about it, he said that the staircase itself is something of a period piece. So they won't have cared to touch it. Now the problem is. . . ."

". . . Two. Mastiffs."

"The *safe*, yes, there's a gap in the research there, I must admit. All I can tell you is that it's twelve years' old and of Spanish manufacture; and, of course, if it's on the Olmedos analogy, it ought to open if we blow on it. And I can truth-fully say that, given time, I can manage most of the makes that one comes across."

"Given time. We agreed on four hours."

"As a minimum."

"I doubt if we'll manage the entry in much under forty minutes. Dogs can be the hell of a time-waster."

"Four hours is a long time, Michael. Longer than the longest job you've ever done. . . ."

"More coffee? . . ."

"Agreed, then. It has to be Saturday or Sunday. And the sooner the better. We could drive out there tomorrow morn-ing, look it over in the afternoon, and if everything's right, go in at ten o'clock. Don't you think?"

"If everything's right," Jeye said. "Yes."

"Then I think we might call it a day."

. . . On and on and on. For longer, much longer than the proposed operation; a technical, impersonal discussion from out of which, tomorrow, the final brief would emerge in a matter of minutes. The curtains rasped back on the rail as Fé pulled down the cord; the afternoon overwhelmed the room in a sudden rush, startling in its effect. Jeye blinked at it; Moreau, hunched over the papers on the desk, emerged from his mood of abstraction as from a dream. For all they had known or cared, it might have been midnight. Only now was Jeye reminded that he hadn't yet lunched.

Moreau began to collect and re-arrange the papers. "It isn't a matter of a week's work . . . all this research," he said slowly. "Or even of months. No. It's been years. It sounds idiotic, I know, but in some ways I enjoy the research as much as the actual results of it. Studying people . . . their intelligence or lack of it . . . their habits, their morals, their bank balances . . . it fascinates me, all that. It really does."

"I remember," Jeye said. "Psychology. You told me."

"So I did. You don't feel that?"

"Not in the same way, no."

"Well, there it is." Moreau unlocked the deep drawer of the desk, slid the folders into place inside. "When I've finished with any of these files, I feel rather as though I've . . . I've had a tooth out. . . . No, that's a very inexact comparison. Very inexact. Perhaps more as a doctor feels when one of his oldest patient dies. These are my medical files." He patted the drawer gently, dreamily, with the flat of his hand. "I might do well to bequeath them to posterity. Sociological interest, you see. A whole cross-section of fashionable society filed away, analysed, dissected. All the richest men in Spain are tucked away there; de Cabo, the Marches, Salinas, Ramirez Costa. . . . Capitalism in the deep freeze. A novelist could really make use of something like that. Cela, for example. As a matter of fact. . . ."

121

He stopped short. Then closed the drawer; locked it; put the key-ring away in his pocket. "Anything the matter, Michael?"

It was acute of him. Nothing much had happened; other than that, at a certain point, Jeye's mental exhaustion had vanished, his attentiveness been turned on as though by the flicking of a switch. ". . . You said Salinas."

"Yes?"

A long pause. It was Fé, still standing by the curtains, who broke it. "I have a funny idea about Michael. I have the feeling he wants to *do* Salinas."

"I see," Moreau said. "And why not?"

"Because it'd be suicide. That's why."

"Suicide?"

"Yes. You know it would."

"Perhaps for you and me. We're merely professionals. We're in it for the money. But Michael's a genius. He *may* do Salinas one day, who knows? But not with us. No. Not with us."

"I was asking," Jeye said coldly, "if you had anything on Salinas. That was all."

"Yes, I have: I've done research on a great many subjects I shouldn't dream of attempting. One piece of research helps another; one learns. One learns so much."

"I see."

". . . Were you thinking of asking to *see* my research?"

"No," Jeye said.

"Ah, I'm rather glad of that. After all, you're a practical man and I'm a theoretician. And as such, I'd feel a certain sense of responsibility——"

"I said *no*," Jeye said, "didn't I?"

"Yes. You did. So let's just think about tomorrow. That'll

be a big enough hit, in all conscience. So big that if it comes off, maybe we can forget about the third."

"It'll come off all right. It has to." The razor edge of Jeye's hostility had turned away from Moreau, and he smiled as he spoke, though thinly. "They always have to," he said. "That's the point."

Aranjuez.

Fifty-odd kilometres south of Madrid; the first long pace of a journey towards Africa. Jeye knew the town, but not well. He knew the road better; but Fé was driving, anyway. He sat in the passenger seat beside her, seeing no more of her than her grey-gloved hands on the steering-wheel; Moreau sat behind, for the most part in silence.

They passed the Cerro de los Angeles at ten o'clock, the tall statue of Christ on its summit gleaming in the morning sunlight, and shortly afterwards Fé began to put on speed, edging the speedometer up to the hundred-and-twenty mark; fast enough, Jeye thought, to be pleasant, fast enough for one to feel that sympathy between man, machine and unwinding road that forms nine-tenths of the attraction of long-distance motoring, but not too fast to divert the whole of one's attention from the fields, the hills, the rivers. This was the open Castilian country, streaked with brown and green to the horizon; above it the sky, pale blue of the morning and flecked with bars of cirrus. He thought of the sanatorium, of two-one-two, of watching the cars float down the road; that had been long ago; now he was free, free if only in the sense of going somewhere, going somewhere with Fé. And with Richard, too. Why not? . . . That morning he found himself in a mood of acceptance; he had no questions to ask of the sky, of the road, of the meseta or of anything else. He found him-

123

self almost happy. He had no worries.

The wheels that drummed on the road brought them to Aranjuez. Trees in the hollow, vibrant with greenness; the slow-moving river; Aranjuez the oasis, a patch of the Ile-de-France planked down on the burning road to Andalusia. The shadows of motionless branches were picked out with a startling clarity on the white walls of houses; tree-trunks grew like silver ghosts out of a gloom of their own creating; the Citroen, nose held low to the road like that of a questing hound, swung slowly past the grey-and-white walls, rolled through the arches, came to a halt outside the Parador de los Jardines. Fé leaned back, stripped off her gloves. And Moreau, the back seat complaining slightly as he moved his weight towards the door:

"You know this place, Michael?"

"Only by sight."

"I thought we might lunch here later. It's about the only place I know of outside Madrid where you can get genuine Moka coffee. I don't know if you care for the stuff. I do."

"Well," Jeye said. "That's worth knowing."

"I suggest we leave Fé here while we take our little stroll. Half a mile or so, that's all. Just enough to whet our appetites."

The lane turned to the right, following the line of a ditch and of a low ivy-grown wall; as they strolled down it, Jeye had occasional glimpses, through the trees and above the much higher wall that marched inside the other at some thirty paces' distance, of the grey tiled roofs of the house, and each of its different aspects was accepted, recognised, sorted into its proper category, tabulated and finally punched by the silently active Hollerith inside his head. Moreau walked beside him, glancing from side to side with an interested air that was belied, however, by the casual swing of the walking stick in his right hand. They passed a narrow drive-way, leading to a wooden gate in the inner wall. "Back entrance," Moreau said. "Remember? . . . Padlocked, I understand, when they're not in residence."

"This outer wall's certainly nothing much."

"All it really does, I suppose, is mark the extent of the grounds. I'm told that up to a year or so ago, the dogs had the run of the whole area at night. But then a couple of girls from the Training Centre"—he pointed with his stick to the low red roof with the bare flagstaff in the middle distance— "they tried to take a short cut. Stayed out later than they should have done, no doubt. And they got rather badly mangled. Well, of course they'd been trespassing, but local feeling ran rather high and as a result, now the dogs stay within the inner wall. Just as well."

"Mastiffs, you said?"

"Yes. Nasty brutes. I don't much care for dogs, really. Not at the best of times."

"When ten o'clock at night isn't."

"Precisely."

They walked on, following the wide semicircle of the lane to the main entrance gate; where they paused for a moment, staring towards the house. "Imposing, isn't it?" Moreau said. "But then there's something so divinely *age de raison* about Aranjuez. This place, in particular, was well worth recapturing for contemporaneity. Don't you think?"

"It's well laid out," Jeye said, "certainly."

"Oh, a masterpiece. Landscape gardening, after all, is an art so little appreciated in Spain that an arrangement such as this fairly strikes you in the eye. And with just that touch of desuetude, of neglect, that it needs to show that the

125

Romantics have been and gone. Don't you agree?"

"Not altogether," Jeye said. "*Il fût gallican, ce siècle, et janseniste.*"

Moreau's eyes moved in surprise from their consideration of the house and the gardens, settled on Jeye's face. "I used that once at school, in an essay," Jeye said. "The thing seems to have stuck."

"Of course," Moreau said, the corners of his mouth turning downwards. "Let's see. How does it go? . . .

C'est vers le moyen age, énorme et delicat,
Qu'il faudrait que mon coeur en panne naviguât,
Loin de nos jours d'esprit charnel et de chair triste.

I'd no idea that *you* were a medievalist. It's not a thing I should ever have suspected."

He had found it necessary, as certain people seem to, to come to a halt in order to grant his proclamation a due importance. Jeye leaned his weight for a moment on the wall, sensing the damp smell of the ivy, of the mouldering brickwork heavy in his nostrils. "I like Verlaine," he said. "But I can't quote him like that. I wish I could."

"I have what is called an eidetic memory, Michael. Phrases, numbers—I read them, they remain with me. Sad to say, it's not so valuable an accomplishment as those who lack it tend to believe."

"All the same," Jeye said. He pushed himself away from the wall; together, they walked on again. "I had a private tutor once with the gift. History, his line was."

"Oh? You're intrigued by history?"

"That was a long time ago. I was supposed to be good at it, that was all. History and languages. The other's been more useful."

"That's not the only criterion."

After a while,

"Have you ever heard of Ruiz Salvador?"

"Yes, I have. Why?"

"I know him quite well. I could introduce you to him, if you liked. A delightful fellow."

"He writes damned long books," Jeye said.

"I understand he's the greatest living authority on the Catalan trovadores. Is that *your* estimation, also?"

"While he's alive, yes. When he's dead he'll be a dead historian, like all the others. And of all dead things, there's nothing deader."

"Just thought I'd mention it," Moreau said pacifically.

"Well. Very kind of you."

Jeye reached out, pulled thoughtfully at a projection on the wall. It came to pieces in his hands, crumbled into fragments as fine as sand. He dusted his palms. They walked on.

They climbed over the wall.

The sky was full of stars, but there was next to no moon; only what the Spaniards call a *luna mora*, a pale yellow sliver hanging on its back above the hills. The close-cropped grass felt hard as a billiard-table under their feet. Ahead of them, the dark mass of the trees and the sharper, nearer outline of the inner wall. The air was warmer than in Madrid. They reached the wall and stood in its shadows, listening. Jeye's nostrils, wide open, were testing, probing that temperate air; the scent of the Spanish moss hanging phantom-like from the branches overhead, a sharper smell of sage brought down by the night breeze from the sierra; these two alone determinable amongst a thousand others. He could hear nothing, nothing at all.

127

Moreau, fumbling in the pocket of his raincoat, brought out a brown paper package; opened it. Inside were chunks of raw beef. He stabbed deep notches into the meat with a penknife; shook a fistful of colourless capsules from a small glass bottle into his palm, pressed them one by one into the dark gashes, pinching their apertures closed afterwards. His movements had a quick, almost satisfied deliberation about them; he looked up now at Jeye and nodded. "Right?"

"When you're ready."

Moreau unbuttoned his raincoat, took from the breast pocket of his jacket a small steel tube. He blew into it experimentally. Nothing happened. *"Mierda,"* he said, shaking it. He tried again. From his mouth a cicada bubbled a series of rattling screeches, punctuated by quick whistles; the whistles, however, pitched at too high a frequency to be audible to the human ear. Moreau took the tube from his mouth and stood motionless, head cocked to one side; from behind the wall there came a distant whine, then a volley of barking. He tossed the meat, piece by piece, over the wall. Furious growls, an angry yap; slobberings. Jeye's hands on the edge of the wall groped for fingerholds; found them; he paused at the top to break away the jagged edges of broken glass, to spread his raincoat over the space he had cleared. Not until then did he look down. Beneath him, dark shadows writhed on the grass, thrashed to and fro and were still. They had been mastiffs, all right.

"Come on," he said, reaching down for Moreau's hand.

They dropped together to the lawn below; crossed it in silence, moving in the shadow of the huddled trees. They reached the path that flanked the house (crazy paving, flags of heavy granite brought down from Despeñaperros in the panniers of weary brown mules) and walked quickly along it, their heads on a level with the crenellated pillars of the long stone balustrade, the deep balcony that had served as a flirting-ground to countless nineteenth-century duquesitas on just such quiet and almost moonless nights as this. They stopped at the point where the pillars halted and the old stone wall of the house reared upwards; old stone, very old stone. Jeye stripped off his raincoat, his tool-belt, his gloves; rested his naked hands with their long, muscular fingers on the cool granite, assessing somehow the quality of the material, the resistance—or the lack of it—this obstacle would offer. He wore the same grey trousers as before, a light blue cashmere sweater and no jacket. Moreau watched him and said nothing. Still with no word spoken, with no preliminary movement to show that he had reached his decision, Jeye hauled himself smoothly upwards and began to climb.

He climbed at an astonishing speed. Moreau, taking five paces backwards to the edge of the lawn, found that by the time he had taken those few steps Jeye was already twenty feet up and was no longer visible, other than as a vague, prehensile shadow on the face of the wall; that shadow and the dark outline of the nearest first-floor window seemed to move together, to merge and then to draw apart again. Moreau stepped yet further back, taking care to remain within the shadows. When he looked up again, Jeye was a black, blurred patch moving sideways now, using the invisible ridge at the top of the window embrasure as a traverse; then inching imperceptibly upwards to reach for the shelf of the second-floor window above and then to flow on upwards, roofwards, as silently as smoke. Moreau took the torch from his pocket, checked the alignment of the shield; bounced it loosely against the palm of his hand.

Jeye, sixty feet up now, reached the skirted overhang of

the roof and began to travel to the right; his weight well outwards, his toes pressed against the friction-hold of the weathered granite, his hands becoming in rapid succession levers to push him onwards, hooks to support him against the ever-constant pull of gravity, suction-pads to absorb for brief seconds the foreign reality of stone into tensed and straining muscle, flesh and bone. He breathed deeply and steadily. Moreau, far beneath, kept pace with him as he travelled sideways; once he heard the sharp click of Jeye's fingers calling for light and, aiming the torch upwards, sent a narrow beam of brightness through the air to envelop a crumbling patch beneath the gutter. He saw the black shadow of Jeye's hand and arm enter that hollow halo, move to and fro; then the hand flap loose from the waist in a gesture of dismissal. He switched the torch off. Loose cement rained gently on the paving-stones in a three-second shower; then the dark shadow was moving onwards again in its steady traverse, moving onwards to a point above the narrow black slit of the guest-room window. There it stopped.

Moreau waited, biting his lower lip. He felt the perspiration cooling under his collar and in the loose folds where shirt tucked under trouser-belt. The metronome at the back of his mind kept up its rigid, unstoppable swinging, ticking off like a pendulum four-seven-seven, four-seven-eight, four-seven-nine, four-*eighty*, setting off the answering chime *eight minutes gone* even as the count went on, four-eight-one, four-eight-two. . . . Eight minutes, and for the last two of them that shadow had been riveted into place as aimlessly as though pricked into the wall by a giant pin, moving, yes, occasionally twisting itself from side to side as though in agony, but returning always to its point of crucifixion, what was the *matter*? Uncertainty? Vertigo? Couldn't he see?

And if he wanted light, why didn't he signal? Five-oh-three, five-oh-four, five-oh-five. . . .

He knew well enough, really, what was the matter. Of course the situation had already been envisaged. There was Jeye, clinging to the roof-edge; there was the window, some twelve feet beneath him. He had got up all right; now he had to come down. How he did it was up to him; but he had to do it. Otherwise the whole thing was off.

Five-oh-eight, five-oh-nine. . . .

Then it came again, faint, almost inaudible yet reassuringly definite; a snap of the fingers, like a breaking twig. Moreau focused the torch again, and once more that bright tiny ring of light blazed against the roof-edge, fractionally clear of Jeye's shoulder. And the hand entering it at once, pointing downwards. Downwards? . . . The window, then. Moreau dropped his wrist a fraction, began to circle the beam around the window embrasure. At the top of its circle, Jeye's shoes were brought into dim focus at the edge of its aureole; the narrow sill at the bottom seemed all of eight feet beneath them. Between, no suspicion of a foothold; nothing but smooth stone, untrustworthy stone, and the blackness of the window aperture. No way down, Moreau thought. Jeye had been wrong. . . .

Then suddenly, etched into that blinding Giotto's circle of swinging light, bisecting it with the pure and untouchable beauty of Euclidean geometry, a falling figure; a body freed suddenly and unforgettably from all the trammels of earth, surrendered to the binding law of the universe, a diving body pure and of itself, arching downwards with an unbelievable slowness, knees together, arms swung out wide, dropping feet-first into infinity; a moment of a beauty so clear and un-distilled that Moreau gasped aloud, numbed into aweness as

131

he might have been by the impact of Gauguin's colour or a cadence of Mozart. The torch-beam dropped also; caught that figure in the incredible moment of its check, of the perfectly-timed slap of hands, of hairsprung fingers, on the four projecting inches of windowsill, of the unwinding coil of the long body, stomach and shoulder muscles taking up the impetus of the fall, reaching the point of inertia at full stretch and springing back again; a check so exquisite as to have seemed the product of a thousand rehearsals, like that of a great trapezist, so difficult and so dangerous as to make it seem impossible that its execution had been impromptu, its object merely to overcome an incidental difficulty. There it is, Moreau thought; the moment of genius. The whole sequence was there. Surrender to the binding law of death, then withdrawal, instant withdrawal at the moment of acceptance; a withdrawal as satisfying, as cathartic as the acceptance itself would have been. There it was again; first Dubos, in all the arrogance of his nineteen years, in whom the act had last been consummated; now Jeye, Jeye still alive, and that was what genius meant. There was no mistaking it. Moreau's eyes were moist, were damp now as the skin of his neck and back; he switched off the torch, raised his knuckles to them.

Jeye, in that sudden darkness, rested with his hip on the edge of the sill, his twisted body relaxing, his eyes closed. His forehead was pressed against the coolness of the window-pane; he breathed through his mouth now, but silently as ever. Eventually he raised himself up on one elbow, took the glasscutter from his sweater pocket and scored two deep diagonal strokes across the glass. Then holding the cutter in his mouth, he ran strips of adhesive tape the length of the cuts; took the cutter again and pried the putty loose from each corner of the pane The glass snapped inwards to the pressure of his elbow, sounding no louder than had the clicking of his fingers; the diagonals collapsed, hung down from the tapes. Jeye slid the cutter back into his pocket, thrust his arm shoulder-deep through the open pane.

Beneath the sill he found the expected roughness where the alarm cable had been let into the wall; he probed at the plaster, first with his fingers and then with the blade of the rubber-handled penknife, until the wire was severed. Then he freed the catch of the window, raised it a couple of feet and rolled inside.

He went through the room and down the great staircase, treading cautiously, close to the wall, and following the pencil-beam of his pocket torch. In the hall, to the left of the main entry, he found the copper alarm-box; turned the calibrated knob to break the connections. He went to the front door, slid back the heavy bolts, edged it open; Moreau stepped inside. ". . . You know you're mad? . . . A lunatic? . . . You *must* be."

"Why?"

"Taking that kind of a risk. I thought you were a goner."

"I have to take them," Jeye said. "Calculated risks. You know that as well as I do."

"But dropping like that——"

"A deadfall isn't so difficult. It's just a matter of balance and of falling straight. Look, we haven't got time."

. . . For a chat, he meant. That was true. Moreau switched on his own torch and walked quickly over to the library door, a tall arch-shaped door of Spanish oak. He knelt down beside it, taking the probe from his pocket; the lock clicked open in a matter of seconds. They stepped into the room, sweeping

133

the walls with their torches; a big room, lined with long shelves of heavy leather-backed books, except where, on the far wall, a huge picture glowed in a welter of sombre colour. The curtains, massive full-length curtains of red velvet, were drawn across the windows.

Moreau paused for a moment to stare at the enormous canvas in front of them. ". . . Pity we're not in the art racket, Michael. That's a Velazquez and a good one, too. Still . . . every cobbler to his last. . . ."

He had left Jeye's raincoat, belt and gloves draped over a chair to the left of the door; Jeye put them on, unhurriedly, while Moreau, with equal composure and very systematically, searched the upper inside corner of every shelf, from knee-height to the uppermost. Eventually, he grunted in satisfaction; there was a click, a subdued whimpering sound, and a section of the bookcase swung sideways on noiseless rollers. Behind, in the wooden panelling, was the safe. Jeye heard the sudden insuck of his breath, and moved forwards.

"Look at *this*." Moreau's voice seemed to die, as of inanition, on the final syllable. The grey-blue steel of the safe door shone dully in the light of the twin torches. "A bastard," Jeye said. "A right bastard."

"It looks like a Chubb to me. And a modern one at that. Well, we live and learn." Eight-three-eight, eight-three-nine, eight-forty, said the small unceasing metronome within his brain; he turned the torch down towards his wrist. "Fourteen minutes gone."

"Check," Jeye said.

"Well, let's see."

Moreau rubbed the tips of his fingers against the cuff of his coat, delicately touched and spun the tumblers. Silence hit the room with an impact like that of a hand grenade.

Jeye watched for a few moments, then switched his torch off and went to sit in one of the chintz-covered armchairs by the long red curtains. Moreau had placed his torch on the carpet so that the safe remained visible in the reflection of its beam; but light wasn't really necessary now. Now it was a matter of the infinitesimal adjustment of rotating tumblers, a matter of sound and of vibration and of intuition. Jeye sat very still. Time became like an elastic band that stretched and then went slack; a continuous tautening and relaxing related no longer to minutes or seconds nor even to the beating of the human heart but only to the inaudible whispering on invisible bearings of inaudible ratchets, all inside half-an-inch of tempered steel. Jeye thought of many things. He thought of green corn in the valleys of the Downs, somewhere beyond Brighton, moved by the wind in slow, soft-rustling waves; he thought of the stolid march of olive-trees over the hills of Córdoba, the earth red and powdery-white between their trunks. He thought of the taste of young strawberries served with beaten cream and a little white wine, of the grain of well-cooked rice against the palate; he thought once of his father, once of a girl he had met in a train travelling from Hamburg to Innsbruck, once of a man called Mario Cruz and several times of Fé. Indeed he thought mostly of Fé, though he had no wish to do so. He imagined her standing by the Citroen in the shadows, looking towards the great house some four hundred metres distant; and at other times he thought of her body, outstretched on the rust-coloured carpet, unfolded by the act of sex, uncurled by the warm currents, like the tentacles of a sea anemone at the bottom of a deep clear pool. And he imagined himself speaking to her then, the whisper of his voice in her ear falling into her rich world of images and instantly becoming part of them, circling both

135

upwards and inwards from her like rings on the water's surface. And where those circles overlapped, a stillness, a silence, Nirvana; her flowing limbs, contorted trunk metamorphosed into water, into stone; like the love goddess carved on the wall of an Indian temple, voluptuously straddled on eternity. A heart of stillness. Time, tautened to breaking-point. And death, perhaps, that stillness made absolute.

This, while Moreau crouched beside the safe. Crouched and listened. The muscles of his inner ear were contracting the receptive surface of the drum to a tiny pulsating point the size of a pinhead; against that point, sound waves irrhythmically impinged and sang away again into space, except for those that were absorbed and captured by the bulk of that heavy lowered head, symbol of another and an unknown world, planted in their inevitable and self-centred part. He listened, then, while his fingers moved. His brain had shut out everything that was not sound or touch, had curtained off sight and smell and taste and, as far as possible, thought itself. That is what "listening" means. You may have forgotten; more probably, you've never tried it. It isn't easy.

Moreau stopped. Sat back on his heels. He looked at his watch. An hour and five minutes. Slowly, he wiped his hands with a handkerchief.

"*Nada*," he said. "*Nada*."

Jeye came across to stand beside him. "You'd better take a spell."

"No. This one's too good for us. That's all. We could spend a week on the bastard and still get nowhere."

"Bust it," Jeye said tonelessly.

"Impossible. Just look at it."

The surface of the safe shone in the light as it had done

now for an hour and more, lustreless, untouched, untouchable. The jambline was so fine that one could hardly detect the outline of the door. "The drill's hopeless," Moreau said. "You might as well scratch it with a knife. It's a jelly job, if I ever saw one. And even then. . . .'"

"I never use the stuff," Jeye said.

"Nor do I. This isn't a job for us. That's all there is to it."

"There's a six-inch recess."

"That's no help."

"We can dig it out. Take it with us."

"One metre by sixty, at least, and we've no idea how deep, we'd need a *crane*."

"We've got this far," Jeye said. "We can't stop now, we've got to try it."

He took off his raincoat and the tool-belt; laid them on the floor. From the belt he took the small crowbar and the sledge-hammer. Moreau touched his shoulder; felt the nervous energy come surging through like an electric charge. "It's no good. It's just not possible."

"Get me one of those curtains."

Moreau took his hand away. "What?"

"Tear down that curtain," Jeye said; tonelessly still, but his voice rasping like the edge of a file. Moreau took the nearest of the great curtains in his hands and threw his weight on it. The cloth tore free from the rings and Jeye was waiting for it as it fell, carrying it over to the recess in which the safe stood, jamming it hard into place with his hands and the crowbar. He picked up the hammer, began to smash with all his strength at the sides of the recess; the heavy velvet muffled the sound of each impact, but the vibrations seemed to shake the room. "For God's sake," Moreau said.

"Get back to Fé. Tell her to bring the car round to the side gate." Jeye, pausing, stood tensed against the torchlight, the hammer clenched in his lowered hands. "Take the tools with you. My coat as well. Give me ten minutes and if I'm not there, get the hell out of it." He dropped his head; the hammer swung up, came splintering down against the wall; the strength of the blow was horrifying. Moreau found it so, at any rate. For a few moments longer he watched, as though hypnotised; then turned and went, walking fast and no longer silently; the sound of those terrifying thuds, regular as heart-beats, chased him through the hall and the door, out on to the lawn. Like that story of Poe's, he thought; *The Telltale Heart*. Frightening. Macabre. A lunatic. He stopped as he gained the shadow of the trees, turned to stare towards the servants' building not a hundred yards to the east. Light showed now in two of the rooms; past a window, someone's head and shoulders moved quickly; as the night breeze died against his face, he heard a faint cross-rhythm to the steady drumbeat behind him, dance music, a radio turned on. A stroke of luck, he thought; but even so. . . . The hammering went on without a pause, with a near-pathological insistence; soon someone would hear it, would *have* to hear it. Ten minutes. . . . It was mad. *He* was mad. Moreau took half a pace back towards the house; turned; ran on towards the wall. His shape merged into the darkness under the sleeping trees.

Jeye's face, contorted with a rictus of effort. The torchlight showed the cracks in it, like in a loaf of bread that has been baked too long, deep dark creases twisting the sides of his mouth and pulsing like wounds. His hands, wielding the hammer, smashing a way through the wall to the left of the safe. The wall on the other side had been blasted apart as though by a charge of dynamite, the stone blocks cracked and pulverised, the iron side-arm of the safe sprung loose from its concrete setting. The hammerhead moved at the speed of a projectile, the breath jerking from his lungs with the crunch of its final impact. Flakes of stone, of concrete whipped through the air; a chip cut open his forehead; blood dribbled with the sweat down into his eyebrows.

It was the other side-arm at which he was swinging now; the iron bolt twisted and bent, yet still resisting. The snap, when it came, was loud as a pistol-shot, or seemed so. Jeye dropped the hammer, stooped to pick up the crowbar, used it to loosen the rubble; finally thrust it in deep to find its purchase against the safe itself. He braced himself against the floor, exerting every available ounce of leverage; under the sweat and the blood, his face went white. The safe groaned in its recess, moved forwards about three inches.

Jeye released his grip on the crowbar, wiped his forehead with the back of his hand; then tore away what was left of the curtain. The wool of his sweater was wringing wet, the seam of the right shoulder had been torn open; everything he wore was caked in a clinging dust. In five minutes, he had worked himself to a stage not far off collapse; he looked like a miner coming up from an eight-hour shift in a claypit. He stared down at the ruined wall, his whole body shuddering with great gulping breaths; then he took the safe in both his hands, his chest pressed against its hard cold surface, and began to pull. The safe moved another couple of inches; stuck. Jeye changed his grip, tried again. A thick grey vein swelled up in his temple; his eyes began to bulge, to thrust themselves hideously out of their sockets. A sound of creaking, of yielding; the safe came away from the wall in a greedy rush, plummeted out of his grasp to the floor, smashing one of the floorboards into splinters. Jeye collapsed on top of it, his stomach heaving in a desperate effort to retain its vomit, and

139

stayed spreadeagled there for perhaps five seconds. Then he turned on his knees, pulled into place one of the heavy library chairs and, summoning again all the energy and will-power he still possessed, lifted the safe on to it.

He crossed to the curtainless window, threw it open; hung, and this time for a full half-minute, over the sill like a strip of used-up cotton waste, his arms dangling loosely, long threads of saliva looping downwards from his mouth. From an im-measurable distance away he heard the sound of music; a radio playing; the tap of Leonora's high-heeled shoes; between each tap, he heard time passing. He raised his head. Yellow lights swung and gyrated before his eyes. He went back into the room.

The safe was still there, on the chair; the torch still burn-ing. He tilted the back of the chair over, dragged it on its two squeaking rear legs over to the window. A low sill, and that was lucky; a foot higher, and he couldn't have made it. Or could he? . . . Oh, yes. He'd have done it somehow. As things were, though, it wasn't too difficult. He toppled the safe over on to the sill; felt the movement of air as it rolled outwards, heard the sharp, murderous crack as it hit the paving-stones beneath, splitting one of the heavy flags like a mirror. Torch, crowbar, hammer no longer mattered; there'd be no prints; he vaulted out through the window without looking back. . . .

He landed lightly, as always; but the impact sent him into a fit of coughing that curled him up on top of the safe once more, gasping, weak as a kitten. There was no way of stop-ping it; it was a terrifying half-retching noise like a whoop-ing-cough, exploding against his throat and nose like sickness; he jammed his face hard, hard, against the unpolished steel, listening to the sounds he made, watching the yellow lights swell up and recede again, swing from side to side. There were more of them than before, or so it seemed; there was a blurred orange rectangle, too, where a door had been opened. The only way to stop coughing was to move; he realised that; and got, somehow, to his feet. A sharp cord of pain twitched at his chest; a torn muscle, maybe. He stooped. Lifted the safe, holding it poised between arms and stomach and thighs. Then, lurching, ran with ridiculous six-inch paces across the lawn, through the trees, making for the side gate that stood behind them. Not far, he told himself; not far, not far. The safe was falling from him, he couldn't hold it up; his stomach had lost contact, it was down to his knees, was brushing the grass; he couldn't let it go, though, without collapsing himself. His hip struck a tree; he staggered sideways. The weight was now on his back, in the hollow of his back, was ripping his stomach muscles in two, was a leaping furnace flame, burning him up. Not far, not far. . . .

He came up to the gate. He dropped the safe. And reeled, with the release of his swollen muscles, into the wall, the rough stone ripping at his arm, at his unprotected ribs. The shock of the blow almost sent him to the ground; he caught, however, at the wall and held himself upright against it, eyes closed, his head and all his body quivering in a silent scream of pain, throbbing to the blows of the swinging hammer. He pushed himself away from the wall. It was bad, it was hurting him. Came up with a thump against the gate. Locked. Padlocked. He took the chain in his hands and twisted it; twisted it, jerking. The steel tore a slow bloodfilled gouge across his fingers, then the lock gave way. The gate swung open.

He turned, picked up the safe again; came tottering through the gate. The Citroen was there, the rear door open, a dark shape, Moreau, moving forwards, all this mixed up with his counting, four, five, six, seven, eight, the paces to the waiting car, nine, ten, eleven, as the paces grew smaller, twelve and he was there; he pitched the vastness of the weight he was carrying, or was dreaming that he carried, upwards from his knees through to the back seat. "Right," he said, or thought he said; "All right"; and fell, head first, on into the blackness. Moreau pushed the limp body inwards, folded the legs, slammed shut the door. "That's it," he said, getting in beside Fé. "Drive."

6

THE Citroen rolled quietly through the streets of Madrid; a black turtle-shell, carapace and plastron, crawling through the steep shadowy canyons of the city; Lagasca turning right into Padilla, down Silvela and into the Avenida de los Toreros, past the bullring and skirting the Retiro as far as the Puerto de Alcalá, turning then into Serrano. It halted at the parking lot opposite Hieronymo's; Fé got out. Moreau she had already seen, sitting in one of the alcoves outside the restaurant and eating calamares with his fingers; he looked completely Spanish there, she thought, and part of his environment; a lawyer, perhaps, or a fashionable medical specialist; with his great head and carefully-combed white mane poised over his sober black suit. An air of distinction, of unostentatious wealth. She sat down opposite him, not putting her handbag on the table but holding it in her lap; she herself an attractive, well-dressed, brittle madrileña like ten thousand others. "Good morning, Richard."

"Good morning, my love," Moreau said. "And how *are* we this beautiful morning? In particular, the patient?"

"Getting back to normal."

"To normal, eh? The normal man has yet to be found, and when found, cured. An aphorism from the Secret Sayings of Sigmund Freud. Does Don Gregorio agree?"

"I don't know," Fé said. Richard was in great form this morning. Obviously. "He ordered massage."

"And he seems quite cheerful?"

143

"Michael? . . . Oh, yes. I think so."

"He has good reason to be," Moreau said.

". . . You've opened it?"

"Yes. Last night. It had to be blown."

"And everything was there?"

"Yes, indeed. And more, much more than we'd expected. I'm afraid our friend has been trying to cover himself against further risks of inflation." Moreau dipped a golden ring of squid into the bowl of breadcrumbs, eyed the result with vast satisfaction. "He's been buying in," he said, popping the speckled fragment into his mouth. "Secretly, of course. He wouldn't have wanted Ullastres to get to hear of it. Anyway, there was almost as much again as we expected, and *very* handleable stuff. I'd put it at round about thirty million."

His fingers moved amongst the calamares remaining on the plate, selecting another titbit; Fé stared at them as though mesmerised. "But that's fantastic."

"Thirty million pesetas. Yes, quite fantastic. You may have to run them up to Belgium next winter; I can't see our friends in Tangiers handling *that* amount of stuff. At current prices, it ought to translate out into something not far short of half a million dollars. This time we might even go to the Russians, sell in bulk. Yes, it might be worth trying."

"That makes it about the biggest job yet," Fé said.

"It does indeed."

"There's going to be trouble."

"I don't think so," Moreau said. "That's the beauty of it. The way things are, it's almost certain these stones are un-insured, and in any case he won't care to report the loss in full. He won't *dare* to. There's plenty of people in the Cabinet who'd like to know what he was doing with thirty million pesetas' worth of jewellery; the Opus Dei crowd are after him already, and after that Swiss bank scandal he can't afford any more false steps. In fact, I feel better about this than. . . . Would you like to drink something?"

"I would, yes, I certainly would."

"Cognac? Or a liqueur?"

"I'll have a rum-and-coke."

"Good God," Moreau said. He beckoned the waiter, and gave the order rather as though he were arranging an assassination. ". . . Yes," he said, turning back. "And of course it explains that brand-new bastard of a safe. How Michael got it to the car, I'll never know."

"He killed himself," Fé said. "Or damned nearly."

"Yes. While I stood around and watched. All very galling to one's personal pride."

"We brought him in, didn't we, to do the rough stuff? It was *your* research. And it's the research that counts."

"Even the research wasn't satisfactory. I'd no idea that the old devil had got in a '64 Chubb. I'd no idea that he'd been buying up all the best stones in the peninsula. I was ready to call the job off, I *did* call it off. But Michael wouldn't have it."

The waiter arrived with Fé's Cuba Libre, set it down on the table, polished the table with a damp cloth, smiled companionably and went away. "The job came off," Fé said. "That's all that matters."

"No. The *way* it's done, that matters too. You should really have seen him. He climbs like a cat, and I *mean* like a cat. You feel a certain excitement just in watching him. It's beautiful. Like ski-ing. Then when he started striking out with that blasted hammer. . . ." Moreau paused; it was as though he had repressed a shudder. "He frightened me, Fé.

145

He honestly did."

"Frightened you?"

"Yes, he did. Honestly."

"Oh, I see," Fé said. "One of those sex things you get from time to time. I see."

"Oh, don't be *silly*."

"I'm not being. Was that why. . . ?"

"Why what?"

"*You* know. That night."

"All I know is, I was frightened." ·

"It doesn't matter," Fé said quickly. She didn't know what he meant, but she could see that he meant it. No one likes being frightened.

"I don't *like* being frightened," Moreau said; it was as though he had followed her thoughts. "When reason tells me that a thing is impossible, I like that thing to *be* impossible. I've built up my own little prison of unarguable facts, and I'm happy in it. I don't like it when someone walks in and picks up a hammer, smash, smash, *smash*, and says look! you're free! . . . I don't like things being stood on their head. *That's* what frightens me."

"You don't have to tell me all this, Richard."

"You know it already, I suppose."

"Well, I knew you were frightened. You cried that night."

"I *cried*?"

"Yes. In your sleep. You haven't done that for years."

Moreau went on eating calamares. The curious thing, Fé thought, was that throughout all this his air of elation, of internal satisfaction, had remained unchanged; he spoke vehemently, but as though about another person. "I suppose he makes me aware of my own inadequacies," he said. "That's the trouble."

"He's younger than you are. That's all. *That* kind of inadequacy never troubled me much before."

Before? . . . It wasn't what she'd meant to say at all. Her mouth jerked open to correct the slip, but Moreau got in first. He probably hadn't even been listening. That was lucky. "I don't mean *si vieillesse pouvait*. Nothing like that. It's more . . . just that I see I've made a . . . miscalculation. I'm a professional, he's a genius, that's what I've always thought. Two things that aren't just different in quantity, they're different in kind. I knew that, all right, in *theory*. But I never really realised what it *implied*."

"Being young and strong," Fé said contemptuously. "That's not genius."

"Of course not. But is that all *you're* getting out of him? Just youth and strength?"

". . . No," Fé said.

"What, then?"

"I don't know, except that it's something that. . . ."

"Go on."

"All right. Frightens me."

"*Exactly*. There you are, then."

"But that's because I'm not *used* to it. So I don't know. . . . It's not *him* I'm getting frightened of, it's *me*."

"Of course," Moreau said. He pushed the plate away, empty. "That's what one is always frightened of, in the last analysis. Oneself. There's nothing else."

Fé drank, and closed her eyes.

"What can we do?"

"I think we need a good long rest. We'll run down to Mijas next week, and relax in the sun."

"Michael too?"

"Of course."

"He does need a rest. He suffered a lot, you know. He wouldn't take morphine."

"So we'll cancel that last job."

"We can certainly afford to."

"In fact," Moreau said, "we never need do another. That's a thought."

"I'm glad," Fé said. "We've done enough. It's not what I meant, though. I meant about Michael, what can we *do*?"

Moreau raised his eyes, surveyed her levelly for a few seconds. "We can talk about that later."

"You see . . . I keep wanting to tell him."

"About. . . ?"

"Us. Yes."

"No," Moreau said. "You mustn't."

"I keep wanting to, though. It's crazy."

"You mustn't."

"I *know* I mustn't," Fé said helplessly. She brushed her skirt, adjusted the empty glass on the white saucer; preparatory movements to rising to her feet. "No, it's all right. I won't."

"He doesn't ask?"

"No. But he thinks it's odd. He might even guess."

Moreau nodded. "We'll talk about it later."

"I have to go," Fé said.

". . . Give him the good news, won't you?"

"Yes," Fé said. "I will."

She walked away towards the car, her loose skirt swinging, past the table where the three young men were sitting and waiting—politely enough—for her to leave before they moved in beside Moreau. The one in the alpaca jacket she knew to be the latest. Antonio something. He was very good-looking. She pushed out her lower lip in a pout that stopped just short of being petulant. She got into the Citroen, drove off down the wide street towards her flat. It was not quite noon.

Jeye's long body lay outstretched, naked as a copper coin, on the crisp white sheets; face downwards and buried in the pillows, arms held outwards. The hard little hands of the masseuse thumped rigidly against that body, dissolving its solidity into a series of vibrations, of warming waves; moved away to bring drops of golden oil into the hollow at the base of the gluteal muscles, descended again to rub and pound and pummel every square inch of reluctantly yielding flesh. The name of the masseuse was Anita Jimenez; she came from Zaragoza; she was not tall, had black hair and was very pretty. While her hands entered on terms of extreme physical intimacy with her clients, she herself kept well down behind a ceaseless barrier of words, a non-stop commentary of aimless Spanish chatter.

"I was down there last year, you know, and that's where we saw her. Tina Cespedes, I mean. Quite different to on the films, we thought, because she's got red hair and on the films it always looks black, and then she had on this bikini, well my word, and my boy-friend, well of course he's a masseur too, you see, that's how I met him, and he says being a masseur spoils that sort of thing for you, seeing it all professionally so to speak, but all the same I had my eye on *him*, I can tell you. . . ."

"Quite right," Jeye said into his pillow. "I'll bet that's why he became a masseur in the first place."

"Couldn't be that, because he does men usually and he's certainly. . . . He says there's a law against it, really, bikinis I mean, but *I* think it's all the Church and it's just stupid because that's the trouble with Spain, people here just will

149

not take care of their bodies and when all's said and done it's just a machine."

"A what?"

"A wonderful machine," the masseuse said, running a hand expertly over certain of Jeye's more delicate flywheels. "That's what the human body is, a machine, and stands to reason that it has to be looked after. Now yours is in wonderful trim, anyone can see that, so it shows what I mean. Still, we could maybe do with a little more *here*," she said, whacking a brutal little fist into Jeye's right thigh, "couldn't we?"

"Ugh," said Jeye.

He lay still with his eyes closed, feeling those small hard yet agreeably feminine hands travelling like trip-hammers up and down his thighs and calves, half-listening to the unending, not unmusical flow of her conversation. He was in a state of agreeable lassitude, of vague well-being; he wondered idly whether he ought not to make a regular habit of this, as indeed he had done at the sanatorium. Anita's hands had freed him hours ago of that insupportable tenesmus that, stretching like a vice across his chest, had held him pinioned on the bed for a night and a day; he could now sit up, and even walk a few paces, without his stomach muscles clawing up into a ball, toppling him puppet-like to the floor or spinning the room round him like a top. Of those hours that he had spent crucified on the day-bed he had no clear recollection; only dim memories of hands, Fé's hands, on his chest and throat, of grey peering eyes behind bifocal lenses, of the blueish-white of the ceiling and the red and green and red of the drawn curtains. And later, much later, it must have been the following morning, a burningly sharp memory of blue sky seen through the window and in the sky a sea-gull hanging, white, breathlessly white with the sun in its plumage, every feather in its outstretched wings picked out with a supernatural clarity, pink legs and pink curved bill, drifting then turning and falling away, falling, falling, falling. . . .

Anita Jimenez wiped the perspiration from her face and neck and arms with cotton wool; went into the bathroom to (as she would have said) freshen up. When she came out, Jeye was sitting on the bed in his Jaeger dressing-gown and staring out of the window. ". . . Thank you very much," he said.

"Till five this evening, then."

"I'll be here," Jeye said wryly.

"Tomorrow you'll be able to go for a walk. You'll see."

She put on her coat, picked up her bag and moved towards the door. Jeye said, "I wonder if. . . ?"

"If what, Señor Jeye?" She watched him warily but not, as she hoped, too discouragingly.

"Have you ever seen a sea-gull in Madrid?"

"A sea-gull?" She looked rather taken aback; it had not, after all, been precisely the kind of question she had expected. "Good heavens, no. The sea's miles away, miles and miles and miles."

"Yes," Jeye said. "That's what I was thinking. I must have been mistaken."

He rolled over on to his back. Anita Jimenez made her way out of the flat and across to the lift. She wasn't sure if what she felt was relief or disappointment. But anyway, she was looking forward to her lunch. A nice, uncomplicated girl, was Anita Jimenez.

The door of the flat opened again some ten minutes later; Jeye's body tensed itself momentarily, then relaxed as he recognised the familiar click of Fé's high heels on the parquet flooring. She came into the bedroom, already smiling. "Didn't the girl come?"

"Yes," Jeye said. "You're a little late."

"I know. Richard had some good news. I'm going to get you lunch, what would you like?" But she went on without waiting for an answer. "There was much more there than we'd ever supposed, *much* more, and it ought to cut up at something really tremendous. I can't quite believe it."

She sat down beside him, on the edge of the bed.

"Well, how much stuff *was* there?"

"Your part should be something between a hundred and fifty to two hundred thousand dollars. That's if Richard's right. He usually is."

"Yes. I know. That's a lot of money."

"The biggest yet. For any of us."

"Depends on how you look at it, though. Luis Miguel might get that for three afternoons at Valencia."

"Thank God you're not a bullfighter," said Fé, struck by the thought. "That would have been the *end*."

"Not such a disaster nowadays, is it?—socially speaking?"

"It's not that side of things I care about."

"No. Lucky for me. Aren't you being pretty badly compromised, having me *here*?"

"It won't be for long," Fé said.

"No. I can walk quite easily now. I can go back to the hotel when you like. Tonight, even."

"You can't. We've checked you out. Richard got your things yesterday, where did you suppose the dressing-gown came from?"

Jeye looked down at it in surprise. "I never thought about it, to tell you the truth."

"It's safe enough like this. Nobody'll ask questions and

if they do, they'll find an obvious answer. I don't mind *that*."
She took the lapel of the dressing-gown in her fingers, rubbed it gently. "When I said it won't be for long, that's because we'll be leaving."

"Leaving? Where for?"

"Mijas. That place of ours near Málaga."

"Yes," Jeye said. "I remember."

The fingers moved down his arm to his bandaged right hand. "You'd like to go?"

". . . You and me?"

"And Richard."

"Yes. I don't mind."

". . . How soon will it be before you're better?"

"I *am* better."

"But better?"

Jeye's own fingers moved over her hand, squeezed it gently. "Tomorrow," he said. "Yes. Tomorrow. I think."

"You're sure? I don't want to rush you. Yes, I do."

"Tomorrow," Jeye said. He made the word sound like an incantation.

"Yes. Yes, tomorrow. Now I'll go and get you some lunch."

"No hurry," Jeye said.

"It's getting late."

She reached up to stroke his face, her thumb brushing his eyelids, then went through to the kitchen. Jeye lay back on the pillow, listening to the sound of her heels as she moved about, the occasional clatter of a dish or a saucepan. That sound had been there in the dream too, that soft rhythmic clicking; that was how he knew it so well. Her hands, the doctor's eyes, and the sound of her footsteps. All that had been at night. Before the morning and the blue sky, it was odd of course about the sea-gull. . . . Jeye's eyes, wide open,

153

clouded with the opacity of thought.

Not here, though. On the day bed in the sitting-room, by the red and green curtains. Quick soft steps, and other sounds. Her voice, of course: voices. For a very long time. The doctor, yes; Moreau? Had he been there? But the tap of her heels and voices, that was certain. Voices from the distance, behind a door. This door, it would have been. And other sounds. The sound of . . . someone crying? No, that had been later. In his sleep. He had dreamt that he was crying, and had called out, and Fé had come; her hands again, her hands on his forehead, over her eyes, and under the loose blue housecoat she had been naked. No. That too had been later. And part of the dream. It had all been part of the dream, the seagull as well. Because the sea was miles away, miles and miles and miles. . . .

"I've bought you a present," Fé said on the Wednesday morning. She said it shortly after ten o'clock and it was, in fact, her first utterance of the day; Jeye wasn't as yet sufficiently awake to hear her, or to acknowledge having heard her, so she shook him gently by the right shoulder and said it again. "You can't have," Jeye said indistinctly. "Shtoo early."

"I ordered it last week, idiot. And it's just arrived. Come and look."

"Where is it?"

"In the street."

"In the *street*?"

"Yes, come and look."

Jeye rubbed his eyes. "You're *dressed*," he complained.

"It's ten o'clock, damn it. No, be careful."

"I'm all right," Jeye said. "I'm fine."

154

He got out of bed and walked across to the window and together they peered downwards at the road beneath them. There it was. It was blue and shiny and smooth and beautiful, and there was nothing else it could be. "*That?*" asked Jeye, pointing.

"Yes. That."

"You've *bought* it?"

"It's in my name. But it's yours."

"Holy Cow," Jeye said. "You do your boy-friends proud, I'll say that for you."

"You like it?"

"Loveliest job I've ever seen."

"You can try her out later."

"Let's go now."

"You can't go like *that*. I may be dressed, but *you're* not."

"To hell with it," Jeye said. "I can drive in pyjamas, any law says you can't?"

"I'll bet there are plenty. Besides, I certainly *will* be compromised if this goes on."

"That reminds me," Jeye said. He took her by the shoulders.

"What?"

"Today's tomorrow."

"What?" Fé said again. "Oh, yes. So it is."

"A promise is a promise."

"But you're sure you. . . ?"

"Yes," Jeye said. "Shut up."

Her foot twisted slightly as they lay down on the bed. The shoe fell off. It made a little noise that neither of them heard.

The road to Manzanares. Flat and level, grey as a snake in the noonday sunlight. Jeye's foot impassive on the accelerator;

155

his bandaged hands on the ribbed black metal of the steering-wheel. The speedometer needle on one-twenty; miles, not kilo-meters, because this was an English car, an E-type Jaguar, and going like a bomb. Fé at his side, smoking a Chesterfield, strands of hair wisping out from under her scarlet beret, flagellating wildly in the slipstream. And on the horizon the dark spires and roofs of the town, backed by the darker slopes of the Sierra Morena, rushing soundlessly towards them, towed in as though at the end of a glider's cable and about to drop away beneath them and out of sight. Jeye lifted his foot gradually, and the hum of the whirling tyres changed its tone gradually, became more sibilant. "There's half an inch on the pedal I'll never want to use," Jeye said.

"She's only just been run in. Anyway . . . we ought to be turning back, don't you think, if we're lunching in town?"

"We're not going back," Jeye said. The idea hadn't occurred to him until she had spoken, but now was as definite in his mind as though he had planned it all along. "We're going on."

"On? Where to?"

"Mijas."

"But. . . . Are you serious?"

"Of course I am. Wasn't that what you wanted?"

"But not today. We haven't any luggage. Or anything."

"We don't need luggage," Jeye said.

They entered the Manzanares by-pass; still travelling fast, eighty miles an hour or a little less; the chain of roadside garages and paradores went past them like the rattle of heavy rain on an iron roof. "But what about Richard?"

"We'll send him a telegram."

"He won't like that."

"He doesn't have to like it. We're escaping, that's what,

eloping," Jeye said. "From your wicked father."

"You. . . ?"

"Like in the fairy stories."

"Oh."

The mountains were opening out before them, slowly at first then with a sudden flick like a lady's fan. In front, the high sierra, the Despeñaperros gap. Sierra Morena, thought Jeye, the images forming in his brain and circling like eagles; Sierra Brava. Miles of naked rock and of scrub, the farmhouses lonely in that wilderness. Miles of it, miles and miles and miles.

"Anything the matter?"

"No. No, nothing at all."

Jeye was slackening speed again. "You look a bit pale."

"No, it's nothing. What fairy story?"

"Eh?"

"You said, in the fairy stories."

"Oh yes . . . I don't really know. Must have been something I had at the back of my mind."

The lonely farmhouses, the *fincas de recreo*, hunting lodges. Franco's was there; Dominguin's was there; Don Pedro Capdevila's and the Duque de Lerida's. They came in cars like this or in long black *haigas*; they shot; they went away again. It was part of their inheritance; and part, too, of Jeye's own *visión de Castilla*. Because he too was a hunter, and felt at times a hunter's love for the things that he preyed on, making their customs, their traditions his own. And again the idea came to him as something that he had always known, always planned for; the idea that a Spanish wife, should he marry at all, would be for him in no way inconceivable, would be indeed the only choice possible. *Choice?* It wasn't a matter of choice. That was the hell of it.

157

"Would you ever leave him?"

"No. Never."

"I didn't mean a divorce. I know that's not possible. I just meant . . . leave him."

"I know what you meant," Fé said. "I can't."

Jeye nodded. Grey suit, white cotton shirt; he sat slumped back in the seat, nerveless, tranquil. Fé said, in some kind of desperation,

"We can all be together, can't we, until he's dead? Then, if that's what we both . . . still . . . want. . . ."

Her voice faded into uncertainty. Her fingers moved in her lap, folding and unfolding a pleat in her skirt. The car went on, fast and smoothly, through a great sunbaked emptiness. "Forget it," Jeye said.

"It's just that——"

"No. We'll talk about it later."

Driving tired him more than he had expected, and the palms of his hands, the edges of the half-healed gashes there, began to itch intolerably. They stopped to lunch on the far side of the Despeñaperros gap, and after lunch Fé took the wheel. By seven o'clock the light was fading, bleeding slowly from the sky as they mounted the steep switchback hill beyond Córdoba and turned left on to the Antequera road with the width of the Guadalquivir valley extended behind them, smoky with distance, and Córdoba, no longer white but blue-grey city, began to sparkle with pale jewel-like pricks of light, calling them back through the dim unmoving ocean of the evening. Fé drove on, but the impetus of their journey had died; in front of them was the hairpin mountain road that spanned the Sierra Nevada, a bad road to take in the darkness and even in the twilight after four or five hours at the wheel.

"...Lucena?"

"All right," Jeye said.

So they stopped at Lucena, leaving the car parked in the wide village square that smelt of oil and of wine and of the mountains; they ate *flamenquines* and salad with a bottle of Vibora and with *carne de membrillo* to follow, and they slept in the back room of the nearest fonda, where the walls were whitewashed and shone in the starlight and the windows stood wide open to the night air. It was warm there, very warm, and they lay beneath a single sheet, leaving the two blankets that were of coarse wool and smelt in no very tangible way of horses crumpled into a rough ball at the foot of the bed. The mattress was extremely hard and the bedsprings squeaked abominably. Things, in short, they found to be just as they should be.

Next morning at seven-thirty the maid brought hot water in a tall enamel jug; but both of them had been awake for some time before, since in the chill before the dawn the blankets had become necessary, after all; and then, of course, not so necessary. They had heard a canary chirping in the patio, the rattle of a donkey's hooves on the cobbles beyond and the aggravating tin whistle of the milk boy, the voice of the maid herself singing as she got up and dressed, the barking of a dog from somewhere in the depths of the village and the deep clanking roar of a church bell; all these things Fé had heard while inside her body once again the warm tide was receding and his mouth, reluctant as always to leave her, still pressed at the soft hollows beneath her collarbone, between her breasts. She felt him there and within her, his hands shaping the curve of her buttocks, while around them and outside the village came to life, the village and the

159

inn; men went out to work in the fields and the bodegas, maid-servants in stiff black dresses started to sing, and in the end he took his weight on his downthrust forearm and, kissing her, left her, pulling her head at once on to his shoulder and holding it there in a renewed gentle agony of possession; and soon after that, the maid came in with the jug of water. And it became another day; not like all the others, no, but different as yesterday had been. Frightened was still the word. It's frightening to find that you have so much to give.

They breakfasted in the bedroom; hot coffee that was mostly chicory and tortas wrapped up in crinkly greaseproof paper. They paid the bill, went to the car and drove off again, drove very fast along the road that travels, straight as an arrow for much of its length, to Antequera and towards the mountains.

They reached Mijas in time for lunch.

7

IN the early evening, they bathed; and later they sat in cushioned chairs on the veranda. Jeye's body was aching a little, not altogether surprisingly, and his hands and face retained the sting of the slipstream, as of the sun and the salt water; this didn't affect the more general feeling he had of an unusually complete physical contentment. Looking down now towards the sea, he could make out the white houses along the beach shown each one in brilliant clarity by the rays of the low-lying sun; and behind them, a shiver of uncapturable colour, of colour with the purity of light, where those rays dripped liquid gold and silver across the sea. He could hear a lark chippering away somewhere in that great anesthetised swell of blue that stretched overhead, and other sleepy sounds from the village to the west. The evening extended from where he sat to embrace the whole of Spain; like something everlasting, everlasting as death. Sometimes he looked towards the chair where Fé sat, reading a book; beside it a chess-table, the red and the white pieces drawn up in readiness for battle; the sun glinted off them, off the black-and-white squares of the chequerboard, as it glinted off everything. Eventually, Jeye got up and went into the house.

It wasn't, in fact, so much a house as a *cortijo*, a series of rooms arranged apparently at hazard round a central yard. The yard had at some comparatively recent time been paved with grey Granada marble, great pieces of hewn rock in which

161

the veins of quartz and jasper were twisted into threads of bright green and purple; in its centre stood a trough where fountains played, after the style of the Generalife gardens, but using, as Jeye had already seen, the same water over and over again. The drops fell into the shadow of a central trench with a soft, incessant patter, unchanging in tone, though at times they reached out, lifted by the breeze, to stain the marble slabs around the trench with a darker design, random yet suggestive of symmetry. Basically, the place was an eighteenth-century farmhouse that had been modernised and redecorated; the windows had been widened, electricity brought in, the heavy oaken doors replaced with canvas shutters that moved on well-greased rollers; there were Granadine rugs on the tiled floors and modern Swedish-style furniture in every room; the window blinds were of coloured plastic, adjusted at the touch of a cord. All this, Jeye thought, without affecting notably that air of Andalusian bareness appropriate to the place's origin; it had remained simple, single in design and in function. But it now represented that form of simplicity which requires a very considerable capital outlay. There were servants, of course; Jeye didn't yet know how many, but . . . three or four, at least; maybe five.

He crossed the patio, went through the new french window into the library. A long, low room, where the nineteenth-century panelling had been left untouched; the books ran along one wall only, the inner wall, but there were certainly more than five hundred. Not all old ones. On the opposite wall, three portraits. One of the late Juan Carbonell, whom Jeye easily recognised from his recollection of the frontispiece to *La Esperanza*; another of a girl of fourteen or fifteen whom, not quite so easily, he recognised as Fé. Both portraits had clearly been executed by a painter of resounding mediocrity.

He crossed the room to look more closely at the third; a woman of astonishing pallidity, perhaps over-emphasised by the artist, and of a no less astonishing though unconventional beauty; a beauty based on a certain delicacy of the facial bone structure. She had demanded a certain effort, obviously, and been duly granted it. She was dressed in deep black, with high comb and mantilla. The religious type. Jeye reached out and swung the painting to one side; replaced it with no change of his expression. He stepped back a couple of paces.

"How did you know?" Fé asked.

He didn't turn round. "I was looking at the portrait," he said. "And then I must have smelt them. It's a funny place to keep them, though."

"Too obvious, you mean? . . . Richard's an admirer, you see, of Edgar Allen Poe."

"Oh, yes," Jeye said.

"What made you come in here, anyway?"

"I don't know. Maybe I heard the diamonds calling."

Fé perched herself on the oak table in the centre of the room. "Were you bored, out there on the veranda?"

"No," Jeye said. "Not bored."

"Do you think you'll like it here?"

"Yes," Jeye said. "Very much."

"There are lots of parties here, you know. Málaga, Torremolinos, Fuengirola. Plenty of gaiety."

"And sailing, of course. For a change. Remember?"

"Yes," Fé said. "It seems a long time ago."

She swung her right foot to and fro in the air, and they stared for a while at each other.

". . . But I like this place," Jeye said, sitting on the table beside her. "I didn't realise you had . . . roots. Know what I mean?"

163

"Yes. They're useful, sometimes."

"Useful?"

"To be able to meet the right people. On their own terms."

"I wasn't thinking of that so much."

"No?"

"No. I was just thinking of it as . . . roots . . . as something I hadn't got. That's all." He nodded towards the portrait. "Your mother?"

"Yes. The house was hers and she left it to me. Otherwise my father would probably have sold it."

"Did you live here when you were small?"

"Yes. When I wasn't in the convent. At school, you know. I lived here with my mother. But it wasn't . . . like it is now. It was rather tumbledown, to tell the truth."

"You did it up when you got married?"

"Well, no. Before, mostly."

"Before?"

"Yes. Oh, two or three years before, I'd have been . . . sixteen, seventeen. . . . Why?"

"I understood you hadn't much money," Jeye said, "when your father died."

"Not a bean. Richard advanced it, you see. He was my legal guardian, in charge of the estate." She waved a hand in the air. "This was the estate."

"You mean your father named him as. . . ?"

"I thought you knew."

"No," Jeye said. "How *would* I have known?"

"You've been asking questions, haven't you? I was sure that you'd have gone to the Probate Office."

"No. I started asking questions, yes. But then I stopped."

"I see," Fé said.

"Anything you want me to know, I suppose you'll tell me. The rest doesn't matter."

Fé looked suddenly downwards at her knees. "It would be wonderful," she said, "if you really *meant* that. If you really did."

"But I mean just that. I really do."

He probably believed this himself.

Moreau had received their telegram the previous evening at about the time when they had been looking down from the hill road on to Córdoba, *lejano y solo,* and its fanned-out lamps and smoke-ruined spires. After that he had dined at the Riviera with Antonio, had listened to a number of short verses that the other had written—somewhat in the style of Juan Ramon Jimenez, but not devoid of merit—then had returned to make his arrangements.

Two days later he and Antonio drove down to Fuengirola and the Hotel Cataluña, where Antonio was to stay at Moreau's expense. Then, after taking a coffee alone in the casino, he took the Citroen on up to Mijas, stopping for a few moments on the way to watch the crescent moon tangled in the boughs of the olives. He found Fé sitting on the veranda.

". . . You're not cross?"

"Cross? Of course not," Moreau said.

The next morning he spent mostly in the small room off the library that served him as an office, rearranging the files that he had brought with him from Madrid and checking, against a typewritten list, sixty-seven assorted items that represented about three hundred thousand dollars' worth of jewellery. Certain of these he examined minutely with a twenty-x, but the list stood in no need of correction. A little before noon, he locked away both list and jewellery in the library safe and the files in the oak escritorio that stood in the corner. Then for fifty minutes he sat at his desk, smoking three cheroots.

They had lunch, the three of them, on the balcony. They ate *almejas al ojo*, pungent and steaming; they ate huge Mediterranean sardines that had been roasted over coals in the kitchen; and they ate some chumbos, hard green fruit of the cactus expertly pared with a sharp knife so that the insides, watery and white, nestled inside four pointed green petals like the calyx inside an open rose. The sun shone down on them from above the blue and wave-wrinkled sea, not strongly enough for its heat to become oppressive but with enough strength to flush the skin of Fé's arms and shoulders with a new suggestion of colour, a pinkness beneath the smooth tan, subtle as the bloom on a peach. "So here we all are," Moreau said.

"Again."

"Yes. Again. And very pleasant too, if I may say so."

"Yes," Fé said. "Very pleasant."

"Why, it's almost spring."

"It always is, down here," Jeye said. "You don't have to wait. You can jump in a car and drive to it."

"You don't like waiting?"

"No one does."

"Oh, I don't mind," Moreau said. "I don't mind." He wiped a dribble of juice from the side of his mouth with a napkin. "And after all, April is the cruellest month, just as Eliot says. There's no doubt about it."

"Why do you think that?"

"It's true. The suicide rates, for one thing, of almost every country. They rise in the spring. And April's usually the peak."

"Anyway," Fé said. "Here we all are."

"Again," Moreau said, spreading out his hands. He chuckled.

"And how's Antonio?"

"His driving is improving immensely."

"He'll be wanting you to buy him a sports car before long," Fé said, looking at Jeye from under her lashes.

"I'm afraid his ideas *are* rather derivative. The stuff he's doing now is sadly juanramonesco. Though he does touch at times on an ironical vein I feel he'd do well to exploit."

"I'm very glad Michael's not a poet."

"You're glad I'm not a poet. You're glad I'm not a bull-fighter. Isn't there anything that you wish I *were*?"

"I don't think so. What do *you* wish you were?"

"A sea-gull," Jeye said instantly. Then, having thought about it for a few moments in the silence that followed,

". . . Or I don't know. No, maybe not. Not really."

Both Fe and Moreau were looking at him oddly. "You sounded very *definite*," Moreau said.

"It's just a thing I've . . . sometimes imagined."

"Being a sea-gull? Really? What does it feel like?"

"Wonderful," Jeye said.

Rather to his surprise, Moreau now nodded. "Of course, there *are* people like that. People with a peculiar insight into the feelings of animals and children. Juan Ramon himself was one, obviously. And D. H. Lawrence. Have you read any of Lawrence's poems about animals?"

"No," Jeye said. "I don't think so."

"You should do. There's a copy in the library some-where."

And Fé said suddenly,

"Let's all go to the beach. Let's go down to the beach and

167

have a swim."

Jeye found that he liked Antonio more than he had expected. It was hard to say why, though. Maybe it was a certain quality of enthusiasm that the boy conveyed, a kind of vitality rather rare in Spanish youth, an echo, perhaps, in more positive form of the genial quarrelsomeness of Juanito Salinas. They took coffee, all four of them, at the beach café and later drove round to the cliffs behind Los Boliches to swim and sunbathe. Lying on striped towels thrown out over the warm sand, they talked about islands, all kinds of islands, for almost an hour. Then, with the evening approaching, Antonio ran off barefooted for a second swim and Fé in her lemon-yellow one-piece bathing suit ran after him; leaving Moreau and Jeye, whose muscles were still not fully returned to their normal pliability, behind them. "This," said Moreau, who was lying at full length with his great white head pillowed on his forearm, "is pleasant. Isn't it? *Dolce fá niente.* Even though in many ways I prefer the night."

"Um," Jeye said. His eyes were closed, the lids a warm red curtain of membrane holding off the sun.

"And you?"

"What?"

"Do you agree?"

"I like it here," Jeye said. "I quite like it here."

"You don't suffer from the Nordic urge to be always up and doing?"

"We've just done two, haven't we? We meant to do three. But two's enough."

"As things have turned out, yes. It may be a long time before I shall want to do another. You know that, I suppose."

"That makes sense," Jeye said.

"I'm glad you see it that way."

". . . Or are you trying to tell me the partnership's over?"
Jeye turned his head sideways; sand rustled in his hair.
"Gently? Tactfully?"

"It isn't that kind of a partnership. It never was. You must
stay here in Mijas for as long as you wish, that goes without saying. You're all right for money?"

"Money?"

"If not, I'll make you any advance you like on your share
of the, er, takings."

"No hurry," Jeye said.

"Good. We'll probably be able to realise some of the assets
almost immediately, but the greater part'll go next winter . . .
I should think." Moreau placed a cigar between his lips and
struck a match; the flame burnt invisibly in the bright sunlight, his fingers wavering behind it as in a haze. "My own
view is that I should retain control of our account, as far as
is convenient. It's better that way."

"Why?"

"Oh, I'm sure you'll have covered yourself extremely well.
But when all is said and done, you're a foreigner here. So am
I, if it comes to that. But nobody's likely to inquire too closely
into how the daughter of Juan Carbonell comes by her money.
Fé's accounts are damned nearly invulnerable."

"I see," Jeye said. And after a pause, "Is that the reason why
you married her?"

"Not the real reason, no."

Moreau looked towards Fé's black-capped head, breaking
the surface to disappear again beneath the white fluster of
an incoming wave; his gaze followed that wave as it continued its course, broke at last on the brown boulders in sudden shavings and slivers of leaping light; in the beauty and

169

impermanence of that moment something touched him, some feeling of sadness or of sorrow, making that moment right, perhaps, for the first hint, the first partial revelation of that other, future moment in which he and Jeye and Fé in the sea would become not peripherally, but inextricably, involved, king and pawn and queen checkmating each other in some way the rules of the game could not envisage or explain. "If I were to tell you the real reason, you wouldn't think it was a reason at all. That's why you find it so perplexing."

"I didn't say I found it perplexing."

"One day I'll tell you, Michael. I promise you. But meanwhile we'll both have to wait. You don't like waiting, and I do." Moreau shrugged. "That's the luck of the game."

"What game?"

"The game we've all come here to play."

Jeye lay now propped up on one elbow. He picked up a handful of sand, tilted the grains out from his palm in a whispering stream. "You said you'd be selling some of the stuff . . . almost immediately."

"Within the month. Yes."

"Fé'll run them?"

"Yes."

"It's a bloody dangerous game."

"Yes, it can be."

". . . Why bring her into it?"

"She wanted to do it," Moreau said. "She has what you might call a natural aptitude. Many people in the trade would rather deal with a woman—you know that as well as I do—and I'm no good at salesmanship myself, no good at all. Besides, this way the percentage stays, so to speak, in the family. We can trust one another."

"Who did you use before?"

"A woman. She was French. She died."

"Died?"

"She was murdered. Yes."

"Helga." Jeye nodded. "I rather thought so."

"I'm cautious with names."

"Was it your stuff she was pushing when they caught her?"

"No, no. I'm glad to say, no. Yes, I suppose one *has* an indirect responsibility."

"*Indirect*," Jeye said. "Jesus Christ. If someone like van der Velde or Petersen cottons on to Fé in Antwerp, we've an indirect responsibility, have we? Jesus *Christ*."

"It's hardly possible," Moreau said.

"*You* cottoned on to *me*."

"Yes, but my information service is unique. Research is my speciality; you keep forgetting. If you were to look through your own file, you'd find it very interesting. There are things there you'll have forgotten about yourself, and others which maybe you never knew."

"Then you can do me a favour."

Moreau nodded. He didn't smile. "Tonight," he said. "You can set fire to them yourself, if you want."

"You should have done it before."

"To tell you the truth, I've been saving them up . . . in case the need should arise for some sort of gesture. To make an occasion of it, if you know what I mean."

To tell you the truth, Jeye said; Fé was always using that expression, too. Yet neither of them would. "Yes," he said, sitting upright. "To dissolve the partnership. Or perpetuate it, according to how you look at it. Well, maybe you're right. Maybe you are."

Fé was splashing up from the slope of the beach, adjusting

the top of her swimsuit as she ran; the water boiled at her ankles, sucked at them, receded. "We'll talk more about this later," Jeye said.

"Of course we will. We've plenty of time. We have all the time in the world."

8

TICK tick tick, said the clock in the bedroom, nearing midnight.

"A week."

"What?"

"We've been here a week. It seems longer."

"Uh-huh."

"When are you going to Tangiers?"

"Soon."

Naked, she was propped up by the pillows; half-seated, so that her breasts lost none of their depth of contour and the muscles in her thighs stayed partly tensed. She seemed none the less to be on the verge of sleep; her eyes had closed some minutes ago, her lips were slightly parted. Her face was shaded by the hang of the curtain from the moonlight; there were soft shadows also on her body, contrasting with the darker pools in the folds of the white lamb's-wool blanket on which she was lying. Jeye, in slippers and dressing-gown, sat on the end of the bed; he looked at her without really seeing her.

Between the cats and the fences, the diamond pushers. They have their exits and their entrances. In New York they gather off Forty-Seventh Street, men in slouch hats and loose linen trousers leaning against the beetling walls of red brick buildings; in their hip pockets, black wallets that smell of tobacco and bourbon and that contain at least one chip, one multifaced chip of compressed carbon, and maybe more; maybe four or five. In Antwerp they stand at the river end of the Suikerrui; in Tangiers, dressed in burnous or djellaba, they sit on the benches round the Place de Paris. These are the outcasts of the diamond world, the Mr Two-per-cents; others in a higher class, the Krugers and the Petersens, often operate from well-appointed offices, perhaps as a sideline from legitimate, or terrifyingly illegitimate, business. But these, too, have their exits and their entrances; and the former, once in a while, may be sudden and violent. Jeye thought, as he had thought before, of Helga, whose surname he had forgotten and whose photograph he had seen on one occasion only; he had been reading a newspaper on the Métro between Sèvres-Babylone and Austerlitz, travelling to take the morning train to Irun, and Helga had been there on the front page, heading a full column of excited print, her raddled, middle-aged charwoman's face criss-crossed with the pattern of blood that the shivs had drawn. He had studied that photograph for a few seconds only, but the memory of it had remained with him as a perpetual reminder of the other side of the medal, of the world of which he knew much by hearsay yet had had few dealings with, as few as possible; a world, however, which he and the other cats created, made possible. Indirect responsibility; of course, it was no more than that; were there no such things as diamonds, people would kill each other for something else, and would do so, as always, under the cloak of . . . yes, legitimate business, as it's called, the continuation of war by other means. That was all right. One could escape all the implications by living inside a jewel, thieving for thieving's sake, l'art pour l'art. Inside a diamond, light is graduated by such subtle degrees that the change to darkness is never fully perceived; never, indeed, fully comes about; that tone of deepest purple is only attained in the very depths of the stone, too far in for any human to hope to reach. To live in a diamond is to live entirely in a state of free fall, free of the pull of morality; is to be granted a kind of secular sainthood.

On a woman's body, though, light and shadow are clear. Are never clearer.

Inside the diamond, the atoms circle in endless orbit. Coming out of orbit, that is what's dangerous. Exciting, though, to feel that gradual pull, the swing of the deadfall, the suck of the air, with the whole of space between you and the four-inch ledge of safety. It's all a matter of balance, Jeye thought. To *fall* in love, we always say; well, that's exactly how it happens. You mustn't miss the ledge. That's all. Not just to fall, but to drop and to drop *right*; that is what's important. Otherwise, there's no way back into the diamond again.

He crossed the patio, awash with silver and with shadows, past the trickling fountain; entered the library; switched on the lights, both the overhead lamp and the reading-lamp on the table. The book also was on the table, where he had left it. He sat down, leafing through the pages until he had found the place. Then he began to read.

And there is nothing else, throughout time and eternity,
but the abyss, which is bottomless,
and the fall to extinction, which can never come,
for the abyss is bottomless....

The truth is, thought Jeye, I don't know what it means. I don't understand it. There's a sea-gull, hanging in the window, white on endless blue, and I don't know what *that* means

175

either. White stands for purity, doesn't it? Virginity and all that jazz? Yes, but shrouds are white. And snow. The falling snow. No, I don't understand it.

> *... yet never finds an end,*
> *for there is no end,*
> *it is the abyss of the immortality*
> *of those that have fallen from God. ...*

He looked at the white lady in the black dress. Fallen from God, he thought; haven't we all? What about *you*, señora? Yes, I know, it's Holy Week, you're in mourning for Jesus Christ. And black sets off that lovely pale complexion. Your face under the shawl. White as a sheet. But Fé belongs to the sun; her face, her body, long slim limbs are brown. Only once have I seen her white like you; that time driving down here in the car. Driving too fast, perhaps. Not fear, though; of course not; she's not afraid of anything, any more than you were. Courage can't be painted, but there's something that shows. People who have it recognise others who have it; in a painting, a photograph, anywhere. You were brave, señora, I can see that. And you married a coward. A man in a white uniform with nothing inside it. Me? ... I'm brave. Or I try to be. I work sixty feet up, eighty, a hundred. At sixty feet, nobody's brave; there's sweat on my hands when I jump. But it doesn't stop me. I'm in love with your daughter, señora. I've fallen, I'm still falling; I'm a brave man, you know that, but I'm sweating, I'm afraid. And you know why. You could tell me why, if you wanted to. You know all about it. You could tell me just what it is I'm afraid of.

Moreau's a brave man. He may be sweating, too, for all I can tell. But still, he *knows*. He knows and I don't. It isn't fair.

Only man can fall from God,
only man.
No animal, no beast nor creeping thing. . . .

No good. It didn't make sense. Jeye closed the book, went back to the bedroom. In the bedroom, Fé had switched on the light. She was wearing some frivolity in pink chiffon and, still sitting up in bed, was manicuring her nails. "I thought you'd be asleep," Jeye said.

"Why, is it late?"

"Not really. Why don't you ever wear a watch?"

He sat down again on the end of the bed, loosening the sash of his dressing-gown. The clock was on the bedside table, anyway. It seemed to him that nowadays they were always asking each other questions that needed no answer; perhaps, he thought, to avoid the others, the questions that *had* no answer. The manicure case lay on her knees, file, clippers, scissors all in place, as carefully arranged as his own tools. She had, for a woman, a very orderly mind.

"Richard's not back yet," he said.

"No."

"Does he always go out at night? In Madrid, yes, but what does he do *here?*"

"He doesn't sleep," Fé said.

"Insomnia?"

"You might call it that. It's just that he doesn't seem to need it. It used to worry him once, but not any more."

"So he's not just being tactful."

"Tactful?"

"Keeping out of our way."

"He doesn't have to be. He's got his own room."

"He has *now,*" Jeye said.

177

He watched her put the orange-stick away, close the case, slide it into its recess under the night table. The room, after all, was hers, really. The whole house. It wasn't *that* he wanted to talk about.

"He says I shouldn't go with you. To Tangiers."

"It'll only be for a couple of days," Fé said.

"I went last time."

"That was different."

"Why?"

"That was so you could see how things were for yourself. You didn't really know us, then."

"I'm damned if I do now," Jeye said. "That's the trouble."

"What do you mean?"

"You know what I mean."

"It makes it more dangerous, your being there. Not less."

"I never said——"

"You didn't have to say it. You worry about me. I don't like that."

"Of course I worry."

"Richard doesn't."

"That's one of the things I don't understand."

"It's very simple," Fé said. "He respects me. It's very simple."

"But I respect you, too. It doesn't have——"

"No. You don't. With you, it's different. I'd hate you if you did."

Jeye sighed. "There you go again. Your own special way of using words. You know what you mean, but I don't."

Fé said,

"I could have had a husband who respected me. You know what that means in Spain, don't you? . . . who'd have put me on the shelf. Who'd have bought me diamonds for my birthday and a mink coat for Christmas. Who'd have left me to pick up dust, like Leonora de Lagranja, to do what I dam' well liked, provided I could always be taken down and brushed up for special occasions. Well, when I married Richard I knew what I was doing, I knew *just* what I was doing. I knew that whatever happened, it wouldn't be like that. Because whatever he was doing, I'd be in on it just as much as he was. All the way, all the bloody way, which is as far as you can go. Respect. *That's* what I mean by it."

"I wonder if that's true," Jeye said.

"I'd have thought it was clear enough."

"It's clear, yes. But I don't know if it's *true*. I heard once that no one would marry you because you didn't have any money."

Fé leaned forwards and slapped him very hard across the face. Then swung round on the bed, her feet going down to the carpeted floor and her back turning defensively towards him; she stared through her fingers at the far wall.

". . . That could be true, as well," she said.

"Oh, of course you're different," Jeye said. "You're different to the women we rob, of *course* you are. But it could be that you've been made different. You felt that you weren't wanted, that people despised you, so you decided to hate people back. But you don't have to be that way underneath. There are plenty of wives in the world who love their husbands. There *have* to be."

He took his hand from his pocket, rubbed his cheek. He hadn't been surprised by the slap so much as by the force of it.

"And that coming from *you*," Fé said.

"Why not from me?"

"You're the man who said the world was a brothel."

179

"Yes," Jeye said, and rubbed his chin instead. ". . . I really thought that, then."

"God, you're a fool," Fé said, turning round.

"I don't think so."

"Being so sure about everything. Then letting it all go. And all for why? Because of me?"

"Because of *us*. I don't understand *anything* any more, you know. I was thinking that just now."

"Neither do I."

"But at least, more than I do."

"No, I don't. That's why I . . . you made me so cross then. It's awful when you think you're a certain kind of person and then find out you're not, you're just the opposite. Respect, you see, I've always thought it was *that* I really wanted. And now it's turned out to be the other thing, it's just too damned humiliating and that's why I was. . . . I'm sorry I hit you, though. Really, I am."

"Fé."

"What?"

"Look. I love you. Oh, God." Jeye got to his feet. "No, *you're* right, too, it sounds ridiculous."

"It just needs practice. Like everything else."

"You think so?"

"Oh, come on," Fé said. "Let's *get* some practice."

"Fé."

"Oh, no. Don't stop."

"Fé."

"Yes?"

"I love you."

"Yes," Fé said. "Oh, yes, that's so much better."

The lights of the fishing-boats, pools of warmth on the sea, trailed out in an almost motionless procession. The night lay not behind them but all around them, lapping them in a solitude clear as wax; though farther to the east the moon shone, the waters rippled, and the darkness beyond the moon was that of the low hills of Africa. The lights of the boats glowed softly, fervently, like candles, against great patches of black nothing where holes had been torn in the universe; above them a scattering of pale stars that echoed coldly, distantly, those living flames. Behind Moreau, the radio was playing quietly; people were talking; a clink and subdued rattle of glasses, of knives and forks on china. He turned and went in from the veranda, walking back to his table.

His mind remained curtained in heavy blue velvet; bright points of light still winked there, pulsed to an unsteady rhythm; and as he sat there, slowly came into focus, coalesced into an image as clear as a colour photograph. It *was* a colour photograph. Against that blue velvet background, great diamonds shone like a moonburst in a setting of liquid gold and silver; rubies flowed across them in a river of blood. In his mind was a masterpiece, the greatest masterpiece of an unknown medieval craftsman; an achievement as marvellous in its way as the altar-piece at Ghent, as the rose window of Chartres. St. Elizabeth of Hungary had worn it; the Hapsburgs had owned it. Goya had painted it once on the brow of Maria-Luisa de Parma. One of the oldest crown jewels of Europe; the royal tiara of Hungary; rubies, diamonds and gold. Moreau pressed his hands to his forehead for a moment; then, slowly, took the cigar-case from his pocket. Once there, he thought, in his mind, it was always there; it couldn't be forgotten. Jeye was quite right. It was immortal.

That, after all, was Jeye's gift. To close one's eyes, and see a certain image; that must be wonderful. Just to see diamonds,

rubies, gold. But when I close my eyes—he thought—what is
it I can see? . . . Music is different. Power may be an illusion.
Yet I have no choice. There is a plan and there has always been
a plan, and at the end of the plan is the kill; yet the plan
isn't really mine and the kill won't be made by me. A pistol
of diamonds and of rubies; all I have to do is place it in another man's hands. Why? . . . That's the question that's
never asked. But, well, why, Iago? More fell than hunger,
anguish or the sea? . . . It's life, that's why. It's fulfilment.
Hunger and anguish are part of life, and the sea waits at the
end of it, a blue solitude, dark, unenvious. It's what he wants.
He's come out of the shell because he wants it, white scuttling
body and waving claws. He wants to die. The kill will be
made, but not by me.

In the sky, a pale echo of living flames. Not in the stars,
but in we ourselves; that's the whole point. Michael is a
genius. Fé has an orderly mind. My kind of mind. Fé recognises inevitability, just as I do. Michael can't or won't; that's
why he's a genius. I'm thinking too much. It's all very clear.
But I'm thinking too much. That's why my head aches.

"Todo a su gusto, Señor Moreau?"

Moreau looked up. The head water. Black tie, folded napkin
tucked over elbow, professionally wearied smile, as though
his mouth had buckled at the knees. "Everything as I expect
it, Pepe."

"As always, señor?"

"Of course. As always."

The head waiter bowed and padded away. Moreau opened
his cigar-case, took out a cheroot.

No, he thought. That isn't why my head aches. I know why
my head aches and that isn't the reason. Two years more,
Don Gregorio had said; but then all doctors are optimists. It

would be less. I dislike pain. When the moment comes, I'll take the pistol and I'll go where Michael is going. Though that's a metaphor, of course. The sea is always waiting, blotched with shadows; but only those shadows give it shape and form. Beyond, there are no shadows. Nothing.

Rien que le néant, he thought, striking a match. *Et le néant c'est tout.* There's nothing. Nothing at all.

"He really was a policeman."

"I know," Jeye said.

"In the Sûreté, too. Special Branch."

"Yes."

"Well, maybe that's it."

"How d'you mean? It?"

"I mean when a policeman comes over, he comes over all the way. Because when he stops being a policeman, it's as though there's nothing. It's almost like losing his identity. . . I'm not putting it very well, am I?"

"For once," Jeye said, "I know what you mean."

"Well, that's it."

"And of course, he starts off with the know-how. That's a big help."

"Yes. You know how it all *really* started?"

"No."

"I know you don't, but if you shut up, I'll tell you."

"Sorry."

"There was a man called Dubos." She lay face up to the ceiling, so that Jeye, beside her, saw her now in profile; the long outline of her nose, pout of her lower lip, firm, lifted chin. ". . . Dubos. Very young. Nineteen or twenty. He was a cat. A very good cat. But Richard caught him."

Jeye, reaching out, switched off the light. Her profile now

183

silhouetted against the moonlight that splashed off the wall, her hair lost in shadows where his fingers were entwined. "He was working with the Gestapo then, on and off. Richard was. There were safes in the Gestapo offices full of jewellery. Confiscated jewellery. Stuff they'd taken from people they'd had shot, waiting to be taken off to Germany. So instead of putting Dubos in the jug, Richard went in with him. He had the information; Dubos did the work. They cleaned out the safes in town after town. There were papers, reports and things, as well. The papers went to the Resistance and the Resistance passed them on to British Intelligence. They were heroes, Dubos and Richard. You know. Patriots. But the jewellery . . . they salted that away."

"Not much else they could have done."

"Maybe not. But the Germans got very angry. They put two or three Special Branch men on to catching Dubos, and one of them had to be a cat specialist. Naturally. It was Richard. A comic situation, wouldn't you say?"

"Stranger things have happened," Jeye said.

"So Richard caught him. Dubos was caught one night in the act, and at dawn next morning they shot him dead. On Richard's orders. That was in the winter of '43. The year after that, just before the Normandy landings, Richard left for Spain."

"And that was how it started?"

"That was how he started."

Jeye grunted. "A smooth boy. Right from the beginning."

"You could call him that. He was in love with Dubos," Fé said. "An idyllic affair, from what I gather. Oh, he kept the jewellery all right, but he talks as though it were the other thing that mattered."

"He *talks* about it?"

"To me. Yes. How else could I have known?"

"Well, what happened? A lover's quarrel?"

"No. It wasn't that. In a way, you could say he'd had an ultimatum. From the Germans. He had to catch Dubos, or else."

"They could *both* have done a bunk, couldn't they?"

"The thing is, it was like a part of himself that he felt he had to destroy. And when he'd done it, then it turned out to be damned nearly the whole. At one time I thought I could understand that, but I understand it less and less as time goes by. At one time," Fé said, "I felt the same way. That was why I married him. To destroy a certain part of myself for ever. But it didn't work out."

She felt Jeye's fingers tighten slightly in her hair.

"Marrying someone and killing someone are rather different things."

"It's not the *someone* who matters. That's the point. It's you yourself. You have to do something you can never turn your back on, so that all you can do . . . is go on from there."

From Jeye's fingers, some nervous impulse seemed to travel towards his brain and explode outwards with tremendous speed. Understanding came to him of a certain bewildering truth, and came—again—with a strange sensation of being something he had fully known, had realised before; but the knowledge this time was agonising, vertiginous as a precipice, and his mind couldn't hold it. He closed his eyes and as he closed them, it was gone. He had understood at last, and yet he hadn't. There were things that it had to do with; that was all he could remember. It had to do with pain and cold and with his parents' voices in another room. With voices and with hands. That was all he could remember.

"That time I cracked up," he found himself saying. "That

185

time you took me home in the car and put me to bed in the sitting-room. What happened that night?"

"A lot of things happened."

"I meant between Richard. And you."

". . . Oh."

". . . Well?"

"He was in a bit of a state," Fé said, rather slowly. "Over-excited. It was really rather odd."

"So you had to quieten him down."

"Yes, I did."

"*That* way?"

"Yes. *That* way. If it matters."

"I don't know," Jeye said. "I suppose it oughtn't to."

"I *am* his wife, damn it. There's not much I can do about it, if. . . . Well, *is* there?"

"No."

"He's no good, you know."

"No, I realise that."

"And it can't happen while you're here. That's what matters."

186

9

THEY drove through Torremolinos and on towards the airport. The motor hummed quietly on a note that seemed electronically rather than mechanically conceived, the tyres spinning almost soundlessly; Fé was at the wheel, Moreau and Jeye in the back. It was not yet quite dark. A little before the Churriana sideroad they turned sharp right towards the beach, under a huge stone arch and down a well-gravelled drive; at the end stood Las Arboledas, the yacht club, grey and leafy, with cars strewn as though at hazard in front of its tall stone walls. The sound of music came faintly to them as Fé cut the engine and opened the door; a woman was laughing very loudly by the front steps, harsh Spanish peals of laughter that seemed unlikely ever to stop.

"You've got your mask?" Moreau asked, and Jeye nodded.

He took it from his inside pocket, put it on. It fitted well enough, though the eyeholes were a trifle too wide. Masked balls were supposed to be forbidden in Spain, as a result of some antiquated but not forgotten ordinance; a ruling, however, that couldn't reasonably be held to apply at the social level that the members of the Club Nautico represented. Moreau certainly looked remarkably distinguished in his, the black velvet admirably setting off his mane of white hair; while Fé looked kittenish, absurdly young, in spite of the alarmingly sophisticated hair-do she had acquired that afternoon at Conchita Alba's. For a moment the three of them surveyed each other as though they had to deal with strangers.

"Isn't this fun," Fé said uncertainly.

Jeye wasn't too sure. He was wearing a glen-plaid suit of orlon and wool with a four-button front and narrow lapels, with a grey silk tie by Vega de Madrid; on his head, a deer-stalker cap of matching plaid. He took now a meerschaum pipe from his pocket and clenched it defensively between his teeth. Identification symbol from Dunhill, thirty-five shillings. He was Sherlock Holmes.

"Ah, well," Moreau said. "It's all in a very good cause." He took Jeye lightly by the elbow as they moved towards the main entrance. "By the way, if a lady with a face like a bulldog should attempt to interest you in a raffle ticket, I advise you strongly to buy. That will be the Duquesa."

"I have my cheque-book."

"Very wise. She's a useful contact. Sits on the committee of just about everything. Call her Mimi."

"Mimi?"

"She'll be flattered."

A retired ambassador in evening dress took their invitation cards and bowed. They went through into the main hall. It was crowded. Even the dance floor. The orchestra sounded like a good one. A younger diplomat in a plum-coloured dinner jacket led them to their table. There were lilies, yellow- and blue-streaked, in a tall glass vase at the centre.

"If you'll excuse us for a moment . . ." Moreau said.

Jeye nodded and sat down. The Señores de Moreau made their way towards a table to the left, where a thin man in a black cloak was wildly signalling to them; Dracula? Jeye wondered; surely not. . . . He took the pipe from his mouth and, leaning back in his chair, took in the scene; the ornate chandeliers overhead with their glass beads faceting a thousand points of dull pink light, the writhing baroque figures adorning the stone pillars along the walls, the long benches of the buffet table-clothed in gleaming white with their long pallid rows of silver dishes and hotplates; the heavy leather divans paralleling the benches; the deep blue carpet underfoot. The orchestra dais, in a recess some forty feet to his right. His table was a good one. The aristocracy had taken the best, as usual, but Moreau, as a resident, clearly rated. Mimi had obviously received the right donation.

Salinas was there all right, and not so far away. Jeye watched him unobtrusively. He resembled his son not in the slightest; he was a small brown man with a low-lying thatch of black hair and a long mournful Andalusian nose. His age, like that of many Spaniards in his position, might have been anything from forty to sixty; though Jeye, of course, knew it to be fifty-three. His party was quite a large one. Rich men are rarely left unaccompanied on these occasions, and Salinas was supposed to be the third richest man in Spain. He sat not at a table, but on a couch drawn up close to the wall and discreetly screened from the orchestra dais; Jeye beckoned to one of the waiters, who came up alertly. "Tell me. . . ?" Jeye said.

The Marquesa de Villalobos was on the right, Tina Cespedes the actress was on the left. Opposite was Teniente-General Carlos Capdevila, Father Gregorio Sanchez, SJ, Don Miguel Barbudo and Don Artoro Nuñez de Soto. Father Sanchez represented the Missionary Church, Capdevila the Guardia Civil, Barbudo the world of commerce and Nuñez the Falange. The Marquesa represented Acción Catolica and Tina Cespedes, by common consent, the oldest profession. Salinas' party seemed a remarkably adequate cross-section of the well-heeled, as Jeye himself conceded with a nod; the waiter, politely

189

smiling, withdrew. His services were often called for in this direction. Everyone wants to know who everyone else is, at this kind of social function; what else is there to talk about?

"Hullo," someone said.

Jeye rose courteously to his feet. "Oh, hullo."

"You don't remember me, do you?"

"Please sit down," Jeye said. "It would be from some previous incarnation, of course? Didn't I once have the pleasure of ravishing you, when I was Atila the Hun?"

She giggled; he at least had struck the right note. Whoever it was, he didn't think it was Mimi. "No. Last month in Escorial. You drove me in to Madrid."

"So I did," Jeye said, sitting down again beside her. "Carmen, isn't it? I *am* sorry. It's the mask, of course."

"I recognised *you*, though."

"I'm not quite so heavily disguised, though."

"Oh, come now," Carmen said, elevating her bust. "It's for *real*."

"That wasn't what I meant. It's the veil thing on top of . . . on top."

"I'm the Sultan's favourite."

"Are you, by God."

"Sherry something. Comes out of a book."

"I must read it."

"Not really my idea. What's happened is, I'm trying to get into films. But it doesn't look as though it's going to work out."

"I didn't know you were an actress."

"I'm not. He said it didn't matter."

"Yes," Jeye said. "He was quite right."

There was a man over in the far corner. Not a footman, not a waiter; not quite a guest. It didn't take me long to spot

him, Jeye thought; and then, But why should I bother?
Just force of habit? Or professional pride?

"He can go jump in the sea, anyway. For all I care. I'm not
all that keen."

"I'm afraid I don't know much about films," Jeye said.

"Nor do I. But he's an American, so I thought. . . . You
meet the right people. That's the thing."

"The right people?"

"Yes. Look. You know who that girl over there is?"

"Her name's Tina Cespedes."

"*She's* a film actress."

"Yes," Jeye said. "Very popular, they tell me."

"And you know who that is with her?"

"His name's Salinas."

"You're quite the little mine of information, aren't you?
Well, that's what I mean. That's what I *call* a meal-ticket.
He's worth millions."

The man in the corner was alone. He wasn't rich. Jeye
didn't know his name. It was Ballastero. He had a rank, which
Jeye would have guessed to be Captain. Jeye would have been
right. He was Captain Ballastero of the police.

"Would you like to dance?" Jeye said.

"Love to."

They went over to the floor; Jeye pressed his left hand not
too purposefully against Carmen's near-naked back and they
began to circle round, their knees bumping together from
time to time. As a dancer, Jeye was nothing great. And
then the touch of his fingers on her skin reminded him of Fé,
which was distracting.

"I have a friend says he's too old."

"Who?"

"Salinas."

"Oh, I don't know," Jeye said. "They're never too old."

"I know what she means, though. It's disgusting, sort of."

"You think so?"

"Old men."

"Oh, I don't know."

"Sometimes they want.   Oh, well. It may be just what people say."

They passed the corner table. Captain Ballastero, scratching his left ear, gazing past them with an air of infinite boredom. No, thought Jeye; never seen him before. But I'll know him again, if we ever meet. Odd, the way they always bring the police in on these functions. Nobody in his senses would try anything in a place like this, with the odds fifty to one in favour of your walking off with a piece of paste . . . if you walked off at all. You'd think they'd know that. Still and all, it couldn't cost them much. And what's it matter to me? Why do I bother? . . . Better, perhaps, to think about that than the other thing. I have a friend says he's too old. Disgusting, sort of. You have to quieten them down. *That* way. Yes. Disgusting. The noises.

"Hey."

"Sorry."

"It's all right."

"I know his son quite well," Jeye said.

"Juanito?"

"Yes."

"They say he does nothing all day but lap it up."

"Um."

"And then nothing all night."

"You're hard to satisfy."

"How do you mean?"

"You don't like it when they do. You don't like it when

they don't. So where does that leave you?"

"Now *you're* being disgusting."

Past their table, a bucket of iced champagne now beside the lilies; Fé sitting there alone in her white powdered wig and tight-waisted blue dress, smiling, waving. "Who's *she*?"

"I think she's meant to be Manon Lescaut."

"But she's with *you*?"

"Oh, yes."

"Silly of me, I thought you were alone. Oh, blast."

"No, come and join us."

"Oh, I can't, I mean, what's-his-name will be wondering what's happened to *me*."

"We'll meet again, I expect."

"I expect we will."

To hell with it, Jeye thought, as she walked away. Fictional characters, we're supposed to be. That's just what we are. None of it's for real, except Fé and me; Carmen isn't, Salinas isn't, why do we have to come here and pretend otherwise? Useful contacts, yes, but to hell with it. It's all a game, when all's said and done, and there are times when you just don't feel like playing. He sat down beside Fé, squeezed her hand.

"Who's *she*?"

"Oh," Jeye said. "Just a useful contact."

"I came back as quickly as I *could*, damn you."

"You were gone for ages."

"Yes, I thought so, too."

"What the hell are we *doing* here?" Jeye said. "Why aren't we out sailing somewhere, you and me? Why all these other people?"

"It was only five minutes."

"I know."

"Oh, God, I'm going to be three *days* in Tangiers."

"I know," Jeye said. "I know. Don't talk about it."

Their hands clasped together under the table. Ten feet away, a champagne bottle exploded noisily, amid much laughter. A chair fell over, and somebody with it. Applause. This was fun.

10

SOUTH of the port of Tangiers the sand begins. Jeye sitting on the veranda at Mijas or lying on the beach, thought at times of those other sands, vast and mindless, striding downcoast from the woods of eucalyptus and of cork towards distant Casablanca, of the heat haze rising and of the slow surge and thunder of the sea; not there the tamed and tideless Mediterranean, but the great Atlantic rollers, green and foam-flecked. He thought of the hill country inland, where the narrow roads are littered with loose stones, where the pique-boeufs fly down the dry valleys with lazy, listless beats of their white wings. He thought of the Zoco and of Dean's Bar and of the Hotel El Minzah; of a white room free, in the winter months, from the hum of the air conditioner and the chirp of the cicadas, where he would lie again on a bed with turned-down sheets and feel Fé's sleeping body return to life against his mouth, twist to and fro there, pinioned. Her hand in his.

In Tangiers once, for the space of forty-eight hours or so, he and Fé had been free. Free, somehow, of the pressure of events and free, as yet, of each other. Since then something had happened, something had changed. Of course it was absurd to think that by returning to Tangiers with her, he could re-experience that simplest of all forms of solace which, at the outset, they had offered each other, the solace of the demand and consent of the flesh; that in any case was still with them in Mijas, was the firm base on which stood everything else. Absurd, then, to try to return; Jeye was not even sure that he wanted to; everything was what he now demanded, nothing less would do. And yet . . . the obscure sense of having lost something, of having been pinioned, trapped. . . . A sense of misgiving, perhaps, like that which affects every bachelor on his wedding-day, yet not quite the same. Somewhere along the line, Jeye knew that he had offered something as a hostage to fortune; he didn't know exactly when, he didn't know quite what. He didn't believe in destiny as any kind of assessable or recognisable force. Something had been started that needed to be completed; that was about the size of it; and the terms of the completion were for other people, not for him, to decide. That was the hell of it. Going to Tangiers, he knew, would provide no kind of an answer. All the same, he wanted to go.

Fé packed her case the night before. She took with her her manicure set, the diamonds screwed up inside the hollow handles. She drove off at eight in the morning. She would lunch at Algeciras, leave the Citroen garaged there and take the afternoon boat. All very simple. From the window, Jeye watch the plume of dust moving down the valley towards Fuengirola, a grey plume glinting with gold in the early sunlight. He was still in his pyjamas, hadn't yet shaved. He turned away and lay, face downwards, on the empty bed.

He hadn't slept well and so he felt tired, though tired mentally rather than physically. He wasn't sleeping well at Mijas. Maybe because of this uncertainty he felt; maybe because of his nearness to the sea; maybe, and most probably, because of the after-effects of muscular strain. The reasons hardly mattered, anyway. Fé would be on the main road now and driving west. Algeciras. Then Tangiers. Three days.

Fé was so damned young. Time was the trouble. Things that happen before you're born. Dubos, Richard. The war. How could she talk about it all like she did? It was very odd. Dubos had died in 1943. She'd been born when? . . . '45? . . . So where was the connection? Richard, yes; but that was too obvious. No. Time. Time came into it somewhere.

In 1943, Jeye had been eleven years old. Ten, and then eleven. Two days before his birthday, the bomb had fallen. There were things about the bomb that he remembered vaguely. Late evening, clear but dark; London blacked out, searchlights in the sky. And Jeye, the boy, walking down the street towards the office, his father, his mother who worked there, too, as a secretary for the duration, whatever that meant. Walking down the street, when it had come. Then the office, the shop, the whole building a heap of bricks and of rubble, red-edged with flame; the iron grille blown out of the window and the muddy pavement outside scattered with bits of jewellery. His parents, amidst the rubble. And other bombs falling now, slow irrhythmic crumps pulsating from somewhere down by the docks. He had begun to pick up the jewellery, carefully, systematically, as though collecting the shattered pieces of a life that had been blown into fragments. Others were helping him. Someone with a torch, the sharpness of its shielded beam blurred over with tears. Not when he had finished but before, with diamonds still lying there in the dust, they took him by the elbows and led him away. In the dark side-street they emptied his pockets, the soldier and the man with the torch; he fought back; they held him and hit him hard in the face and tore the coat off him and, when he fell, stamped on his fingers and kicked away the last fragments clenched in his fists. They were thieves, the soldier and the other. They took the lot. So he lay there for a long while, face downwards, on the empty bed, knowing that his father was dead and the diamonds gone and that now in the darkness no more bombs were falling; it was all over. So he got up and walked away down the dark street, and the dark street had had no ending.

He had thought about it all; not often, but sometimes. Because, looking back on it, it was a strange thing to have done. Choosing to pick up the diamonds, rather than to scrabble —however stupidly, however hopelessly—among the bricks and rubble in search of his father. But his father's passion, while he lived, had been for those stones; and it was as though the diamonds had become, at the moment of his death, a symbol of the man himself, of the man who had been the object of Jeye's own passion, Jeye's undiscriminating ten-year-old's hero-worship and admiration. The love of diamonds Jeye had perhaps inherited; much of his knowledge of them had by then already been transmitted to him, he sitting on the office table while his father talked. But perhaps not till that moment had the passion, the *need* for the stones become real in him; so, having lost father and diamonds together, he had started again; had got up and walked away down the dark street.

Now there was Fé. Fé and Tangiers. Was he, no longer ten but thirty-three years old, seeking now as then to set out in search of the irrecoverable? Or was it just that he, like Richard, had experience of an act from which there could be no turning back? The death of Dubos, that had been something else. Had *meant* something else. To Richard. But what? . . . He had no means of knowing. Other than by asking.

He rubbed his chin; rolled off the bed and put on his shirt and trousers. It was time for breakfast.

"I suppose," Moreau said, "she had the right to tell you all that."

"That's hardly the point, anyway."

"What *is* the point? You're shocked?"

"No. Puzzled."

"Still?"

"Of course."

"Oh, no. Not *of course*. One reaches the stage where one stops being puzzled by the things that people do."

"One stops caring, perhaps. The problem remains."

Crumbs of fresh bread on the tablecloth; Moreau brushed them away with his fingers, then helped himself to another roll. Sliced it carefully in two with the knife. ". . . Let's say, then, that one stops looking for an answer in human terms. We live in a world, don't we? . . . that doesn't take much note of humanity as such. There are forces that shape us, and nowadays they're mostly forces of destruction. So we ourselves seek to destroy one another. Unconsciously, perhaps. But none the less, yes, to destroy. Inevitably."

"You and I?" Jeye said. "For example?"

"Yes. You and I. For example."

"Now that Fé's gone, there's just you and me left."

"That's so," Moreau said.

"So there's no need to wait any longer."

"You speak as though it were simply a matter of choice."

"Isn't it? Isn't that why you sent her away?"

"I didn't exactly *send* her. It was agreed that she should go."

"And now she's gone."

"That worries you?"

"Yes. It does."

"You think I should worry, too. And you wonder why I

don't. But you have the explanation already. After the first death, there is no other." Crumbs fell again from Moreau's fingers to the tablecloth; he munched reflectively. "You know who wrote that?"

"No," Jeye said.

"It was Dylan Thomas."

"Look," Jeye said. "To hell with whoever it was."

"All the same, he made my point remarkably well. Dubos, you see, was the first death. All other deaths for me can be no more than a part of his. Do you understand that?"

"No," Jeye said.

"No. You wouldn't."

"I don't understand anything. But I want to."

"Badly?"

"Very badly."

"That's the main thing. That's a good sign. The thing is that you want permanence, too, Michael, just as we all do. But you look for it in too simple a form. Diamonds are permanent, yes, or nearly. But permanence *itself* . . . that's something different."

"All right. What is it, then?"

"I think of it as a fight, as a kind of war. Time wants everything to be permanent; to be level, identical, symmetrical, a complex of perfect structure like a snowflake . . . yes, or a diamond . . . while *life*, you see, life is irregular, irregular, it's ungeometrical, it's a kind of inconsequence. It's a *disease*, in fact, like a cancer on the lungs of eternity. And death, well, death is a return to normality."

"It's still too abstract," Jeye said.

Moreau took no notice. His eyes stared out now across the sunlit valley. "You can't escape, you see. You think I should have tried? . . . Well, in some ways I did, I tried to get away. When I first came to Spain, I tried to fall in love. I tried to love women. Or *a* woman. To forget someone— that's the easiest form of escape there is, wouldn't you say? But I didn't succeed. I suppose because all directions become the same. That was really the irony of the attempt."

"And the woman?" Jeye said.

". . . Was Carbonell's wife. Fé's mother. Though not, of course, at that time."

"I see."

"Doesn't surprise you, does it? Yes, I thought you might have guessed. Carbonell was possibly my best friend in Spain, so even in my escape the choice was consistent. Choice? . . . Well, if that's the right word. . . ."

"You destroyed him, too, then?"

"Oh, no. No, I hardly think so."

"He died."

"Yes," Moreau said. "He died."

"And he left you as Fé's legal guardian."

"Yes. He did. Oh, he wasn't an intelligent man. But one can't make an ideal of the forces of destruction—as he did, politically speaking—without getting to understand something of the way in which they work. And his idea may have been that we too should destroy each other, Fé and I. He was a stupid man, but there are some things. . . . Fé hated him, of course."

"Yes. I know."

Breakfasting on the veranda, with the valley stretched out in front of them. The house was high, very high. Looking now where Moreau was looking, Jeye felt a sudden wave of vertigo, of near-dizziness; he looked down, down at the floor between his knees.

"Even quite normal children," Moreau said, "like to pretend, sometimes, that their fathers only exist in a sort of protective capacity . . . that their *real* fathers are somewhere else, in another kingdom; more exciting, more dashing, more romantic. . . . Of course you can't see me as a Prince Charming. I'm not saying that Fé did either, when at last she found out. But at least, she saw me as someone different from Carbonell."

A wind now came from the valley, stirring Jeye's hair. He still looked down and the ledge was still there, between his knees. This time he knew he was going to miss it.

"And there it is. I *am* Fé's father," Moreau said. "And that, I suppose, is what you wanted to know."

. . . But when you miss it, nothing happens. There's a sensation of breathlessness, almost of euphoria; and that's all. Jeye wanted to laugh. Some of the crumbs had fallen on to the napkin on Moreau's lap; he shook it out, the crumbs fell and the wind blew them gently away.

"When she found out, you said. She knew? Before?"

"Before she married me? Oh, yes."

"But then why? Sleep with her, all right, Christ, but why *marry* her?"

"Well, on a prosaic level," Moreau said, "to stop people talking. But I suppose you could say it was really more of a gesture. Gestures have more value than most people think. In any case, as I told you, it's no good talking of *reasons*. Perhaps it was her way, her *only* way of becoming what I already was."

"I don't see that. She was born a bastard. *You* became one."

"Yes." Moreau's eyes turned now towards Jeye, mirroring nothing but a very faint concern. "You think perhaps I shouldn't have told you? That this wasn't the moment, after all? . . . No. You were right in the first place. It was necessary."

The air was moving faster now, so fast as to have created on the veranda a huge vacuum; that vacuum sucked greedily at Jeye's stomach as he walked away from the table. The roaring sound in his ears was like that of a huge waterfall; the pick-up had gone haywire, was flooding his brain with booming sound, with the dizzying swirl of the vortex. He caught at the concrete post at the end of the veranda, tried to hold himself upright. The whirlpool was inside him now, hot and angry. He went down on to hands and knees and vomited. The roaring didn't stop.

He took the car down the hill in a series of fast and curving sweeps, his body angling to the bends like that of a skier; letting it gather momentum, letting it take each successive curve a measurable moment faster than the one before. The sea was flung out before him like a great jewelled blanket, alive with light; the shadowy olive trees flickered past him, row after indistinguishable row. Eighty miles an hour as he reached Fuengirola, blank streets of sleeping houses in mid-morning stupor; he swung the car west on to the Algeciras road, fixing his attention patiently on the swerving steel-grey ribbon of its surface. The speedometer needle continued its slow and effortless climb up the edge of the dial. High rocks to the right echoed the hollow whine of his passage, bouncing it back across his slipstream so that its sound became a fierce snarl of turbulence; to the left was the beach, the open sea a thirty-foot drop away from him, and the thrum of the motor drifted out across the tumble of the waves, higher-pitched, more penetrating, sadder. In the woods of umbrella pine where the night still clung to the tree-trunks the sound changed to a rushing like that of a powerful wind; the car moved faster,

203

even faster, faster still. The sun caught them as they howled into sight of Marbella, Jeye and the Jaguar, flashing blue-black dot against the cracked ash-grey immensity of the mountains, moving at the speed of Icarus at the peak of his flight, at that moment when his waxen wings commenced to melt and the fall began; the sun clawing at them with its vast jagged shadows with Fé now waking, the moonlight tangled in her hair and on the pillow, and turning quietly over, one hand outstretched. . . .

Time had come between them. He would never catch her up again.

He sat on the dry earth, where the bare hill fell away from the veranda. The soil turned to dust in his fingers, was blown away by the wind. He watched the ants move in long procession across the path and into the shade of the trees, disappear at last among the heat-twisted roots, their red-black burnished bodies glittering like metal. He had still the savour of sickness at the back of his mouth.

He cleaned the mist from the mirror with a wipe of his towel, leaned forwards to examine his face, his hot grey eyes, heavy-lidded. It was a disembodied face, seeming to have lost all connection with the hands that moved in the water that was splashing down from the tap, hands that tested the temperature automatically, like mechanical recorders. Behind those eyes, an emptiness, a vacancy; he was a ghost, perhaps, some nonvisceral, non-cerebral being, or maybe a god; Melmoth the Wanderer, condemned to an age on the earth, an eternity of listening to stories, to other people's nightmares, to weird and Gothic adventures, impossible as the Gioconda, meaningless as coal. Sherlock Holmes or Scheherezade: a fictional character, just as the invitation had said. His hands moved busily now with the shaving brush, soaping, lathering his face; a mask of foam; masks, he thought, why masks? . . . and picked up the Schick razor with its blade fresh from the injector and with it ploughed a clean swathe down the side of his neck. What shall we do, what must I do to be shaved? Nothing. Nothing to do. Nothing to say. Go, yes, but where? How *can* I go?

Salvation. Forgiveness. They're words, just words. I don't know what they mean. Human beings are capable of anything, and anything that's human can be forgiven. All right. But where's the limit? How can you draw the line behind you, once you've gone all the way? Or say, what about murder? What about Helga, what about the blurred photograph with the ravaged face and the staring, sightless eyes? What about Dubos, and the crash of the shots at dawn?

Murder, incest, adultery. They're all words. Adultery, I take that in my stride. I never even *thought* of it in that way. So why should I have to think about the other? Her husband, her father; what is there *about* that second word? In the word, nothing. So it's something in me. Or something that I lack; a kind of courage. Richard may have it. I haven't. It's been bled out of me; when I was a child, someone turned the tap on and let it all drain away. In the last resort, I depend on morality just as all the others do; I'm a moral parasite like them, though a little bit more intelligent perhaps and with a correspondingly greater skill in self-deception. Illusions, why, they may be necessary. For where are you without them? In Moreau's world of death, of mutual loving destruction. And that wasn't true, either. Destroy us both? . . . No, that was an exaggeration. It had to be.

205

He said to Moreau,

"I have to go."

And Moreau,

"Don't you think we ought to talk about it?"

. . . This was in the library, where Moreau sat writing a letter and where Juan Carbonell and his lady wife stared down at him from the walls; a girl whom Fé had once been also. The door leading into the patio was open, and the sound of trickling water was just audible. Then Jeye closed the door. Coming in out of the sunlight, he felt the coolness and the dimness of the room press in on him, as he might have felt the coolness and the dimness of the sea; he walked across to the table where Moreau sat writing. Moreau still wore his black silk pyjama jacket over well-pressed grey flannel trousers.

"It'd be better," Jeye said, "if I did my thinking before we started to talk. That's what I want to do."

"We have three days before Fé comes back. There's no need for you to go away."

"I've packed my case."

". . . Just as you wish," Moreau said.

"There's something I want before I go."

"Yes?"

"The Salinas file."

The sound of the water could still be heard, when neither of them spoke. Moreau's chair squeaked as he pushed it back, four or six inches; his fountain-pen he placed on the letter pad in front of him.

"You'd better do a *lot* of thinking, Michael."

"I know where you keep the files," Jeye said. "Over there. In that desk. I could take them, if I wanted. But it's polite to say please."

"I have the Salinas file to hand."

"Good."

". . . Because I thought you might ask to see it."

Jeye said nothing. Moreau watched him for a few moments more, then got up, taking the key-wallet from his trousers pocket. He went over to the bureau, opened it. There was none of the usual decisiveness about his movements.

"How about money?"

"You asked me that a week ago."

"That was a week ago."

"I don't need money," Jeye said.

The folder was, as Moreau had claimed, to hand. Fastened with a paper-clip and neatly pigeonholed. Moreau picked it up and weighed it in his hand; as he did so, Jeye leaned past him and took the pistol from the right-hand drawer. "It's loaded," Moreau said.

"You said you never used one."

"Nor I do, on a job. That's for the legitimate protection of my personal property. I have a licence for it."

"And you keep it there?"

"Yes. Of course, I wouldn't use it. Except as a last resort."

"A last resort," Jeye said. "I see."

He held it loosely. The barrel pointed not at Moreau, but not very far from him, either. "In Spain," Moreau said, "people go to extreme lengths to guard their personal property. Salinas keeps one of those in a drawer of his bedside table. At night, he employs a house guard, and the guard carries another. You'll find it all in here."

He dropped the folder on to the table with a little slap. He turned round. Jeye was still facing him.

Behind Moreau, directly behind him, was the portrait of Carbonell. A bullet fired now, Jeye thought, would pass through them both. The pistol was a great deal heavier than it had seemed at first, and his hand felt soft, clammy, around the butt. Now that his eyes had grown used to the dimness, he could see more clearly; could make out the colouring of the rows of books to Moreau's right, could even make out a few of the titles that gleamed there in letters of gold. From there he looked back at Moreau; who hadn't moved; who was standing very still. The folder lay on the table.

"If you were dead, she'd marry me. She said so."

"Not, I think, if I died in that particular way," Moreau said.

"In what particular way?"

"In the way that you're thinking."

"I'm not thinking," Jeye said very quickly. "That's why I'm going away, isn't it? . . . to think. I shan't start to think until I've gone. Right now, I'm not thinking. I could do it, you know, like that—without thinking. That way, it's easy."

"No," Moreau said. "Believe me, it's never easy."

He was watching Jeye's thumb. Which moved. The safety catch clicked forwards. Moreau stood still.

"Well, perhaps she wouldn't," Jeye said. "Marry me, I mean. And that mightn't matter. She'd still be free."

"No," Moreau said. "I tried to explain that to you. Very carefully."

The barrel rose maybe half an inch.

"No," Moreau said.

Behind the sound of the water, a sparrow was singing.

"Why not?" Jeye said. "You want me to. Don't you?"
Again, Moreau heard the muted click as the safety catch

went back. Then Jeye leaned forwards, placed the pistol on the table and, with the same movement, picked up the Salinas file. He went out of the room without looking back. There was phlegm in Moreau's throat, a ball of saliva that felt as hard as a knot. He swallowed painfully. Then, rubbing at the base of his throat, sat down at the table.

Something (Jeye thought) that had to be completed. That was the way to look at it. Something that had to be completed at once, without delay. Why? . . . He didn't know. It wasn't a matter of having reasons. After all, there would be nothing random about it, nothing impulsive. This job had five years of patient study and work behind it. Study of things, of people. Two summer months in a chalet near Alicante with one of Salinas' ex-mistresses; three winter months in a sanatorium with Salinas' son. He knew more about Salinas now than either of them. And over those five years, a plan slowly taking shape; there had been many diversions from that plan, much time spent in other jobs, other amusements, but only during the past few weeks had the secret blueprint been allowed to fade from his mind. Now it was back, sharper and clearer than ever. Now he had Moreau's folder. There might be a few details there that would be new to him, but they would be very few indeed.

The most complete of files won't tell you everything. Sometimes one can think of these things in military terms. In war, there's a limit to what you can do with equipment; sometimes one side, sometimes the other has an advantage, but no matter how good your equipment is, it'll always fall short of perfection, because the people who operate it are human. So when the chips are down, it's never the system you have to break; it's the person who uses it. Two people only

209

were in on this hand; himself and Salinas. That was the beauty of it.

An intelligence service wins no battles. Intelligence is just what you must have before the battle can begin. You want it on paper, but most of all you want it in your brain. Jeye was not memorising the contents of the papers spread over the table in front of him; he was checking them, tabulating them, against that knowledge which he already possessed. High up by the whitewashed ceiling, a fly buzzed. Otherwise the room was silent. Jeye sucked at the end of his pencil.

Take the grounds first. Not too much of a problem there. Two acres only, backing on the slope of the Gibralfaro and well below the road that ran down to La Caleta; no skyline, next to no chance of being overlooked. Roughly rectangular, only one side fronting on the street; Baños de Marmol, a cul-de-sac, very little frequented. No dogs, but an armed guard, from twelve at night to 8 a.m. No trouble there.

Next, the house. Almost square in plan; a broad front, and two comparatively narrow wings at the back partially enclosing an open patio and a swimming-pool. Local granite base, then mostly concrete and steel; almost as much reinforcing steel as structural, which was a healthy sign. Walls that you'd never get through in a month of Sundays, that wouldn't take a piton, but walls, on the other hand, that a climber could definitely trust. A cat's job, all right. That much had been clear from the first.

Four stories high, with a roof garden of sorts. On the ground floor windows, traditional Spanish-style bars, *rejas*, of cylindrical steel. The plate-glass southern frontage had a Gordini lock; the windows on the other floors, simple flanges that screwed down and lightweight steel shutters. Drainage to the rear and minimal, as you'd expect in Málaga; no pipe, just the projecting overflow tube at roof level. The layout's pretty conventional; the operative section is the fourth floor of the west wing. There's a small reference library, two offices— owner's and secretary's—a photographic darkroom, a w.c., and the Collection Room. Yale-type locks on the office doors, the Collection Room a 1954 Challoner. No photograph, but that didn't matter. Nothing there to break anyone's heart.

The alarm system, that was what mattered. Conventional Bell on the first three floors, but the fourth floor was something shocking. Mostly covering the roof entries and the fire escape exit, as one would expect. Magic eye coverage to the Collection Room only, but that from two separate cells. The wiring was beautiful, just beautiful. Impossible to cut; double relay from door to windows; FPA was the one thing they'd missed out on. And the whole system completely independent of the Bell, with a separate ground-floor monitor and running from a master in Salinas' bedroom. Brandt of Zurich had been the contractors. They weren't what you'd call skimpy workmen.

Last of all, the safe. Lombardo y Gutierrez, installed 1961, inspected annually. Weight just short of half a ton. Eight-figure combination, Swedish tumblers. And inside. . . . That, again, didn't matter. It wasn't some young lady's set of toys, but a private collection; assessment, 1959, just short of two million dollars. The collection didn't matter; there was just one item that did. The Hungarian tiara, assessed at one hundred and ninety thousand dollars. That was selling it cheap, of course; but insurance agents have to say something.

It's tough (Jeye thought), but it isn't impossible. The reason it hasn't been done before is that no one's ever tried; the goods are unsaleable. But this is the way I like it; just me and Salinas; a nice clear straightforward issue. All you have to do is work out the odds the way you've always worked them out before, and if they're right, and now they *are* right, then in you go. It's crime, it's all in black and white, like these photographs on the table; not like the other thing, not like . . . not knowing. . . .

He leaned forwards, adjusting the focus of the magnifying glass on the uppermost shot. West wing, third storey. The weakness was somewhere there, the crack in the armour-plated shell; and he knew just where to find it. In the silence of the room, his breathing grew heavy.

Moreau heard the car drive up and halt a little after five o'clock. He was taking his afternoon coffee at that moment, and paused with the cup half-way to his mouth. He hadn't expected Jeye to come back so soon; he hadn't expected Jeye to be back at all. And the motor hadn't sounded like that of the Jag. So it was probably someone else; Moreau didn't like that much, either. He didn't welcome any departure from the expected.

He finished his coffee slowly and poured himself out a second cup. The door opened while he was doing so, and Fé came in. Moreau stared at her.

"What the hell went wrong?"

"Nothing went wrong. I came back. That's all."

The corners of Moreau's lips became compressed.

". . . You'd like some coffee?"

"No. Where's Michael?"

"He left."

"You told him. Didn't you?"

Moreau tipped a spoonful of candy sugar into his coffee, then another. Fé, outwardly as calm as he was yet giving a strange impression of being out of breath, sat down opposite

212

him; rested her hands on her lap.

"I had a feeling. That was all. And so I came back. Feminine intuition, would you call it?"

"I'd call it a mistake," Moreau said. "I don't see that there's anything we can do. Not yet awhile."

"I'd have thought *you*'d done enough already."

"I knew you'd be angry," Moreau said. "It's only natural. But it really doesn't——"

"Where's he gone?"

"I don't know."

"But what did he *say*?"

"Nothing. Just that he needed time to think." Moreau shrugged. "What did you expect him to say?"

"That would depend on how he found out about it."

"I was very tactful."

"Oh, I'm *sure* you were," Fé said. "*Very*."

Moreau picked up a spoon and stirred the coffee, leaning forwards as though something were to be seen, something vitally important, in its steaming depths. "He had to be told, sooner or later. And being told, well, then he had to do what he did. Or to do whatever it is he's *going* to do." He made an impatient gesture with the spoon. "The point is that you can't fight against the inevitable."

"I found him once," Fé said. "I could find him again."

"It wouldn't help."

"You talk about people having to do things. Well, I'm going to have to try."

"No," Moreau said. "You're too sensible. You have too orderly a mind. Oh, you could talk to him, yes. But you'll never change his mind. You'll never stop him."

"*Stop* him?"

"I said I didn't know where he was," Moreau said. "That was the truth. But he's gone to take Salinas." The coffee was too hot. It burnt his lips. He wiped them, very gently, with a white handkerchief. Fé said nothing, nothing at all, and in the end he found himself compelled once more to look at her.

". . . Would you like me to explain?"

"Yes," Fé said. "I think perhaps you'd better."

"You see, I understand it all so well. You take a man who suffers from a certain obsession, or," Moreau said, "since Michael himself wouldn't like that expression, let's say a man who lives for a certain purpose. Someone whose whole life, professional and personal, is built around a certain objective. A man who doesn't steal to live, as we do, but who in a certain sense lives to steal. How would you set about curing such a person?"

"That's doctor's language," Fé said with contempt. "Not ours. Or at least, not mine."

"Well, curing, changing, whatever you like to call it. I'd say there were two ways. The first is to find the root of the obsession and cut it out. Make him become aware of it and, through that awareness, able to combat it. That's what a psychiatrist might do. We're not psychiatrists, though, as you rightly point out. We're not doctors."

"No. We're thieves. Like him."

"Thieves, yes. But not, I think, like him. The other way," Moreau said, looking now down at his coffee, "is to transfer his obsession to some other object. To some more *natural* object. Such as a young woman. The disadvantage of that method is that if—when the transference process is almost complete—something happens to make him question, or force him to deny, his new set of values, he'll return to his original obsession and it'll be stronger than ever. He feels safe with it, you see. It's tried and trusted. So he jumps for it, he leaps back into his shell. . . . It could happen at any time, Fé, and

214

for any reason. Today, next month, next year. Better for him and for us to make it today."

"Anyway, that was how you planned it."

"No. I didn't really plan it, I foresaw it. That's not the same thing."

"You make it sound all very simple," Fé said, "all very logical."

"It is. It's the end. And the end of anything is always logical. The difficult thing will be for you to realise that. Michael saw it at once, in a flash"—Moreau clicked his fingers —"just like that. For you, it won't be so easy."

The echo of that click seemed to hang in the air, to create there an uneasiness like that of some obscure demand, while Moreau picked up his coffee-up again. ". . .You'll manage it, all the same," Moreau said. "Of course you will. You've no alternative."

On the white walls of the house, black specks moved; lizards in the sun. Above them, the shadow of the balcony speared to the plaster. Jeye lowered the field-glasses, rubbed at his eyes.

The Cespedes walked across the patio. Blue two-piece swim-suit, a towel over her shoulders. She stood at the edge of the swimming-pool, shrugged off the towel, and dived, the field-glasses bringing her so close at the moment of impact that the flying drops of water seemed to splash the lenses. Jeye sighed enviously. He had been sitting there on the hillside for almost four hours, and even in the shade of the low scrub it was very hot. He stretched out his left leg, flexed it. A bird flew away, twittering, from the nearby bushes.

Foot-stamping; the hot sharp prickling of tears; the tautness of the muscles of eyes and mouth. Symptoms of what, for

215

heaven's sake? What loss of a proper objectivity was this? The girl in the portrait in the library, miserable creature, had known all those sensations; such emotional tantrums had been part and parcel of her daily existence. But Fé-in-the-mirror was different, was composed, was an Integrated Personality; was someone, in short, who knew how to recognise the inevitable. So why should the mirror now show the tear-stains on the cheeks, the quiver of the lips? It wasn't fair. Was neither fair nor true.

The mirror was misting over with the rising steam; Fé dipped the round sponge into the hot water and carried it to her forehead, squeezed until narrow gleaming rivulets ran down her face, her shoulders, and past her breasts. She towelled herself dry, standing with her slippered feet a little apart on the bath mat; left the mirror fogged over with vapour, drops like tears condensing on its surface. She worked her arms through the sleeves of her dressing-robe and walked through to the bedroom, tying the flannelette sash around her waist as she went. Then she sat down on the bed.

Michael wasn't there. Michael had gone. Had gone, because he couldn't take it; that was what it all added up to. Because of something he had been told, Fé for him had ceased to be a person, a human being, a woman; a string had been cut somewhere, he had dropped away. Had gone like all the others. The Others, like prisoners in a cage. Once you're free of that cage, then where do you stop? Nowhere. You go all the way. That's if you're logical, if you have an orderly mind. *She hasn't any money. She's married to her father.* Why should someone like Michael care about the one thing more than the other? Why should he have left her, like all the others, unless indeed he were one of *them* at heart?

And Richard's right. Even if I find him, what can I tell

him? I was young then, I didn't mean to do it, I never really thought what it implied? That wouldn't be true. I don't regret it. Otherwise I'd still be what I was before, the girl in the portrait in the library, poor little sniveller. Michael's the one I ought to hate. Not Richard. Richard's my father, he *is*, not the other one, and how can you hate your father? I can rely on him, always, always. There was a way to make sure of him, and I took it. And I don't regret it. *He*'ll never let me down. It wasn't Fé-in-the-mirror that you wanted, Michael; it was just her body, her outward appearance that deceived you. What you wanted was the girl in the portrait, and she doesn't exist. Not any more. That's if you ever really wanted *anything*.

Fé rolled back on the bed, buried her face in the waiting pillow. She snivelled.

Shadows on the wall now, long and dark, from roof to basement. The scent of bougainvillea. Jeye stood on the concrete path and peered upwards, his fingers resting lightly on the rough white plaster. From the swimming-pool to his left, a sound of muted laughter; Salinas was there now, with Cespedes and two other friends. A car came down the street, running downhill in low gear; at the first sound of its motor, Jeye stretched easily upwards and began to climb.

"It's getting cool," Tina said. "I'm going in."

Salinas was opening a can of beer. He nodded.

"... Darling?"

"What?"

"Are we going out tonight?"

"I don't think so," Salinas said. "Barbudo'll want to talk business after dinner. No, I thought we might have a quiet

217

night . . . for a change."

Jeye sat, feet tucked up, on the iron balcony. The grille he
sat on was thick with dust, and the railings also. In the corner
was a beer bottle, its label peeling and illegible, the brown glass
invisible under a coating of grime and cobwebs; it had been
left there some six years ago by a boy called Juanito. Jeye sat
there, motionless, and looked at it. He, too, had found the
Secret Place.

He sat there while the darkness gathered round him.

11

THE weakness of all equipment lies in the fact that human beings use it. The best alarm system in the world won't work unless it's switched on; and the fourth storey system was indeed kept that way permanently. But the house system wasn't. Millionaires often have guests and always have servants, and not even the most cautious of millionaires wants to hear the alarm system go off every time someone opens a window; that's a thing that one does pretty often in a hot climate. So the main system is switched on last thing at night, when the owner can feel reasonably sure that his guests have settled down. There's a period of ten minutes or so, maybe more, between the time the guest-room lights are switched off and the time the system is switched on. In that period, you're not likely to bump into anyone by accident but, on the other hand, any noise you may happen to make is likely to pass unnoticed; experts have been known to cover themselves as they move down the passage by going into a convenient lavatory and pulling the chain. Jeye, whatever else he was, was an expert. He was waiting, and he knew what he was waiting for. It would be a long time; not before midnight at the earliest. But Jeye was good at *that* kind of waiting.

The guests would cause no trouble. There were only two; a business contact of Salinas' called Barbudo and his wife. Then there was Salinas' personal secretary, who'd probably retire discreetly to his room quite early in the evening. Those three, Salinas himself and the Cespedes would be sleeping on the second floor. On the third floor, *el servicio*. Three maids, a cook-housekeeper, and the major-domo; all the others slept out. They, too, would be early to bed except the major-domo; he had the actual responsibility for the alarm system and so would be last of all to bed. He was therefore the main danger. He might well be moving around at the moment when Jeye went in. The entry, though, is usually relatively simple. It's when you're inside that your troubles begin.

First thing is to make sure you can get out again. You have to wait until the system has been switched on, so that half-an-hour or so later you can switch it off again; that's unless you're planning to do the job by daylight. Sometimes that's not so easy as it sounds. But if you can't get at the switch itself, you can usually get at the bell quite easily, because that's the only part of the system which, once installed, needs regular maintenance. And quite often a very complicated system is connected to just one single alarm bell, because that reduces time, cost and trouble. You don't even have to disconnect it. A postcard across the trembler will do the trick.

Right, then. That to begin with. The trouble, of course, will be the fourth storey. The system there is on all the time, and the control's in the main bedroom, so that Salinas can check up on it last thing of all. Moreover, there's a monitor light in the patio, so that the night guard can check on it from time to time. That's all he does, though. Take a red-lensed torch with an adjustable shield, a low-power bulb and a magnet on the holder; clamp it on the monitor and the guard won't notice the difference. Unless he looks closely, and why should he? A glance is all he gives it as he mooches past. The Collection's been there for twelve years now and no one's ever even *tried* to nail it. He's got about the most boring job

on earth, and he treats it as such. Has his head down half the
time, if the truth were known. No reason why he should cotton on to a trick that wide-awake and well-paid bank guards
have been fooled by.

The switch in Salinas' bedroom is the hardest point. Its
weakness is a weakness of the system as a whole, that of any
double system yet invented. A question of priorities. The layout assumes that you're going to switch off the main system
before you tackle the other; which is as natural an assumption
as any you could think of. But somehow you're going to do
it the other way round. A simple idea, yes, but then simplicity
pays, you're *always* simple. All the time. That's why less
fortunate people who can only play it simple for *some* of the
time call you a genius.

Take the safe. A real modern bastard, eight-figure combination, weighing half-a-ton. The easiest way to open a safe like
that is to find out the combination. Then use it. And that's
exactly what you hope to do.

It's been going on for a long time, the war. The war between the safemakers and the safe breakers. First there were
four-figure combinations. The fiddlers opened them. Then six-
figure. The fiddlers opened them. It took them longer, that
was all. Then eight-figure. That beat them. A good eight-
figure combination based on one of the shuffle systems is beyond the powers of any fiddler alive, though even *that* defence
may be cracked one day. The trouble is that, in beating the
fiddlers, the safemakers have beat the average safe-owner as
well. No person in his senses is going to trust the key of an
eight-figure combination to his memory alone. The key of
an eight-figure combination is always *somewhere*. Written
down and, obviously, to hand. *Always*. All that you have
to do is find it.

DEADFALL

Salinas had a Collection, and the Collection had a secretary, and the secretary had an office up there on the fourth storey. Occasionally the secretary would have need to open the safe, because Salinas was a busy man who wasn't always around. So the key would be in the secretary's office. It's as easy as that. All you have to do is look, and go on looking until you've found it. It may take you hours; all night; even all tomorrow night. as well. Why not? The point is that it's there, it has to be. And that sooner or later, you're going to find it. All you need is patience. And, maybe, luck.

. . . Not that Jeye thought about it that way. Not that Jeye thought about it at all, now. He sat on the balcony and watched the moon come up over the neighbouring house-tops. He ate bread and Manchego cheese, and he drank a little red wine mixed with water. The empty wineskin he folded and put back in his pocket.

Around eleven o'clock, when no car had arrived and it seemed clear that Salinas and Tina wouldn't be going out that night, he commenced his listening watch. He set his ear to the narrow aperture that his penknife had probed through a slat in the wooden planking, and for one minute in every five he listened carefully. There were cicadas in the garden, and traffic moving down the main street three hundred yards downhill; it wasn't easy to distinguish between the sounds that mattered and the sounds that didn't. But he wasn't worried. Not yet. All this he had done before.

The overhead light in the passage was burning, and in the bathroom of the main guest-room a shower was running. Jeye closed the balcony window behind him, pushed the two planks that he had levered open back into place; one of them had splintered a little against the pull of the screws, but not

222

noticeably. He then walked quickly down the grey-floored corridor, paused at the head of the stairway, walked on to Salinas' bedroom. No light showed from door-jamb or keyhole; no sound came from within. Jeye opened the door, switched on the light.

A large room, wool-carpeted; the windows were closed, but the shutters open. The air-conditioner wasn't in use, but a ventilator fan whispered from a recess in the far wall. The throw-switch to the fourth floor alarm system was exactly where he had expected to see it, to the right and within easy reach of the blue-counterpaned double bed. He walked over and examined it briefly. He could see no complications. He opened the drawer of the night table. Yes. The pistol was there. And a nine-millimetre, by God. No joking matter. He took it in his gloved right hand and pumped the sleeve, spraying blunt-nosed cartridges over the bed. When the magazine was empty, he put the pistol back in its place and closed the drawer; then collected the cartridges, went over to the built-in wardrobe in the corner and dropped them into the pocket of one of Salinas' suits. Then he closed the wardroom door and looked at his watch.

Twelve thirty-seven.

He measured the steps from where he stood to the bathroom door, from the bathroom to the bedroom door. Then he turned out the light and paced out the distances again, this time in the darkness. Near-darkness, really; there was plenty of moonlight; too much. He went through into the bathroom, switching on the light as he went; opened the cabinet over the washbasin and checked briefly on what was inside. Then pulled back the plastic curtain over the window. Between curtain and window was an eighteen-inch recess; wider, if anything, than his guess from the architect's plans had suggested. Jeye almost, but not quite, smiled. He went back to switch off the light, then swung himself athletically up into the recess, tucking his knees up under his chin. His left shoulder was clear, though only just, of the folds of the curtain; it was an uncomfortably cramped posture, certainly, but not one that he expected to have to maintain for very long. He looked down once more at his watch; the luminous hands showed twelve-forty, exactly.

Four minutes later, the bedroom light came on. Jeye could see the chink of brightness at the base of the door; the gap at the edge of the curtain through which he was looking seemed a little too wide, and he closed it fractionally. In the bedroom, Cespedes was singing very softly, insofar as a Spanish soprano ever can be said to sing softly; she was perfectly audible, though the door was closed. A few moments later, though, it was opened and the light blinked on; Cespedes came in. She hadn't bothered to slip a bathrobe on and wore, in fact, nothing but black nylon briefs with ridiculous red-and-blue butterflies embroidered at each hip. Jeye felt excitement surge in the pit of his stomach; an excitement not, or only partly, sexual in origin, for she had worn, after all, very little more that afternoon, through that long ninety minutes wherein the field-glasses had observed her constantly and quite dispassionately. What he felt now was rather a sense of intimacy, of that strange intimacy that links the hunter and the hunted the moment before the shot is fired, and of expectancy, an urgent expectancy as keen as any he might have felt had he been watching her not from the bathroom recess but from the bed. An excitement, yes, but a cold and controlled excitement such as no electro-encephalograph could ever have detected. He watched her reach across to turn on the shower, her heavy breasts swinging to the movement with a freedom that somehow surprised him; forced him to think, for the first time that evening, of Fé, whose younger and firmer breasts moved hardly at all, would yield only to the touch of his fingers. The shower wasn't working properly, for some reason, the water coming out in short, uncontrollable spurts; Cespedes wrestled with the control levers for some twenty seconds, getting nowhere.

"Damn the thing," she said.

She pulled down her briefs, stepped out of them and, holding her head back, into the shower. Judging by the gasp she gave, the temperature control wasn't right, either. She reached up again to adjust the lever, tilted nipples hardening to the impact of the water; and in the next room, the door opened and closed again. So here he was. Salinas.

". . . Baby?"

"Uh-huh," Salinas said.

"The shower isn't working properly."

"No?"

"Sort of comes and goes."

"You don't have to take a shower every goddam five minutes, do you?" Salinas said. "You had one before dinner, for God's sake."

"It was all right then."

"Nothing in this blasted country stays that way for long, believe you me. It'll be the pressure, or something."

"What?"

"The water pressure."

"Oh."

Salinas came in, unbuttoning his shirt; went to the washbasin without glancing in Tina's direction. He turned on the hot water tap. "That Barbudo," Tina said.

Salinas said something inaudible under the rush of the

225

water; he had his head lowered over the basin and was splashing his face in a desultory way. Tina looked back at him, turned and got out of the shower. "I don't much care for him," she said, reaching for a towel.

"Business," Salinas said, turning off the tap. "I don't care much for him, either. Or his wife. But that's how it is."

"You know he made a pass at me down there? Under the table?"

"Can't blame him for that."

"Well, aren't you sweet." She stared at herself self-critically in the mirror, twisting at the hips to bring the jut of her breasts into profile; then, still patting herself dry, walked out through the open door. Salinas slapped backhanded at her buttocks as she went past him. "All the same——"

"All the same, it's a bit cool. Right here in your house."

She had left the shower turned on, her panties on the bathroom floor. Salinas sighed and picked them up; then reached over, grunting, to pull down the shower levers. The water hissed to a stop. "Here's the best place," he said. "Where I can keep an eye on you both."

From the bedroom, silvery laughter.

"Don't think I don't mean it," Salinas said.

Silvery laughter, stopping very abruptly. "You're not *serious*?"

He looked down, screwing up the damp black nylon in the palms of his hands. "Let's say I'm the jealous type. And don't you forget it."

Once again, in Jeye's mind, Fé was suddenly present. Bedroom conversations, he thought; what do *we* sound like when we're talking? Talking like this? Surely not as. . . . Anyway. It didn't matter. What mattered now was getting ready to move, and to move fast. Salinas, too, was going out. The light went off. The door closed.

Jeye moved.

". . . Hey, I like *that*," Salinas said.

"Cute, isn't it? First time I've ever worn it."

"What's the fur stuff?"

"Mink."

"What I thought. God, mink on a nightdress. That's the craziest thing I ever heard of."

"But you said you liked it."

"I like what's under it."

Jeye had the bathroom cabinet open, the cord of Salinas' electric razor in his hands. Now, in the darkness, he was searching desperately for the plug. He found it; made the connection; from the bedroom, the sound of another comparatively gentle slap. His left hand put a steady, gentle pressure on the water tap, easing it round; his right brought across the end of the electric cord. . . .

"Oh, *no*," Salinas said.

"What——"

"Bloody light's fused."

"But what happened?"

"I don't know. Not a damned *thing* in this house that works."

"Maybe it's just the bulb gone."

"Yes. Just a minute."

Confused movement. Jeye, beside the bed now and close to the wall; his eyes, lowered to take advantage of peripheral vision, catch the blur and swirl of Salinas' dressing-gown as he moves clumsily towards the door. Jeye's hand is on the lever of the alarm switch. Two clicks sound as one.

"No, it's fused. The other one's gone as well."

227

"Well, never mind, honey. It doesn't matter."

"What the blazes d'you mean, it doesn't matter?"

"Can't it wait till the morning?"

"Of course it's going to bloody well wait till the morning, I'm not having Manolo pottering round the place at this hour of the night. That's not the point."

He pads furiously back towards the bed, stubbing his toe on something or other. Jeye, already moving away, doesn't allow for Tina's sympathetically outstretched hand. His sleeve brushes against her fingertips.

". . . Pablo?"

"The point is it's a bloody nuisance. That's what it is."

"Pablo, where *are* you?"

"Here, of course, where did you. . . ? Of all the damned silly questions."

"Oh."

"You'd think, having paid all of twenty thousand blasted pesetas——"

"Choo, choo, choo." Her mouth against his shoulder. "It doesn't matter, baby. What do *we* want the light on for?"

"That's all very well."

"Aahhhhhh. *Come* on."

"I like to see what I'm doing to you."

"Yes, but just this once. . . . There. There now. That's not so bad, is it? . . . Even in the dark. . . ?"

The bed creaks, very faintly, once. Jeye stands in the shadows, motionless. His luck has held good. The second hand of his watch sweeps noiselessly round the dial; other words come from the bed, other noises. Jeye motionless, unconcerned. This, too, he has heard before. He, the thief, is confidant of all the world, participant in all human passion and weakness, yet completely detached from it. He moves now,

228

timing his steps to the slow, anguished rhythm of their coupling, to the hoarse, fervent rasp of Salinas' breath. Moonlight, but not too much, comes through the windows; he keeps to the shadows. He sees, as the sheets are abruptly thrown back, the plunging darkness on the mattress, the blur of their locked and heaving bodies; he waits, one hand on the doorknob, for the moment of completion. The woman cries out, not very convincingly; but it's enough, the spring-latch is back, the door opens silently and Jeye is through it. Soundlessly again, the door moves shut. In the passage, also, there is moonlight; he takes the torch from his pocket, but has no need as yet to switch it on. He makes his way down the landing, pausing to listen at every door. Every room is silent. At the head of the stairs is the switch of the Bell system; for a moment it is ringed with light as the torch flicks on. No trouble there at all. Darkness jerks back again; the click as the lever falls is loud, but not too loud.

Jeye walks downstairs, keeping close to the wall, testing each tread before committing his weight to it. He opens the side door of the hall, goes into the patio; the night air is cold against his face, because already he's sweating a little. The monitor light is out. He takes the other torch from his inside pocket, switches it on; a red, unmoving glow-worm in his fingers. The magnet sucks it into its place against the mechanism of the monitor. Jeye stands still and listens. The cicadas are still chirping, but there's no traffic now. He goes back into the house, closes and locks the side door again. The whole house is helpless, at his mercy. He walks upstairs again; quickly, quietly. Now, sitting patiently outside the Collection Room, he will wait in the stillness for another hour. Tina and Salinas, Barbudo and his wife, the servants and the secretary, all will be asleep before he moves again.

"Let's say," Moreau suggested, "that he's the jealous type. And leave it at that."

"But jealous of what?"

"Of us. Of what we are. To each other."

One o'clock now. Not late, by Spanish standards; most certainly not, by Moreau's. Tonight, though, he felt strangely tired; it was almost as if he needed to sleep. Yet here they were, Fé and him, talking; again, talking; in the empty library, talking. Voices in the night. His head was aching.

"But what if he gets caught? Or killed?"

"Either way," Moreau said, "he won't talk about us. You can be sure he won't. That's the least of our worries."

"So much so that I wasn't thinking about that side of things at all. I was thinking about. . . ."

"Well, what?"

". . . Of what *we* are to each other. Michael and I."

"He'll have thought about that, too. But it wasn't enough. Not for him."

"It still might be for me."

"No," Moreau said. "You look at things too levelly for that. It's not just the physical thing. . . . You know that. Michael knows that . . . that matters. Between us. It's just that when that happens between two people who think alike, who believe alike, who behave alike, who in the end *are* alike . . . then that's the most powerful union of all. Stronger than marriage, stronger than friendship. That was why Aquinas was opposed to it. If you take the myths, the Greek incest myths, for example." He squeezed the bridge of his nose between his fingers. It was no good. He had lost the thread. "I'm sorry. That's not what I wanted to say at all."

"I'm going to look for him," Fé said.

"Believe me——"

"I'm going now."

"It'll do no good."

"I don't care."

Moreau lowered his hand; his face creased painfully into a smile. "You can't be *serious*."

"I've packed."

"But——"

"I'm not coming back."

Moreau shook his head. "I won't believe it."

"Whatever happens. No, I'm not coming back."

His hand reached across the table, rested on her elbow. "Look," he said. "Obviously, we have to talk about this. We have to . . . discuss it. I never expected you to react in quite this way, it's so completely illogical——"

"Talk," Fé said contemptuously. "I don't think so, Richard. There's nothing to talk about. You've talked already."

"But if you go——"

"Talk about what? There's nothing left. Is there?"

His grip on her arm tightened convulsively, painfully. "Fé, if you go, what about *me*?"

"You'll manage," Fé said. "You managed before."

"That was different. We can't stand alone, not *now*. Either of us. Because of what we'd. . . . No. What we've *done*."

"I don't see what's so irrevocable about it. It was just that you hypnotised me into thinking so. You thought it'd be fun to screw your daughter and I thought it'd be fun to go along with you. A crime, like any other. That's all. That's all it is, nowadays. People laugh at it. Oedipus—that was two thousand years ago."

Moreau stared at her. For once, for once when it really mattered, she had the words and he had none. She stood up; he realised she was leaving, and stood up too.

"But who else? Look facts in the face, won't you? Who *else*?"

"There doesn't *have* to be someone else, Richard. I can be alone, if it's necessary. Goodbye."

"Look, Fé...."

"Let go of me, please."

"I *can't*," Moreau said. "That's the one thing I can't do, I can't be alone. You've got to realise that."

"No, don't, that ... *hurts*...."

"You've just got to *understand*."

The strength of Moreau's fingers had once again surprised her; indeed, almost frightened her. So that the violence of her resistance was in large part a response to the sudden stimulus of fear. Moreau, for all his bulk and strength, had some little difficulty in subduing her; for a few moments they struggled in silence, Fé twisting her back towards him, Moreau's forearm pinioning her from behind, so that they seemed to be moving to and fro in the steps of some novel and complicated dance. The effort, physical and mental, involved seemed to be such as to prevent either of them from speaking, though from time to time Moreau's lips moved, as if in rehearsal of something that needed to be said, but couldn't be. The room was whirling round him as they wrestled; he was conscious of a tremendous, excruciating pressure against his eardrums, not from outside but from within, and of the vicious drumming of the blood in his temples and forehead. Fé's mouth was half open, her lips moist and contorted as if by panic; she swayed dangerously on her high heels, almost fell, and Moreau, caught off balance, trying not to prevent but to direct her fall to his own advantage, loosened his grip; Fé, thrusting her elbow hard into his midriff and levering herself forwards, twisted free. She picked up her bag from the table and ran for the door, left without a word; Moreau, head lowered, one hand on the back of his chair, gasped for breath.

". . . All right," he said. "But wait. Phone me in the morning. . . ."

He looked up. It was no good. She had gone.

". . . She *can't* have gone," Moreau said, and sat down at the table. The pain remained there in the room, hovering darkly over his head. In a few minutes' time, he knew, it would descend. . . .

Salinas' secretary. The secretary to the Collection. Well, what was he? An imbecile? Or smart? Jeye turned over the typewritten card, stared at its blank obverse; then turned it over again. The rows of figures were in red and black:

  3 a la izquierda a 8
  5 a la derecha a 2. . . .

. . . a familiar pattern of evenly-spaced columns, eight of them in all, a form as simple and elegant as that of an algebraic equation. Drawing-pins had held the card tacked to the top of the locked drawer in the office desk; handy, but not too handy. It could be right. It probably was. And yet Jeye couldn't be sure. It could have been placed there on purpose, could be the jamming pattern that would render the safe completely unopenable for so many hours. It wasn't likely, no. But it was possible. And Jeve had to be sure. With the key there in his hands, in his coat pocket, he would have to go on looking. Go on searching the office. That was the only sensible thing to do.

233

The silence in this the fourth floor was almost complete; not even the penetrating chirp of the crickets reached this high, and in any case, with the deepening of the night, most of them had fallen mute. There was dust in the little office, like dust on the floor of Pharaoh's tomb; and there was indeed a hermetic, sealed-off atmosphere to the west wing that the moonlight, breaking through the window glass, emphasised rather than relieved. From this height, looking out from those windows, one could see the glint of that moonlight on the patiently moving sea, and nearer, but well beyond the dark roofs of the clustering houses, the refulgent glow of the yellow lights of the port and the harbour wall. The spire of a nearby church stood out against a sky fogged with stars, black and portentous; bell-tower and buttress silhouetted, clear as a cut-out in a child's picture-book. The northern windows gave on to darkness, on to the slope of the Gibralfaro where nothing moved amongst the bushes or on the road; farther north was another road, the road to Antequera, and farther still to the north was the whole of Spain, the oil and the olive and the wheat, dark mountain, sleeping village and then the leaping lights of Madrid, hotel and sanatorium, echoing corridors, river valleys, hare, partridge and wolf, pale horse and black rider. The slow sierras metalled in the moonlight, snow-capped, gleaming with diamonds. The great steel box waiting, waiting....

Jeye worked quickly, methodically. The flat roof directly above him had retained the heat of the day, and the air in the office was warm and dry; the fourth floor was itself like a safe into which he had entered, from which he seemed now to be seeking a way of escape. On his shirt, dark sweat stains grew invisibly. The narrow beam of the torch moved over open registers, open folders, open filing cabinets, the open

234

desk. The time? . . . Was almost three o'clock.

He had found nothing else.

Sitting there alone in the moonlit stillness, he stretched out his arms across the desk and rested his head against its hard well-polished surface. Well, he thought, I've looked. This has to be it. And there's no point in putting it off, even if I'm wrong; because there's no coming back. This is the last time. I've no regrets, though, whatever happens. I'm glad I went in. Down there in the bedroom it was business as usual; but up here, here in the fourth storey, it's different. I've been in some strange places, have been among strange people; but here there are no people and this isn't a place. Any more than a tomb is a place, for the fellow who's inside it. This is where the end is, and I'm glad I came.

Sitting up, he took off his gloves; wiped his hands carefully with a handkerchief; replaced the gloves once more. Then he stood up and went out, leaving the door a fraction ajar behind him.

The Collection Room wasn't large. There were portable showcases, glass and metal grilles, stacked against one wall; opposite, a glass-fronted cabinet, empty, and a glass-topped display table. Jeye had his torch on now; in here there was no moonlight, it was pitch dark; the steel shutters were clamped in place over the windows and let no crack of light filter in. Beside the west window, set in the solid wall so as to receive, under normal conditions, the afternoon light, was the safe. Jeye walked over to it, kneeled down beside it. He opened it. Shone his torch inside. In a blue Morocco leather case on the top shelf was the Hungarian tiara. Jeye took the box, snapped it open, tilted diamonds, gold and rubies into the palm of his hand. That was when the alarm went off.

He didn't believe it, of course. It meant that whoever had

235

designed the safe had had one last trick up his sleeve, the card with which to trump the safebreaker's ace. It wasn't the main alarm bell, downstairs; it was a small bell high up in the wall above the window, hidden in what he had taken to be, what *was*, a ventilation shaft. It made the dickens of a row. Jeye didn't, of course, believe it, but he acted as though he did. He spent five seconds in examining, by torchlight, his capture; this because he was a great believer in making sure. Then he thrust it into his pocket and went out. He kicked open the office door, switching off the torch as he went and dropping it to the floor; went over to the windows and pulled them open. The steel net of the shutters outside took him thirty seconds longer; people were shouting downstairs, doors were banging. He leaned over the sill. Fifteen feet below him was the balcony, Juanito's secret place; not too difficult a drop. Even that last trump card he had tried to allow for.

Pressure alarm, he thought, half-way through the window. Another goddamned PA; could be nothing else. Simple contact. You lifted the jewel-box, a hairspring made the contact and off it went. Running from a battery, obviously. No cables, no leads; no way of spotting it. Moreau might have thought of it. Damn him. But *I* didn't. All the same, this is different to that other job. I've got what I came for. That's the difference.

Spreadeagled on space, his fingers hooked on the sill, he glanced downwards. The balcony, iron railings projecting. Dark, very dark; but I know where it is; I've seen it, I've measured it. Not a four-inch sill this time, but all of twenty. Must take the rail itself, hands and stomach together. It'll hold all right. I've tried it. And the rest should be easy.

236

Easy.

Up his stomach muscles crawled a faint reminiscence of pain. God, no. Not that. I mustn't go tight. Just the swing, and then the deadfall. No voices in the night. Not again. Nor Fé's hands, caressing me, stroking. Wait. Here's the pain. Sweat on the palms of my hands, pouring down my body. No. Don't look again. You've looked already. All you have to do is drop. And drop right.

He dropped.

Air clutched at him. The dark balustrade, slow-moving at first, coming up at him. Feet swinging back, stomach muscles tautening smoothly, hands swinging down to waist level. With the whip of the air, a moment of sheer, unrepeatable physical pleasure, keen as a knife-blade; the intoxication of the drop. The last time, and this, the climax; this, the best moment of all.

Who saw him fall?

Fé, through the night glasses. *She* saw him fall.

The Citroen was parked high up on the La Caleta road, in the shadow of a clump of Spanish oaks; not very far, in fact, from that hollow in the scrub where Jeye had spent most of the afternoon. Fé, too, had been there a long time; had been sitting in the driving-seat for nearly three hours, since half-past one; and her eyes had grown tired and sore through peering past the rolled-down window into the darkness. In all that time, only one indication that Jeye was indeed at work below; shortly after half-past three she had seen, for a few seconds, a faint and fugitive glimmer behind the shutters of a room on the fourth storey, a hint—no more than that—of torchlight reflected from a wall. It wasn't much, but it was as much as she had expected. It was enough.

At four fifteen she sensed, as much as saw, those same

237

shutters swinging open. They were in the deep shadow, for Jeye, even in that moment of emergency, had chosen a window on the dark side of the house to leave by. Even the powerful night glasses picked up nothing other than a dim blur of movement as he slid down from the sill; and he hung there, poised, for so long that Fé—thinking in a moment of panic that she had lost him—turned the glasses downwards to scan the even deeper obscurity at the base of the building. Finding nothing there, she raised them again; and that was the moment of the drop. That was how she saw him fall. One moment there was movement; the next, again, there was nothing.

She rammed the binoculars into the glove compartment, started the motor. A thread of blood ran down her lowered chin; she had made no sound, no sound at all, but had bitten deep into her lower lip. She flicked on the headlights, eased back the clutch pedal and rolled the car out on to the road, moving quickly through second to third as it gathered speed downhill. For once, her movements were clumsy; the gears gritted. The strung-out street lights of La Caleta came up towards her.

In the house at Mijas, the lights were burning, too; though only in one room; in the library. The desk in the corner stood open, empty, its shelves and deep pigeonholes gutted; in the fireplace, a mound of dark grey ash still sent up wisps of smoke. The charred corner of a cardboard folder burst suddenly, cheerfully, into flame; burnt brightly for five or six seconds, then became dull ash. Ash, like all the others. The desk in the corner was empty. Completely empty.

A modern revolver cartridge of .38 calibre develops a muzzle energy well in excess of two hundred and fifty foot-pounds, and a muzzle velocity of round about eight hundred and fifty feet per second. Fired at the head from a range of two or three inches, the impact of the bullet is such that the head hardly moves; the entrance hole of the bullet through the skull is as neat as though bored with a surgeon's auger; there's no splitting, no fragmentation. The days are past when a bullet, carelessly aimed, would literally blow your brains out, spatter them over the wall. A modern cartridge in a Smith and Wesson Special makes a tidy job of it. Only with the exit wound is there perhaps some superficial tearing of the skin, or a fragment of splintered bone, perhaps, poking through the blood-matted hair.

Moreau looked much the same, therefore, after the shot as before it. The fingers of his right hand jerked into rigidity as the result of some neural reaction, and the pistol fell away from them to clatter on the floor; then his hand fell heavily on to the desk and his great white-maned head toppled forwards. Slowly, then, trickles of blood welled out from the temples, ran down his cheeks. He sat very still, as though enveloped in thought, as though puzzling over the letter that lay, uncompleted, on the desk before him.

The ink of the last two lines was still wet.

Of course one sees from the beginning that a certain end is inevitable. The novelist's viewpoint, one might call it. Therefore comes the illusion that the inevitable is controllable, that one may aim to secure it. One thinks, one plans. Forgetting, in so doing, one's own essential role as victim.

We seek to destroy one another, all of us. And those of us who refuse to recognise this truth destroy others none the less effectively. To recognise it gives one no advantage. So we, too, Carbonell and I, are victims of those others, of those who think themselves innocent. I believe that you knew it would happen, my dear Dubos. At least at the end.

Excuse this letter. It is disturbing for one who has always seen so clearly in others the hidden need for death to find, at last, that dark passion overbearing in himself.

There is so much pain. But pain is not the cause. No. Quite the contrary, my dear; tout le contraire.

He had written, for some reason, in Spanish; all but the last three words; the handwriting as evenly formed and dispassionate as the language of the phrases itself. The shot that had eventually put a period to that final sentence had shaken echoes from the book-lined, portraited library walls; Rosario, the senior of the maidservants, had heard it and had hurried from her bed across the whispering patio. She opened the library door; she saw the desk, the letter; Moreau; the blood. In a high, whistling voice, she began to scream.

For Jeye there had been no shot; nothing but the whip of the air in his ears; and now, nothing but pain. Pain was all that he could be aware of. Not localised pain, not describable pain; pain as total reality; everything was pain. His body was being exploded outwards by it, as a shrapnel shell is shattered to fragments on impact; but somehow continuously, constantly; there were no waves, one distinguishable from the other, no ebb and flow. There was simply pain. An eternity of pain across which he crawled. There were no thoughts in his mind; his eyes, half-open slits in the darkness, registered nothing. Across a concrete sea he moved, snake with a broken spine, helpless, purposeless; there were strange shapes and lights around him, figures that had burst through the yawning split in his own skull to bob and float on the endless, the slowly heaving sea. No thoughts, no memories. Nothing but pain. Pain, and one single item of what might have been called knowledge; the knowledge that while pain lived, so did he. That was why he moved, continuously, constantly, dragging the great weight of his legs behind him, over the granite chips towards the shore. The rumbling of waves as tall as cliffs, huge waves of crunching boulders, beat in his ears; naked to their onslaught, he refused to drown.

That was when he remembered the street, dark, forbidding. Sharp-faced walls like the edges of a canyon, red-rimmed with flame; the slow retreating rumble of the bombers, searchlights pencilling the sky. An endless street; no doors, no windows; blank walls to either side. Cobbles, hard against his hands, his torn hands. Shouting, coming from somewhere outside the dream. Shouting, but not to him. He was dead now. Would be dead, if it weren't for the pain. And for the street, stretching onwards and onwards. It had no ending.

The bombers went away. There were no more shouts. The street was silent, now that he lay still. Beside him, in the gutter, ran a thread of water, sparkling; purling into the sunken drain just clear of his outflung hand. There were diamonds in the water. He picked them out, one by one; muddy child's fingers, groping, uncertain. The diamonds smelt of burning, of dark grey ash; of London burning. Footsteps on the pavement. Coming closer, coming closer now. He opened his fingers, let the heavy, scintillating drops fall from them through the grille of the open drain; red drops went with them; redness of blood. There. Now he was safe. Now no one would beat him. Now no one and nothing could hurt him. There was only pain.

Shouting to him. Not shouting to him. No, not shouting now but whispering. Michael. Michael. His name. He tried not to move. He made himself very small; became a stone; a very small round pebble. A noise came from his mouth.

". . . Michael. Don't move. I'm going to bring the car."

241

They had found him, then. Now the pain would begin. He lay there, waiting for it. The bombers were turning round, would soon be back. And the car. The car, she'd said.

Hands pulling at his shoulders, turning him over. Tears rolled down his cheeks.

"Oh, my God."

"Yes," he said. "Michael."

". . . I'm going to call an ambulance."

He was safe now. He had thrown them away. Nothing could hurt him any more. He tried to tell her so.

"Listen, Michael. You fell out the car, that's how it happened. We've been up there on the hill all night. I was driving down and the car door wasn't locked. You understand?"

The car, she was talking about. Jeye's fingers groped in the dust.

"Oh, God. Just tell them that. Leave the rest to me."

She went away. Going to bring the car, the ambulance, the dark street. No, not dark. The street she walked down was grey now. It was almost dawn.

12

DOUBLE compound fracture of the right leg. Three broken ribs and major contusions. Laceration of the scalp and severe concussion. A few other minor items, and that was it.

"A kilometre or more from the place you're talking about," the police doctor said. "That's where the ambulance picked him up. And best part of an hour after you say it happened. So if you're right, then just how the hell did he get there?"

"It's possible, surely."

"With a broken leg and three broken ribs? You're not suggesting he *walked* it?"

"There was a car."

"Did anyone report a car at the scene of the crime?"

"Nope."

"And there was a night guard, wasn't there?"

"Didn't see one. Didn't hear one. Yes, that's the trouble. He knows his job."

The police doctor wiped his hands on a paper towel. "No," he said. "I don't like this one, Captain."

"I didn't say I *liked* it," Ballastero said. "I think he's the fellow who pulled it. That's all."

Jeye was in five-seven-one. It wasn't the best room in the hospital, but it was better than most. When his bed was rolled close to the window, as it was for most of the day, he could see the Mediterranean blue of the sea beyond the green

243

of palm fronds; he could see the rocks of the eastern coast and the sea-gulls that drifted past outside, white in the morning sunlight; he could see from his window a world of colour. From six in the evening onwards, when they rolled his bed away again, he could look at the cream-tinted ceiling and the red canvas screen and, under the blankets, at the swollen hump of his right leg, bandaged and cased in plaster. There were bandages round his head and right forearm, too, and his ribs had been tightly strapped. The pain that came to him at times wasn't intolerable, having, indeed, upon his exhausted mind almost the effect of a blood transfusion upon a body drained to the point of collapse. The pain gave him, so to speak, a personal awareness of being alive, sharper and more definite than his awareness, during the day, of objective beauty of colour and form in the world beyond the window. *I'm hurt, therefore I am.* The street, the dark street that he had traversed had been a long one, a very long one indeed, but not, as he now knew, endless.

He had come round from the anaesthetic and Fé had been there. She had been there, sitting on a chair beside the bed, and he had known who she was; she was Fé; but as far as he could remember, they hadn't then spoken. The following afternoon, when once more he woke up, she was there again. No one else was in the room. That was when he had learnt about Moreau.

"That time I came to see you in the sanatorium. That was where it all began."

"Not really," Jeye said.

"No. Not really. When I came here just now, though . . . walking up the steps . . . I couldn't help thinking about it."

"I wonder why he did it."

"Why did you run away? Why did I go after you? Why

does anyone do anything? I don't know," Fé said. "I don't know."

"Perhaps he was right," Jeye said. "There *are* reasons. The thing is they don't much matter."

She held his hand while they talked. All the time they were each aware of the light, firm contact that the one held with the other, reassuring in its very fragility. The scent of the sea came in through the open window, and the shadow of the clouds.

"I've thought about it before, you know. About that time I came to see you."

"Yes," Jeye said. "Me, too."

"And I thought, if ever I had to visit you in prison . . . how awful it'd be. I couldn't do it. I'd rather be in there with you. If I wasn't, I don't know what would happen. It'd be terrible."

"In the end, there'd be somebody else."

"I don't know. That's just what's terrible, not being sure. But I don't think so. Not ever."

"No," Jeye said. "Nor do I. Think so."

"Anyway, it won't come to that. Have the police seen you yet?"

"No."

"They came to see me. But about Richard. The other thing, I just made a statement."

"I'd better know what you said."

"Yes, you had."

She told. Jeye listened carefully. It wasn't good, he thought, but it might stand up. Because there wouldn't be any proof that it had happened otherwise; with any luck, there wouldn't be. For no one could even be sure that the thief had fallen.

"One thing you ought to tell *me*," Fé said.

"What?"

"Not if you don't want to. But . . . what did you *do* with it? Or didn't you get it?"

"Get it, get what?"

"For God's sake," Fé said. "Get what you went for. I went through your pockets, of course. Nothing there."

"No," Jeye said. "There wouldn't have been." By the sudden knife-edge of pain in his ribs, he knew that he had been about to laugh. ". . . I threw it away."

"You did *what*?"

"I threw it down a drain."

"But you'll never find it again. It'll be washed away."

"I hope so."

"You *hope*. . . ? You threw it away. You mean you threw it *away*. I'd have thought you'd . . . sooner have died."

"Something *did* die," Jeye said. "Something died when I did it. Not me, though."

"I could do that, too. Easily."

"The whole lot?"

"Yes. Everything. There's only one thing now I couldn't do."

"I know," Jeye said. "It won't come to that."

"It mustn't."

"There's a chance, you see, if what's left of us can take it. And we have to. There's nothing else."

"No, nothing."

"I'll be out of here soon."

"And meanwhile I'll be careful," Fé said. "Very careful. Oh, I promise you."

"No promises."

"All right. No promises."

She sat there, holding Michael's hand, until it was time

for her to leave. Then she gave him Moreau's letter.

Naturalmente, se ve desde el principio un cierto fin como inevitable. . . .

The paper, fresh, smooth, had been folded once. Not by Moreau. That, thought Jeye, was what he hadn't foreseen; things go on. Something dies, yes, that's true; but something else goes on.

Hay tanto dolor. Pero en el dolor no está el motivo. No. Todo lo contrario, querido mío: tout le contraire.

Ballastero watched her leave the hospital through the big stone gateway. He was sitting at the corner café, a glass of anis on the table in front of him; a glass of anis and a tumberful of water. His linen jacket was unbuttoned. He wore sun glasses. He still looked like a policeman, and he knew it.

"I know one thing," he said. "She isn't a fool."

"I don't suppose she is."

"Hospital incinerator. That's where his shirt and trousers went. Blood on them, she said. Oh, true enough."

"Shoes?"

"You're joking, of course."

"I see," the doctor said. "Took them with her."

"That leaves just the abrasions on his hands to be explained. And of course you're ready to oblige."

"It's quite consistent with his having fallen out of a car." The doctor shrugged. "More so than with his having managed to crawl the distance you suggest."

"They're clever."

"He'd have to be more than clever."

"They're clever," Ballastero said, as though the doctor hadn't spoken. "And they know the right people. By God,

247

they do. And they're stinking rich. If they weren't rich when they started, they are by now. So what can I do?" His head was turned to the left; he was watching the Citroen turn down the Avenida and disappear. "I'm a police captain, that's what I am. Eighteen years now I been a policeman. So I get fifteen thousand pesetas a month and the odd perks. Oh, I eat all right. So does my wife. And the children. Fine. Grand. Well, and then it's a *man*'s life, you know, it's fun having everyone hate you. You write long letters to important people and sometimes they answer, and sometimes they even come round to see you, so you can give 'em a kosher salute before they kick you in the arse. Here's this fly bird walks off with more than I'll ever make in a dozen lifetimes, and what can I do about it? Salute him? Write him a letter? Kiss his bum? No, *you* tell *me*."

"He didn't *walk* off," the doctor said. "Not exactly."

"Drive off, of course I should have said, I do beg his worshipful pardon."

"He won't walk again, you know. Not without a limp. The leg'll set at least two inches short."

"Oh, stop," Ballastero said. "You're breaking my heart."

"You're only guessing, Captain, after all. Nobody saw the thief. Nobody saw him fall. You're just assuming he did. You can't prove it."

"I don't like coincidence."

"Neither do I."

". . . But all right." Ballastero tipped the anis down his throat, picked up the glass of water. "It happened just the way she says it did. She and this boyo ran away together, and that's why her husband shot himself. They spend the night chatting about it up there in the bushes, then round about four in the morning they drive down into town and he falls out the car. Just like that. You really think the story's a good one?"

"The point is, can you break it?"

"I doubt it," Ballastero said. "Like I said. They're clever."

"You're not suggesting they did in the husband as well?"

"Of course they did."

"He left a suicide note."

"I know he did."

"And besides, people heard the shot. It was near as nothing to the same time you had all the goings-on at Salinas' place. Well, how are they going to be in two places at once?"

"Oh," Ballastero said. "They're clever. All I know is, they killed him all right. Somehow. The two of them."

He drank the water, wiped his mouth with a paper napkin. The doctor watched him with a curious expression of mingled amusement and respect, an expression that one sees very often on the faces of professional men in the bars and street cafés of any Spanish town. It's simply the way in which one ordinary, underpaid but thoroughly competent expert looks at another; the recognition, shared by the two of them, that in this world hard-earned expertise is its own reward. There is no other.

Ballastero stood up.

"Just one mistake they may have made."

"What's that?"

"Oh, it's no more than a feeling that I have. A feeling that somehow they may have got the idea that this is the end. But if they think that, they're wrong. This isn't the end." Ballastero looked towards the hospital. ". . . This is the beginning."

He walked away towards the big stone gateway, a small, white-suited figure against the sprawling width of the

Alameda. He mounted the steps, passed through the archway. The shadows of the palms were growing longer; the doctor sighed, and fumbled in his trouser pocket. As usual, he had been left to pay the bill.